3

MO ~~MY 26 '89~~ AG 06 '91

CO JA 10 '89

KI MY 26 '89

RI MR 10 '89

SW OC 16 '89

UP DE 26 '89

- -

4

ER ~~MR 13 '90~~ MAY 15 '90

CS JY 25 '89

HL JA 25 '91

PI SE 29 '88

BE NO 22 '90

BL AG 31 '90

SIL MR 28 '91

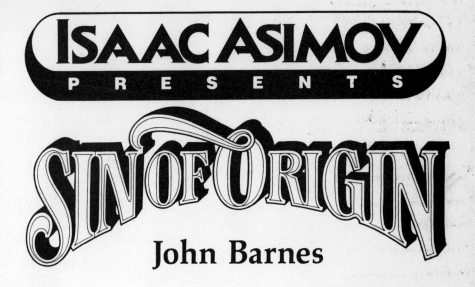

ISAAC ASIMOV
PRESENTS

SIN OF ORIGIN

John Barnes

CONGDON & WEED, INC.
New York • Chicago

In Association with Davis Publications, Inc.

Library of Congress Cataloging-in-Publication Data

Barnes, John, 1957–
   (Sin of origin)
   Isaac Asimov presents Sin of origin / by John Barnes.
      p.   cm.
   ISBN 0-86553-195-1
   I. Asimov, Isaac, 1920–   . II. Title.   III. Title: Sin of
origin.
PS3552.A677S5   1988
813'.54—dc19   87-32999
                                             CIP

Copyright © 1988 by John Barnes
Library of Congress Catalog Card Number: 87-32999
International Standard Book Number: 0-86553-195-1

Published by Congdon & Weed, Inc.
A subsidiary of Contemporary Books, Inc.
298 Fifth Avenue, New York, New York 10001
Distributed by Contemporary Books, Inc.
180 North Michigan Avenue, Chicago, Illinois 60601

Published simultaneously in Canada by Beaverbooks, Ltd.
195 Allstate Parkway, Valleywood Business Park
Markham, Ontario L3R 4T8 Canada

To Kathy Albe—spouse, critic, friend, and creditor—
because she liked this one better

SPREADING THROUGH SPACE
by Isaac Asimov

HOW DID LIFE originate? Biologists have not yet managed to work out a definite scenario. Indeed, the task seems so formidable that there would be a kind of relief in sitting back and saying, "It never happened."

And yet it *did* happen. Here we are. Presumably, very simple compounds existing in the ocean and atmosphere of the primordial Earth, making use of ultraviolet light from the Sun, lightning, volcanic heat, or other sources of energy, gradually built up into more complicated compounds and eventually developed properties we recognize as those of simple life.

The question is whether conditions on the primordial Earth were such as to allow this sort of thing to happen. Even if such conditions did exist, it is possible that the requirements are so tight that only on very few worlds could life develop.

But perhaps very few, or even *one* world is sufficient. Although, it may not be possible for a world to give rise to life, such a world may be hospitable to life that formed somewhere else and arrives here.

Thus, life couldn't possibly have developed on dry land, but having developed in the sea and lived there for 3 billion years, such life was capable of colonizing the land. Again, life couldn't possibly have developed on Antarctica or in the Gobi desert, but having started elsewhere it could spread into those inhospitable areas.

Is it possible, then, that life may start on some particularly suitable planet and then spread through space to colonize other planets? Might we be a starting point and might there be other planets, less favored than our own, that have life distantly related to ours? Or might life have started elsewhere on a world *more* favorable than Earth, and might it eventually have colonized our planet?

The first scientist to take up the notion of life from one planet colonizing another was a Swedish chemist named Svante August Arrhenius (1859–1927). In 1907, he published *Worlds in the Making*, picturing spores escaping from the atmosphere of a planet by random movement and then being driven through space by the light-pressure of the planet's sun.

Driven this way and that, eventually, by starlight, the spores might travel randomly for many millions of years until by sheer chance it would strike the atmosphere of a suitable planet and seed it.

At first blush, this theory looks attractive. Bacterial spores, protected by a thick coat, are very resistant to cold and dehydration and might conceivably last a long time in the vacuum of space. Also, they are just the right size to be more affected by the outward pressure of a star's radiation than by the inward pull of its gravity. To be sure, in 1910, it was found that the bacterial spores we know are vulnerable to ultraviolet light—not to speak of other destructive radiations, such as cosmic rays, stellar x-rays, and magnetospheres full of charged particles.

Perhaps, though, there are some spores resistant to radiation, or perhaps microscopic forms of life arrive at a planet by some means other than simple chance. The English scientist, Francis H. C. Crick (b. 1916) has suggested—possibly half in fun—that an exploring party might land on a planet that is lifeless but is capable of supporting life, if it is introduced. They may leave their garbage behind, the remains of their lunch, let us say, and the microorganisms present may survive and start the vast cycle of life. In that case, the simple cells may have made the voyage under protected conditions.

As a matter of fact, beginning in 1968, astronomers have detected molecules in interstellar clouds, some surprisingly elaborate ones, too, mostly carbon-containing (organic) molecules. One molecule containing as many as 13 atoms has been located. The more elaborate the molecule, the fewer there are of it and the more difficult they are to detect. It may be, if we can only get close enough and study the clouds delicately enough, that molecules on the direct route to life might exist there. In that case, it is possible that a planet may be seeded by these clouds.

To be sure, it is hard to see how material from an interstellar cloud may get to planets, but comets, which are part of planetary systems also contain carbon-containing molecules and some of these may be complex, too. In 1986, a close study of Comet Halley showed that there were long polymeric molecules present.

Not only that but there are certain rare meteorites called "carbonaceous" meteorites that contain small quantities of water and organic molecules. Some of these have been analyzed and have been found to contain certain amino acids that are the building blocks of proteins, as well as certain fatty acids. The nature of the compounds present show that they were not formed through the agency of life, but they might still serve to seed a planet and get bigger things going.

Perhaps the most radical ideas held in this connection are those of the English astronomer, Fred Hoyle (b. 1915) and an Indian colleague, Chandra Wickramasinghe.

They feel that the syntheses in interstellar clouds and in comets may go far beyond what has been detected. Very small quantities of microscopic bits of life may have been formed, they maintain. They suggest that life on Earth may have originated when spores were carried to Earth by comet tails—and in recent times, new and virulent pathogens (like the virus of the 1918 influenza pandemic) may have been deposited on Earth in this manner. (It is only fair to say, however, that the Hoyle-Wickramasinghe notions are not taken seriously by other scientists.)

Nevertheless, the concept of extraterrestrial seeding, while an excellent plot-device for science fiction is not science fiction only. Serious scientists have canvassed the possibility.

Now see what ingenious new possibilities John Barnes comes up with for this theory, in *Sin of Origin*.

SIN OF ORIGIN

PART I
Hauskyld: Randall 2891 A.D.

1

THERE WAS NO reason to suppose that he'd have any more luck with "tmuvam" this time than any other; he had no new data. Still, this was one of two of his original duties left for Hauskyld, and the only one he could do right now, so he ran over what he knew one more time. When the Randallans used it as a transitive verb, it meant something like "love"; intransitively, it meant something like "lives the Tao," always assuming that his translation of "zjirathk" as "Tao" was right. Then again, the gerund form seemed to mean something like "perpetual justice." He sighed, read over the transcript again, and tossed it back onto the tall stack beside his desk.

He had almost fallen asleep over his work, as he did most afternoons, when the shrill alarm came over the intercom. "All hands," Father Sherman's scriptalker ordered, "all hands to sortie positions. Repeat, sortie positions. Quiet procedure. Emphasize quiet. Gate begins descent on landing field in twenty repeat twenty minutes."

Hauskyld grabbed his helmet from its hook and pulled it on. For once he had kept his boots on, as he was supposed to do, so he just stepped out of his cell into the walkway, sliding the door shut behind him.

Everywhere men hurried by, as quietly as possible, staying under the walkway canopies to avoid being seen from the air and thus to let the sortie party get a little farther out before the Randallans could mount an attack. Men were more than ordinarily cautious today—the last sortie had cost two Aquinian Brothers and a badly needed Leonardan.

As always, Brother Gideon and Brother Joshua had gotten to station before Hauskyld. "Mask down, Brother," Gideon reminded him, with just a trace of a grin. Hausklyd pulled down the screen mask and locked it into place; he tightened the chin strap a little as well, then turned to the bolt locker and took a quick inventory.

"Thirty-two shafts," he reported.

Joshua looked up from the swivel. "Could use a little oil next time," he said, "but fine for today, Brother."

"Grab the oilcan and do it now," Gideon said firmly. "We don't want to take a chance on a jam."

Grumbling, Joshua did so. "Hey, Hauskyld. What's that phrase again?"

"*Hataha ji'zjak pha,*" Hauskyld said.

"Yeah, and what's it mean?" The younger man eyed the oil reservoir, nodded, and returned the oilcan to its bracket.

"Loosely, 'Your mother is a slut for the animals,' " Hauskyld explained, for at least the tenth time. "They never hear you anyway."

"*Hataha ji'zhak pa,*" Joshua tried.

"*Ji'zjak pha.* You just said she used to be a midwife until she got a better job."

"*Ji'zjak pha.*"

"Right." Hauskyld exchanged smiles with Gideon; Aquinian Brothers generally had a reputation for being less than brilliant, but Joshua did more than his share to uphold the stereotype.

The loudspeaker crackled. "Radar confirms Gate is on course for landing field. Watch for descent trail at seventy-two forty-one, estimated visible at about fifty-one vertical in about three minutes."

Down below, in the Main Yard, the cavalry troopers were leading their ponies out into the freshly hosed-down yard. The water would keep a dust cloud from rising, giving the cavalry a few hundred more precious meters before the first griffins dove on them. If everything went perfectly, they might only have to fight on their way back.

On the other hand, if the Randallans got wind of the sortie before the gate opened—especially if they got enough griffins into the battle fast enough—the party might never reach the landing ground. "It would be a lot easier if they had four less kilometers to cover," Gideon said, echoing Hauskyld's thoughts. "Especially if they could make the whole run under covering fire. This fort should have been down lower. Sometimes I wonder about the old man."

Hauskyld was about to make some defense of Father Sherman when one of the lookouts shouted, "Descent trail!"

Gideon jumped forward and strapped himself into the gunner's seat, pressing the pedals to make sure the ballista swung freely on its swivel. "Bolt," he said.

Hauskyld grabbed a bolt. It was about a meter long and two centimeters thick, a heavy piece of detempered steel that had originally been a strut of some kind. He ran around in front of the ballista and slid it into the coil. "Loaded," he said.

"Flashes, brother," said Joshua, pointing. Out on the distant horizon, above the redrock mesas and hills, a tiny black dot circled; occasionally the dot flickered into light, becoming a miniature star. The Randallan, mounted on a griffin, was spreading the alarm with his heliograph.

Below, in the Main Yard, the cavalry had mounted. The main gate swung open; the drawbridge slid forward on its tracks, rolling fifty meters out across the minefield. As the bridge locked, the troop trotted forward, swords, lances, and shotguns shining dull red in the afternoon sun. As the tail of each platoon crossed the end of the bridge, they broke into a gallop, heading for the white descent trail.

"Here they come." Gideon's voice was tense and flat. "Prepare for arming."

Hauskyld stole a glance at the horizon; black specks, like a cloud of gnats, were marshalling in the air. He turned to lift the first polaron block from the stockpile; Joshua crouched at the readouts, muttering and swearing under his breath.

By the cloud of dust, the cavalry was almost a third of the way to the landing field now. The oncoming Randallans split into two wings of about thirty griffins each; each wing rushed toward the fort, one rising to meet the descending Gate and the other swinging in low at the approaching cavalry. "Don't think we'll get a shot at them on this swing," Gideon commented. "They'll meet the cavalry out of our range."

The retrorockets cut out on the descending Gate, and the drogue chute popped out. As the griffins swung up toward it, smoke trailed after them. "They're carrying torches," Hauskyld said.

From the inner compound, the fort's two antiaircraft guns crashed. Ordinarily the guns were almost useless—the shells couldn't "see" the body-temperature griffins and Randallans against the hot desert sky—but the sensors could easily spot the flames of the torches. Half a dozen shellbursts sent several griffins tumbling, one apparently torn in half by a direct hit, another losing its rider as it plunged to earth. "That last one blew the head off the griffin," Gideon commented, looking through his telescopic sight. "You should see the way the critter waves all those arms around on his way down."

Hauskyld winced at the use of "critter." But after eight months of war, beginning with a series of massacres, you could hardly expect Aquinians not to be speciesist. Part of it, of course, was that this was an all-human garrison, as Survey Expeditions usually were—there were no cadgers, freeps, or monocorni present to take offense. And although there had been some apparent conversions among the Randallans, there had been no success in organizing a Planetary Legion—all the Randallans were on the other side.

The Randallans were dropping their torches, giving up on trying to ignite the drogue chute. As the main chute deployed, the griffins swung in close to the descending Gate. They would be trying to cut the chute lines, but the iron axes wouldn't even mark spun monomolecular fiber. A couple of them tried to jump off onto the chutes themselves, but there was enough wind to tumble them off before they could do anything; the griffins dove to pick them up before they fell far.

The cavalry was nearing the landing field now, the other wing of the griffins closing with them. Hauskyld couldn't see how it was going at the distance, but he knew that deaths were unlikely on either side—in Randall's thick air, projectiles had little range.

But actual casualties mattered little. The Randallans were fighting to slow the cavalry down; if they could do that, then reinforcements could come up in greater numbers, completely surrounding the cavalry and the people emerging from the Gate. With several thousand troops surrounding the fort, the Randallans could wipe out any sortie if they could cut it off. For reasons that weren't clear, however, they seemed unable to get more than a hundred or so into battle quickly.

The Gate went down onto the landing field. The cavalry rounded the hill and was out of sight. Now all they could see were the swooping, soaring, and diving griffins, the Randallans mounted on their backs waving axes and pistols.

"More trouble coming," Gideon said, pointing at the horizon. Dozens of specks were rising into the air; within minutes there would be hundreds of them on the landing field.

Hauskyld punched his stopwatch. "Two full minutes faster response than we've ever seen before," he said. "Interesting."

"Cavalry's made the break," Gideon said. "Stations, brothers."

There was a change in the whirling cloud of griffins around the field; the nearest end folded up and broke apart as the still-unseen cavalry passed under it. "They got the Gate unloaded fast," Joshua commented.

"They had to. Get ready. The reinforcement wing is coming in."

The cavalry burst around the hill in a cloud of dust, pursued by the Randallans. Gideon bellowed, "Arm!"

Hauskyld lifted the polaron block and dropped it into the MHD well. He slammed the door shut and kicked the foot switch.

"*In Nomine Patri* one two three four armed," Joshua counted, as the MHD hit full power. There was a stench of ozone and a crackling in the air as the capacitors charged.

The coil thrummed as Gideon released the bolt. It fell short of the foremost griffin. "Bolt!"

Hauskyld ran forward to slide another steel bar into the coil, then ran back and moved another polaron block into place beside the MHD unit. He slid the door open, hauling out the blackened, discharged block and throwing it to the side. "Ready!"

"Arm!"

Again he threw the block in, closed the door, and kicked the switch. He had just a moment to look up as Joshua counted off "*In Nomine . . .*"

More cavalry was riding in than had ridden out. At least a whole extra troop had arrived with the Gate, along with supplies and other people—technicians? For once, the apparently random supply system had sent something they needed.

The Randallans must have realized that, too, because they weren't breaking off at the outer accurate range of the ballistae as they usually did. The reinforcements swept right on into the zone of fire, trying to cut off the returning cavalry from the drawbridge.

Gideon fired again, this time piercing the wing of an oncoming griffin, which spiralled screaming out of the pink sky, the Randallan on its back losing its grip and plunging, all six limbs waving, down to the redrock beside its mount. "Bolt!"

Again, Hauskyld ran forward with the steel bar. As he slid it in, something hot went by his face and socked into the rammed-earth wall of the fort. He looked up to see a fresh musket-ball pock in the wall.

"Critters are shooting back," Gideon said. "Arm!"

More musket balls were thudding into the walls now; one gunner a few meters away was hit and fell from the wall as he ran forward to load a bolt. Hauskyld shut the door and kicked the switch; as Joshua began his count, Hauskyld was already running forward with the next bolt.

The first troopers were on the drawbridge now, but the griffins were swooping down on them, trying to force them off and away. Three griffins landed on the bridge itself in front of the cavalrymen, their riders jumping off just before landing, each with pistols in both lower hands and a battle ax in his upper hands. The hand-snakes writhed out from under the poised griffins.

The cavalry hesitated a moment, piling up around the foot of the bridge. That was the moment the Randallans had been waiting for—the troopers were now packed too tight to use their lances effectively. The griffins swooped in, their claws tearing razor-slashes into the crowd as their riders laid into the press below with pikes, flails, and poleaxes.

"Mary's bleeding cherry," Gideon whispered, swing-

ing the ballista around to point down at the bridge.
"Mary's fucking bleeding cherry." He fired; the bolt took
a Randallan through the back of the head, ringing off the
steel bridge and slamming the corpse down face first.
The body flopped frantically; its griffin screamed and
raised its beak toward the cavalry in challenge.

Hauskyld shoved the next bolt in and ran to the MHD
again, but before he could get the polaron block out, the
loudspeaker said, "All hands—scatterguns. Repeat, scatterguns."

Hauskyld whirled; Gideon was frantically unstrap-
ping from the ballista, and Joshua was already running
to one of the scatterguns mounted on the wall. Hauskyld
took his place beside Joshua and looked up.

A huge wave, a thousand griffins or more, was diving
toward them, beaks open and screaming, the Randallans
on their backs clutching javelins and lances. Below him,
Hauskyld was vaguely aware of a desperate fight on the
bridge as the cavalry tried to win through to the gate, and
of the screams of ponies and men still piled up around
the foot of the bridge under the claws and blades of the
Randallans. He swung his gun up; it was really no more
than a piece of pipe given handles and mounted on a
swivel, loaded with an explosive charge and a few fist-
fulls of ball bearings. Scatterguns had little range and
were impossible to aim, but massed together a few dozen
of them could clear the sky.

The waves of griffins tucked their heads and folded
their wings, plunging straight for the wall. "Hold, hold,
hold, hold," Gideon chanted, his own gun now pointed
up at the oncoming griffins. The plunging beasts, delicate in form but big as terran tigers, came nearer for three
agonizing seconds. The faces of the Randallans—bulging seven-faceted eyes above a catlike muzzle—were now
plainly visible.

The griffins reared, opening their wings into a stall,
intent on dropping in among the gunners. "Now!" Gideon shouted.

Hauskyld flipped the switch and his scattergun went off with a terrifying roar. All around him the rest thundered and boomed.

The air was full of screams and blood. A huge griffin, its chest torn to sausage by a scattergun blast, fell onto the wall less than five meters from Hauskyld. The Randallan rider tried to get up, but his leg was crushed under his mount; he drew his pistols and fired one wild shot down the wall before he jammed the other pistol into his mouth and blew his head apart.

"Look out!" Gideon shouted, picking up a ballista bolt. The handsnake squirmed from underneath the griffin, mouth open wide to bite, the claws on its grasping fins extended. Gideon lashed out with the bolt, smashing the snake's head against the concrete. It twisted around, bit itself, and died.

A shout came up from the drawbridge below. The troopers had finally cut down the enemy in their path and were pouring over the drawbridge. A low, foghorn-like noise—the Randallan bugle, an oddly-shaped trombone-like thing with a voice as deep as a tuba—sounded across the desert.

As suddenly as they had come, the Randallans were in retreat. A few futile bolts and shots went after them.

Everywhere, where griffins were down and unable to rise, the Randallans destroyed themselves with blade or gun rather than be captured. Handsnakes flopped and were still, dead of their own venom; griffins ripped their own chests open with their beaks, slashing into the big arteries leading to the heart and bleeding to death in moments. As always, there were no Randallan prisoners—not even their animal companions.

In moments, the surviving Randallans were just specks disappearing on the horizon—then not even that.

"They'll want me at the hospital," Hauskyld said, taking off his helmet.

Gideon nodded. "Go. I'll get things stowed."

2

H AUSKYLD DIDN'T HAVE much of a nurse's touch, so he usually just carried stretchers. This time, however, they put him on filing and recording. About a fifth of the newcomers had been killed or left on the landing field, and a third of the remainder were hurt; all required cataloging, because the officer carrying the manifest was missing back at the landing field.

That fact took a while to establish all by itself; several people seemed to be embarrassed by the number of bodies that had been left behind. "So you think definitely three officers at the landing field?" Hauskyld asked one.

The man started to run his hand over his head, then touched the fresh scrape and hastily stopped himself. "They were in first; I think they got further than the rest of us did. Then those things came at us and they got cut off—"

"You mean you ran away." Hauskyld turned to find himself looking up into the eyes of a Templar captain.

"I'm just trying to find out who we've got," he said, mildly. "Military inquiry will have to come later."

"There's still no excuse for this. Why isn't this man in the penance compound?"

"Because right now we're using it for hospital space. Is there anything you need?"

"Where's the bishop?"

"He was killed a few months ago. You want to talk to Father Sherman. Go across the inner compound and ask one of the guards to show you."

"Thank you." The Templar stared at him for a moment. "What order are you?"

"Mbweist."

"I thought so." He turned and stalked out the door.

Hauskyld turned back to the men he had been questioning, but few of them seemed to know anything. "The thing is, brother, in our timeframe we only boarded the Gate this morning at Arimathea Orbital. And the boarding was pretty confused," one of the unwounded tried to explain.

Hauskyld looked at him closely—he was no more than fourteen. "Confused how?"

"Well—" the boy licked his lips; Hauskyld made sure the recorder was running—"We were late getting started. People were milling around a lot. I think really it was only the Templar cavalry that stayed in line. Everyone else was running around. Then all of a sudden the whistle blew and we were running to get through the Gate, and those things were after us. What're they called, anyway, brother?"

The question startled Hauskyld. "Griffins—the big winged ones. And the intelligent ones, the riders—we just call them Randallans. Their name for themselves is *Thni'tarath-an-k'pha,* which means something like 'wingless walkers.' They call the griffins *Thni-an-k'ba.*"

"*Thni'tarath-an-k'pha* and *Thni-an-k'ba.*" The boy's pronunciation was perfect.

"Right. What's your billet here?"

"Assistant cook and personal servant. And I'm supposed to get some schooling toward a vocation."

Hauskyld nodded and moved on. At least he'd have the boy in his class; perhaps he could interest him in helping out with the linguistic work—there seemed to be a gift there.

With a mental sigh, he turned back to the job at hand. He had just about established that Shorty, Denny, and Sergeant Tang were all the same person, who was dead. If he could find the appropriate corporal or lieutenant—

Joshua tapped his shoulder. "The Old Man wants to see you."

"Did he say about what?"

"No. He just said right away. I'm supposed to take over whatever you're doing."

Hauskyld showed him what to do, then hurried across the sun-broiled courtyard to Father Sherman's office. Since his real duties had effectively disappeared, he was catching everything that didn't fit into a recognized organizational slot, and in a shorthanded fort under siege, that was a lot. Maybe this one would have something to do with xenics, but he doubted it.

3

SHERMAN'S "SECRETARY" WAS the only survivor of a quartet of boy singers that the Archbishopric had thoughtfully sent two Standard years ago. He was blond and slim—the second soprano of the group—and seemed to have a perpetual case of the sniffles even here in the middle of the Spens Desert. As always, it took the boy a few moments to gather his courage and enter Sherman's office.

Hauskyld used the time to look around. Since he hadn't been ushered in right away, it probably meant that he wasn't in trouble; his name had been scribbled into the appointment book right into the middle of Meditation— Father Sherman's daily nap—so it was probably urgent. Further, he was the only one here; that meant something irregular, possibly embarrassing to Sherman.

The sound of a toilet flush told Hauskyld what the delay had been. The boy returned, sniffed hard a couple of times, swallowed, and then pushed the door open. "He's ready to see you now."

As Hauskyld went in, he heard Sherman grunting, struggling to get his robe down and get out of the narrow privy. The old man popped out, doing his best to look as if he had just been contemplating one of the paintings on the wall. "Ahh, Brother Hauskyld, good to see you, good to see you. Just close the ahhh door."

Hauskyld did, and sat without being asked. Sherman sat down at his desk and fiddled with the buttons on the underside panel. The lights went out, and for a moment Hauskyld thought the commander had accidentally hit the light switch and was now fumbling around trying to find it again.

But then the screen lit up. "We got a little bit of ah an interesting recording from today's skirmish," Sherman explained.

The helmet-mounted camera shook hard once and then steadied. On the screen, a griffin swept its head back and forth, beak open to slash. A dead Randallan still clung to its back, one of the big bulging eyes smashed and a shredded hole torn in the chest between the lower pair of arms.

The griffin itself had taken a ballista bolt through its left wing; the little parasol wing at the tip of the main wing had been smashed, and the bolt had shattered the elbow joint. The right front leg was broken, probably from the strain of landing with the Randallan still mounted—normally they jumped off their mounts an instant before landing.

In the lower left of the screen, a hand with a piece of a net could be seen. "Routine," Sherman said, stopping the recorder. "We try to capture any downed griffin or handsnake."

That had been Hauskyld's suggestion. "Sure. Go on."

The picture moved again, then leaped into an enhanced close-up of the griffin's head. The naked scaly face gave the odd impression of a mask; the heavy bone ridges around the big faceted eyes were skull-like, the head like a snake's with a buzzard's beak. The beak was moving; Sherman switched up the volume.

"Thtay back. Thtayback'y'bathtardth'r'wll dropperthnake."

The vid skipped back, playing the sound over and over. Allowing for the high palate, the accent was actually slight. *Stay back you bastards or we'll drop our snake.* The griffin was talking.

"Amazing . . ." Hauskyld whispered.

The griffin backed away. "Stay back," it repeated. "Leave us alone." Then its beak flashed down, slashing through the big muscles on the chest, crunching a rib, breaking the big artery; blood gushed out, it fell forward and was dead. Underneath there was a brief squirm as the handsnake bit itself.

"Well?" Father Sherman asked, switching off the screen and bringing up the lights.

"This is easily the most remarkable thing we've ever found," Hauskyld said slowly.

"Is there any chance that the griffin is just talking like a parrot or a Bukharin clangbeak?"

"Just about none. The use of the phrases is too exact, there are no stray words, and the phrases are too close together in meaning—remember clangbeaks can't remember two phrases that mean close to the same thing. And—" Hauskyld whistled "he made a threat with an 'or' in it, didn't he? Stay back or I'll drop the snake? Sure. That's too sophisticated logically for an instrumental mimic like a clangbeak to act on, and it's unlikely that a pure mimic like a parrot would use it at the right time. No, he was talking. He's intelligent. I guess that shouldn't be a surprise; we knew their brain was a little bigger than a chimp's and a lot more sophisticated."

"How much—ah—do you know now that you didn't before?"

"Well, it clears up some puzzling cultural references, I guess—a couple of things that made no sense before make sense now. But on the other hand, it knocks over everything we thought we knew. It could take a while just to rethink, and most of what I thought would be wrong. What's really needed is a field trip at this point."

Father Sherman leaned back in his chair, his mane of white hair falling over his shoulders. "Yes. Your—ah—standard suggestion. Ahh—what I'd especially like to know—not that your studies are—ah—unimportant, they are certainly, certainly not—is what this might suggest in the way of shifts in tactics?"

"You mean," Hauskyld said, studying his nails, not looking up at the old priest, "that you were wondering if maybe this would help me think of a better way to kill them."

"Well, that's really rather farther than I had intended—ah—to go, but—"

"Well, that's all right. I'll save you the trouble. The answer is no. I have no more idea than I did before about what the war is about, why they suddenly started destroying the missions and research bases, or what makes one of them fight. What I have right now is a lot of questions, and no answers. And aside from that, I'll be damned if I'll assist you in destroying a culture we haven't made a proper study of."

Father Sherman had been quietly digging around inside his nose while Hauskyld spoke; he paused to lick a finger, and then said, "So it would seem—ah-h—that you need more information to be of any help of any kind, I suppose? What would you do if—ah-h—you were to receive my permission for a little expedition? Such as you had proposed recently." Sherman blinked hard a couple of times, as if the idea had startled him.

"What's the catch?"

"Do you want to do it? I know we haven't had much use for a xenist around here—"

"Yes, of course I want to!" Hauskyld was beginning to wonder whether the old commander was actually senile.

"Well, it wasn't clear to me, Brother Hauskyld. Sometimes you Mbweists are awfully hard to get along with. But yes, I think we can see our way clear to ah permitting you. Especially in light of some circumstances that have changed—some recent arrivals."

Hauskyld drew a deep breath. "The Templars. Are they here to—"

"No, not at all. Remember we're, ah, relatively far into the frontier here—it's a simple survey team to determine what desirable sites we might be a pathway to. Silly, of course—"

"No. It's not. Father, we are not going to get anywhere if you won't say what the game is." Hauskyld paused for a moment. Sherman nodded, but said nothing. Finally, Hauskyld went on. "Okay, so they're here to assess us as a jumping off point for setting up bases. Still, when they see the situation—"

"They've already—ah, hinted that sterner measures than the Aquinians take might be, ah, taken to secure this world."

Hauskyld sucked in his breath through his teeth. "When's the ETA on the Evacuation Gate?"

"About half a local year—next winter."

"Oh." Hauskyld thought hard. Though subjective time within a Gate was zero, the universal limit of light speed still held—the new arrivals had left the Archbishopric seventeen years before. If a Survey Expedition was in trouble, by the time word reached its base it would be many years too late to send help. To overcome that difficulty, the Archbishop sent an Evacuation Gate—a Gate with a second Gate inside for the return trip—once the full Survey Team was in place. If everything was fine, the expedition simply loaded documents, samples, and personnel due for rotation into the Gate, which then returned to the Archbishopric. If the situation became dangerous, the entire expedition could leave on the Gate. And if nothing answered the Gate's radio hail, the Gate headed back on its own.

And if either of the latter two happened, the world could be opened to the Templars for "domestication"— ecological reshaping and genocide.

"So," Hauskyld said, and let it hang.

"I think I could depend on you to make a solid xenic case against Randall being domesticated," Sherman said, at last. "And for political reasons, my own Aquinian Order would not care to see that happen either. Now, it occurs to me that in the intervening several weeks, several things could happen if you were to ah sally forth. You could die—at which point there would be no competent xenist to make the determination, and some considerable legal points on our side would be gained. You could find something important—in which case we might enlist the Baconians, Changists, perhaps even one of the older orders like the Jesuits, in our cause. Or, ah, perhaps you might even work out some terms of peace, in which case, the Templar delegation that seems so disturbed about conditions here could be, ah . . ."

"Told to go fuck themselves," Hauskyld finished.

"Yes. Remarkable, ah, grasp of the vernacular. Now, there is, however, one minor matter. While for the ah sake of my order I would not at all want to see this world turned over for such appalling slaughter, ah, I also might face a reprimand if I lost our last surviving xenist. You see how that would look of course."

Hauskyld scratched his head. "It looks a little suboptimal to me, too. But I really don't mind taking the risk. My God—excuse me, Father—do you know what this implies?" He had a sensation of wheels spinning out of control, of plunging into a spiralling whirlpool. "There are still less than a hundred intelligent species known, at least within our local event horizon, and only three of them, counting the Randallans, share planets with other intelligent species—and for that matter, I wouldn't be surprised now if it turned out the snake was intelligent . . ."

Sherman nodded. "More additions to your distinguished career. The Church has of course not forgotten your two other First Contacts."

"Damn it, I mean that this is potentially the biggest discovery in history, no matter who makes it. And if the Templars get called in—"

"Yes. But, as I said, on the other hand I can hardly want to be the commander who lost Hauskyld Gomez."

"That's my risk, the same as always."

But the old man seemed to be plodding along in his usual way. "Certainly. And of course whatever risk is involved in being the commmander responsible for your loss would be mine, as always, and that would hardly be a terrible thing, if, ah, the record showed you, ah, volunteered to go . . ."

"Sure. No problem." If that was all he wanted—

"There's also a minor problem that I truly don't have anyone else to assign to," Sherman said, quickly. He turned to stare out the window at the redrock concrete wall, appearing to be greatly interested; it was not convincing.

However, he could keep it up for a long time. At last, Hauskyld said, "So what is it you want me to do?"

Sherman began to shake. It took Hauskyld a moment to realize that he was laughing. "We had something unusual come in in this last shipment—ah, besides the Templars, that is. I'm afraid it seems to have taken up space that would otherwise have gone to religious instructional materials . . . but then our missionary program has not been an overwhelming success, has it?"

Hauskyld, ready to scream, decided to just sit and stare until the old man told him.

At last Sherman relented a little. "There was a stowaway in a cannister."

Hauskyld shrugged. "Just press him into service—you've got conscription authority and it's the standard procedure."

"But this isn't quite a standard stowaway—not a debt-skipper or an escaped felon. What we seem to have gotten this time is a doctor of xenics."

"Why would a *xenist* stow away, instead of just volunteering?"

"Well, one that wanted to come here, specifically to Randall, from Mars, might—"

"From Mars? A *Communist* planet?"

"Ah, yes. Specifically from Olympia University. What I want you to do," Sherman said, "is figure out what we should do about this. Right now she's being held in the solitary cell in the penance compound—I suggest you have a talk with her. That seems especially advisable since she asked for you when she got here. As soon as you've come up with a satisfactory resolution to the problem, you can, ah, take off on your little, ah, walkabout."

Sherman blinked then smiled, and got up to show Hauskyld out.

The door closed behind him; the secretary, engrossed in something called *Boy's Christian Adventures* didn't look up. Hauskyld quietly walked out the door and across the inner courtyard. "She?" he said, very suddenly and loudly. A guard turned to stare at him. Hauskyld gave him a firm nod and continued on toward the penance compound.

4

THE SOLITARY CELL could better have been called the solitary pit. The former commander of the fort guard had decided he might need to confine someone away from the others. So he had used a directional explosive to blast a hole five meters deep by three across into the redrock, set a grating over it, hung a light inside, and left it there as a convenience against need. Whoever this prisoner was, she was the first occupant of the place.

Hauskyld spoke to the bored guard for a moment; the boy didn't look to be more than fifteen, just young enough to get detailed to less essential duties and just old enough to resent it. Still, he was cooperative enough; with a minimum of fuss, he agreed that Hauskyld did indeed belong there, and got out and rigged the rope ladder. "She hasn't done much but sleep," he said.

Hauskyld nodded, wondering for a moment about the protocol for climbing down into a lady's cell uninvited; it was official business so perhaps that covered the issue. He turned to climb down.

She was still asleep when he got to the bottom. He could see that her hair was dark, wavy, and full, worn loose about her shoulders; like most people from Communist worlds, she was relatively dark-skinned, or at least the part of her arm he could see was. She was using a heavy brown alweather for a blanket, and that covered most of her.

How long had it been, anyway, since he'd met a woman? He'd been on Randall now for six years subjective, and he'd been reshipped from Arimathea Orbital without a home leave, so he could add nine years subjective on Leopold—fifteen years subjective, then. Of course, it would be about a century in Main Track Time; the thought crossed his mind that he had probably lived through a couple of popes without knowing their names. And if this one had come from Mars, with who knew how many transfers between, she might well have been travelling for a hundred years herself.

Well, matters would not be improved by delay; he reached down and touched the back of her head.

She rolled over, brushing the hair out of her eyes. "Hello."

Though he kept his face rigid, Hauskyld mentally gasped; the woman was no more than thirty years old—and, unpracticed as his eye was, she was beautiful, her almond-shaped eyes large and green, cheeks plump, nose pleasantly hooked, mouth very full. "Hello," he said. "I'm Brother Hauskyld Gomez. I'm told you asked for me."

"Yes," she said, blinking hard. "You look a lot older than your picture, but I guess that's to be expected. Sorry, that wasn't polite, I'm still a little muzzy. My name's Clio Yeremenko. What year is this?"

"2891."

"Wow. No wonder. I just did a hundred and twenty years MTT in about two years subjective." She took a deep breath. "Anything to drink around here? Like water, I mean. And what status have I jumped into—prisoner? Trespass? Administrative headache?"

"Definitely that last one, in any case," Hauskyld said. He poured water for her from the pitcher on the cell's one shelf; the glass was cool in his hand, he noted with approval. He handed it to her, and she drank eagerly. "Actually, what I'm here to do, in part, is to determine your status," he explained.

She set down the empty glass, wiped her mouth, and said, "That was great. Well, just what are my choices for status?"

"Good question. Technically, you're a temptation; the Vatican says we have to keep you from tempting anyone."

Clio snorted. "Me? Dad always said they had to tie a hamster to my neck to get the cat interested." She sat up all the way, shrugging off the alweather and straightening her tunic; Hauskyld was suddenly, painfully aware that her figure, if anything, excelled her face. "My brothers always called me 'Fatso' and 'Budgie Face.' "

Hauskyld shook his head. "Ha. What year did you leave Mars?"

"2769, right after Solstice Festival. Why?"

"Well, in a hundred and twenty years a lot of things change. A lot of the younger men here grew up on St. Thaddeus about twenty years ago subjective. At that time your face and," he blushed, gesturing at her, "and your appearance, were, let's say, very much in fashion."

She laughed. "Finally I find a man who likes my looks, in fact several hundred of them, and I'm the only woman on the planet—and they're all monks! My luck is really running true to form."

Hauskyld stifled an answering laugh. "Before you enjoy this too much, maybe I should explain that out here one of the standard procedures is to *shoot* temptations."

Clio shook her head. "But I've got a sterilization certificate."

Hauskyld was a bit shocked; he knew in theory of course that sterilization was not a mortal sin in the Communist system, but as far as he knew he had never met a sterilized person before. "That's a different criminal offense."

"Criminal—" She shook her head again. "Let's go through this slowly. What would they shoot me for?"

"Being a temptation."

"What do I have to do to be a temptation?"

"A temptation is anyone whose presence might cause the men to begin thinking about . . . um, fornication—sexual intercourse."

"They're not supposed to *think* about it? Then how—oh, I see, they're not supposed to do it either."

"Right."

"I didn't realize that you weren't supposed to think about it. They probably don't let you masturbate either, do they? That must be fairly tough—like having to not think of blue elephants."

Hauskyld sat down, quietly. Something about this interview was beginning to bother him. "I don't understand."

"What do you think of when I say 'Don't think of blue elephants?' "

"Blue elephants. I see."

"What about homosexuals?" she asked.

"Well, I don't think you'd be a temptation to them, but we don't have any segregated settlements here, unfortunately. Anyway, we probably won't shoot you. It's in the *Malleus Sexualis* if we need it, but we're supposed to use the least drastic method possible to remove a temptation."

She nodded. "Very comforting. So are they planning to just lock me up, or what?"

"I'm supposed to determine that, as I said. If we can find you a job where you aren't a temptation, and come up with some appropriate quarters, we don't even have to lock you up."

"Oh." She thought hard for a moment. "Would field work be okay—far away from the fort, I mean? It's what I came here to do."

He found himself staring at her. "Is something wrong?" she asked. He shook his head. She pulled her alweather up around herself. "Am I being a temptation?"

"No, I—I think you'd better explain. You stowed away here to do fieldwork?"

"Well, it's not standard procedure, but if I'd followed standard procedures I'd still be waiting—in fact, I'd pretty well wait forever. My project was a little unorthodox."

"Doctrinal problems?" he asked sympathetically. Three of his own papers had had to be rewritten after Paul XIX had made the Doctrine of Unipsychism an article of faith.

"More an administrative thing," she said, drawing her legs up under her. "In the first place, I had three levels of sponsors over me—so I'd never have gotten to do the work—they'd have farmed my idea out to someone further up the ladder. Besides, I was in danger of the Baby Draft."

"Er—what is the Baby Draft?" Hauskyld asked. "The last news I heard from the Home System was from—oh, let me think. Probably the early twenty-seventh century."

She shook her head. "No, you wouldn't have heard about it. It was imposed when I was a little girl. Did you hear that a date was set for recolonization of Terra?"

"No, but I'm not surprised—in fact, come to think of it, it must already be underway."

"Well, when I left, the official date was going to be January 1, 2800. The Three Systems had drawn up a plan for it; how much of Terra you get depends on how many people you can land there. So everyone in range of the Home System is trying to get as many babies as possible born, grown, and on their way to Terra for that date. Was trying, I should say. And if you had wide hips and not too many genetic defects in your past—well, 'On the table, girl, and pop some babies, your future's on hold.' The year I left, CenCom was debating forced desterilizations."

A foot scraped on the lip of the pit overhead.

He looked up to see Father Sherman coming down the ladder. "Excellent, excellent, ah, Brother," he gasped as he reached the bottom. "And you must be the, ah, young lady?"

"That's right," Clio said. "And who are you?"

"Acting commander the Reverend Father Ctesis Sherman," he said, bowing. "Or just Father Sherman. Brother Hauskyld's, ah, boss. You'll pardon my coming down here so abruptly, but the idea of having you ah accompany Brother Hauskyld on the expedition he has been proposing, ah, caught my fancy. It seems to me that it would neatly solve—"

"You were listening in." Clio was incredulous. "You've got a microphone around here somewhere."

"Well, it *is* a prison cell," Hauskyld said, trying to get between them.

"My apologies," Sherman said. "I'm not acquainted with the customs of the atheist worlds. I meant only to supplement the report that Hauskyld was to give me. When I heard your remarkable suggestion, it seemed to me so apt that I wanted to make sure that no chance for it was lost through, ah, for example, any commendable but excessive modesty on the part of Brother Hauskyld." He nodded a couple of times, very firmly, as if affirming the point to a small child.

"Wait a minute," Hauskyld said, "you don't mean that—"

"You will notice," Sherman pointed out, "that it neatly resolves all sorts of problems all at once. First of all, it removes, you'll—ah—excuse the expression, a temptation from the fort here. Further than that, it, ah, makes the best use of the human resources at my command here. As Brother Hauskyld has pointed out any number of times, there is a true paucity of good xenic material upon which to base the decisions I must make; it was for that reason that I had consented to his going out, even though he is our last surviving xenist. Your, ah, expertise in these matters can thus be put exactly where it is most needed, and let it be added under the supervision of an older, highly experienced, and shall we say not without fame person. Thus you get almost precisely what you wish, I gain a second xenist for this expedition—and as it so happens two is normal under the protocols for an—ah—hostile contact, and of course Hauskyld gains some company and assistance for this expedition.

"Now I know," he went on, looking directly at Hauskyld, "that certain—ah—considerations of modesty do intrude here because despite being an older and somewhat more experienced individual, Brother Hauskyld is shall we say not so advanced in years as not to feel a certain temptation. For that reason he might have been tempted, ah, to decline. But as it is it seems to me that this is, ah, so perfect a situation that—regrettable as it might be in ordinary circumstances—I think that we need to consider your generous offer, despite whatever, ah, purely personal though quite commendable motivations Hauskyld might have for declining. So you see, since duty already compelled that I, as you say, listen in, it seemed to compel also that I act on what I heard. And I do apologize for any violation of your undoubted right of privacy that may have occurred." The old man again stopped and blinked a couple of times, smiling as if he had just been complimented on what he had said.

"So I get to go," Clio said quietly.

"Yes," Sherman said. "You do. I'll need your signature on a couple of things—waiver of death liability, application for citizenship in the Christian Commonwealth, and so forth. But as soon as we have all of that, or as fast as Hauskyld can assemble things after that at any rate, you can, ah, head for the wilds. And with my blessings." He nodded once more, firmly. "I take it it's settled then."

Hauskyld bowed; that was as close to a direct order as Sherman ever gave. Copying him, Clio also bowed.

The old man stood there nodding for a moment longer, and then started back up the ladder.

"Er—" Clio said. Sherman turned and looked back down. "Do I stay in the cell or what?"

"Just temporarily," Sherman said. "And, ah, if you'd like, Brother Hauskyld will visit regularly. Until your departure, which should be within a day or so."

Hauskyld was never really sure whether the old man really did move that fast up the ladder, or if it was just his own shock that kept him from complaining about the short time to get ready.

5

I F WE'RE TRYING to get their attention, why did we go out the back gate in the middle of the night?" Clio asked, seven or eight kilometers down the trail.

It was the first thing she had said since they had set out, and Hauskyld had already almost forgotten she was there; it took him a moment to come up with an answer. "Because back there it's a war zone. If the Randallans see anything that looks like us, they kill it without any time for questions. Once we're out of the battle area, things are likely to be different; then we can hope to meet one, surrender, and start talking."

"What if they just decide we're spies?"

"Then we're dead." Hauskyld considered not telling her, but it was after all a xenic problem and she was a xenist. "I think. You could say they don't take prisoners."

She waited for him to go on.

"When they first attacked the missions and the research stations and so forth, they took a lot of prisoners. Once we were bottled up in the fort, they sort of . . . crucified them, out in front of the fort."

"*Sort of* crucified—"

"They tied them to crosses and left them there. A couple of Aquinians volunteered to go out and try to get them. The Randallans didn't shoot at them or anything; they just walked out and untied them, and then several of us went out and carried them in—after a few hours on a cross, they couldn't walk.

"The next day there were more prisoners up on crosses. We went out and got those, too.

"Then Sherman got this idea that perhaps we could use that as a cover for a sortie. When the next group of prisoners was put up, three troops of cavalry went along, and they went into a surprise attack from the ridgeline down into the Randallan camp. It was successful, I guess."

She was looking at him intently; he avoided meeting her eyes. "The next day, there were more prisoners up on crosses, and the Randallans were dug in all along the ridge. We never even got close to them. It took some of them all day to die."

"They died of exposure in just one day?"

"Suffocation. You can't breathe hanging forward by your arms. Sooner or later your muscles get too tired to hold you up against the cross, and then you fall forward. . . ."

"Oh."

"That's how the bishop died. Sherman had to watch that."

"Were they close?"

"Sherman had been the bishop's exec for forty years. And rumor has it they were lovers." Hauskyld shrugged. "He's been falling apart ever since—you saw what he's like. He used to be one of the most competent people you'd ever hope to meet." He steadied her with his arm as they went over a pile of broken rock. "Anyway, they probably won't think we're spies. This has worked often enough that it's worth a shot; it's how I got one of my First Contacts, the one with the gabrieli."

He was hoping that she would ask him about that contact, but she didn't, so they continued on for a while in silence. Isolde, the largest of Randall's three moons, was rising low in the east, a little past half; Tristan, a close-in moon whose synodic period was less than half a Randallan day, was shooting up the sky in the west, visibly moving if you stopped to watch it, waxing as it went. The moonlight was blue-green and barely reflected at all from the redrock around them; the hills and distant peaks appeared in black silhouette against the softly glowing sky. They walked for the remaining four hours before dawn in silence—probably not a bad idea since no one knew how good a griffin's hearing was. There would be time to talk later, anyway; maybe he would tell her about his two First Contacts then.

Though of course she must already know something if she came here to work with him as she had said. She claimed, anyway, that she could have done her research on several different worlds, but she chose the one on her list that had the most prominent xenist assigned to it; not hard to do, since expeditions were planned literally centuries in advance. How she had lived in the Commonwealth, a stowaway and an illegal, she hadn't said.

Just at dawn, they came to the canyon. Redrock was soft and crumbly in any case, held together by small amounts of calcium; "besides, rain here is fairly acidic from the extra carbon dioxide in the atmosphere, and with the slightly lower gravity, you get these wide, deep canyons with shallow sides," he explained. "Erosion is more chemical and less physical than in most deserts."

"Did you ever teach?" she asked. She pulled her hair back and fanned the sweat on the back of her neck. "Like a lecture course or something?"

"No, I've always been in the field. Why?"

"Just wondering. Well, it looks like there's an easy way down. Any risk of a flash flood?"

"Not due for five and a half hours yet."

She stared at him.

He shrugged and pointed to the two moons overhead, now nearing each other. "Three largish moons, and a big sun we're close to, plus a thick, sticky atmosphere and low gravity. Weather here is tidally coupled; you can always predict it exactly. So I knew when the next flash flood was due."

She nodded. He hurried to catch up with her as she started down over a rock fall into the small side gorge.

The sun was full up when they reached the bottom a few minutes later. "Kind of like home," Clio said. "The sun comes up fast."

Hauskyld nodded. "Desert anywhere is that way. If you get up north of here, into the coniferous forest around the Barbara Allen Range, you'll see those long, slow sunrises."

She looked around, scratching the back of her head. "It's hard to remember that this planet has a full biosphere. This desert looks a lot like Mars—I keep trying to adjust my respirator."

"I thought Mars had been terraformed."

"It's in progress, which is a fancy way of saying that maybe by 3000 A.D. there'll be air you can breathe and standing water. Right now—I mean when I left. When I left all there was was a lot of algae, some modified earthworms, and the deep-rooted cacti. Still not even enough oxygen for a lizard." She shook her hair again, lifting it away from her neck and face. "I can tell I should have cut this stuff off. It's starting to get hot."

"It'll get hotter—clear up to twenty-five degrees or so."

"By Martian standards, that's hot, all right," she agreed, pulling her alweather back off of her shoulders. "That's a lot better. I thought there were inhabited places where it goes to thirty-five or forty every day—"

"There are, but they don't have our carbon dioxide content. It's harder for terrestrials to keep their body temperatures in line around here." He waited for her to say something further, but that seemed to be all she really wanted to say. After they had walked a while longer, and were moving comfortably along the flat, hard bottom of the dry river, he decided to just bring it up and see what happened.

"Clio?"

"Yes?"

"Why did you actually come to Randall?"

She looked down at her feet for a few steps, and he was afraid that she was going to ignore the question, but finally she said, "Pretty much the reasons I told you. I had to get off Mars if I didn't want to get stuck pumping out babies."

"And you ran to the *Christian* worlds?"

"I didn't much want to wear five layers of blankets and walk behind a man the rest of my life which is what I'd be doing in the Islamics—and they're hard to get to anyway. And I couldn't stow away to another Communist planet because they'd extradite me back to Mars."

Hauskyld tried to choose his words carefully. "I don't want you to think I don't believe you, but it seems to me that there had to be less drastic things you could do . . . and that there had to be some reason why Randall in particular. There are plenty of frontier worlds, to begin with. And I'm sure you knew you could have simply asked for political asylum—it's routine for people with needed academic specialties. You could probably have gone straight into a university teaching job or government service somewhere, and I'm sure that you were aware of it, because most people don't jump a hundred and twenty years into the future to a just-opened-up planet on a whim.

"Now, what's on Randall? I'm sure it's not me because, flattering as that might be, I doubt very much that you had any basis to decide which frontier world would have the 'most famous xenist' by the time you got here."

He was suddenly, uncomfortably aware of how much he liked it when she smiled. "You were sort of a bonus. I've been keeping my secrets a long time. It's not easy to give them up now." She hooked her thumbs in her lower front tunic pockets. "But here goes. I think I'm going to make a major discovery here—one that'll put my name up there with Chang, Nkaampa, Mbwe, Mossadeq, and—" she winked "—with Hauskyld Gomez. The trouble with it is, it's an idea that anyone can get—if I'd told it to my thesis advisor, or to a funding agency, it would have been somebody else who did the work. And if I did it entirely by myself, it might not have gotten proper attention. So I needed to get out somewhere where I could do fieldwork on it—in the presence of a big name in the field. And without filling out any forms before I went."

Hauskyld slowly chewed that over for a while. By now the sun was higher in the sky, and their tunics were getting wet with sweat—something he tried not to notice about Clio.

By midmorning, it was fiercely hot, and they stopped for a water and food break. "One more set of dry rations and then we start living off the land," he commented.

"Why didn't we do that in the first place?" she asked. "This stuff is pretty tough to chew."

"Wait till you try diggerfish. *That's* chewy. The idea was to not have to look for food during the first day and a half. Same reason we took a big shot of wakeup before we left. That way we get further away from the fort—and the war—faster." He took another swallow from the water bottle and looked up the walls of the gorge. "That break up there looks promising—by that rockslide. It's about time we headed north again—we've gotten around behind the main camps now, and we're already north of what looks like the supply road in the satellite photos, so we ought to have a straight shot into some civilian areas. Better place to start contact."

"I'm glad *some* of the theory they gave us isn't out of date. With the frontier forty light-years away when I left, colleges in the Home System were getting more out of date all the time."

"So am I. I haven't read a journal article in nine years subjective—and more like thirty MTT. There must be seventy more documented intelligent species by now, given how big the frontier's gotten. In fact, I'd love to hear about anything new from the Communist frontier, especially over toward your Islamic boundary—for one thing, you've got most of the intelligent birds." He took another drink and got to his feet. "We're certainly far enough away from the fort, and I hope from the war, to not worry about keeping quiet. If you can talk as we walk—"

"I haven't read much of the recent stuff," she said. She stood up and put her canteen away.

"I thought you had a doctorate in xenics."

"I do. But my specialty wasn't ethno. I do transtellar ecology." She started off in the direction he had indicated; he followed her, catching up in a step or so.

"Isn't that—"

"Yes, I know. That's usually a desk science. Look, I'll tell you about my idea. It's just I've been holding it in for so many years, working all on paper so that nobody can hit the computer files, avoiding getting near the subject in public—it's hard for me to just spill it."

He nodded. In a general way, he knew how scientific funding worked in the Communist worlds—labs and institutions competed for government funds, and within each lab the individual scientists competed against each other. The Jeffersonian Marxist ideal was that everyone competed against everyone to see who could best serve society, and then society rewarded them for their accomplishments. In practice it meant more competition than it did service. The Christian system of simply providing a standard research stipend for each scientist bred deadwood and discouraged large projects, but it didn't create the thievery and sycophancy that was standard in Communist space. "Who would I tell?"

She laughed. "Exactly. This is easier to show you with a map, if you don't mind sitting back down." She hopped up onto a rock and reached into her pack, looking the question at him.

"As I said, we're ahead of our schedule—which isn't a very rigid one. Sure." He grinned at her. "Besides, I'm dying of curiosity. What's so revolutionary?"

She smiled at him. "I just hope you don't laugh when I'm done." She opened a map; Hauskyld saw that it was a map of known space, with the living worlds circled.

"Okay, here we go. It's been known since the last years of the twentieth century that genetic material migrates between solar systems, driven by stellar winds. Mostly it's just stray DNA; sometimes it's something as sophisticated as a virus and on rare occasions a whole spore. When it drifts down into a biosphere, it usually just decomposes or dies, but maybe once per century per inhabited world, the genetic message gets included into some living thing, and maybe once every ten thousand years the virus successfully infects something or the spore actually grows, or whatever. Normally that's the explanation for why life turns out to be so unvaried across all the known worlds—there are only a few kinds of vertebrates, for example, and mammals and pseudosaurians are found on almost every planet. Now, notice that I've asterisked some of the known systems—"

"The ones with intelligent life," Hauskyld said.

"Exactly. Now, we know life didn't arise very often—probably only once—and that the most common cause of a planet's transition from proto-habitable to habitable, the 'Gaia Process,' is the arrival of genetic material from space. The probability of that happening depends on the density of the genetic material in space, which in turn should vary straightforwardly with the square of the distance from the source—because the little bugs and protobugs are being radiated outward just like classical light, right?

"Of course there are all kinds of anomalies, caused by gravity and the presence of more than one star and so forth. But here's the anomaly that interests me—as far as I can tell no one's ever noticed it before.

"The more planets with intelligent life an area contains, the higher its density of interstellar genetic material. I've got that confirmed statistically with everything controlled for."

Hauskyld nodded slowly. "I see what you mean. This probably *is* the kind of thing that people with more money and resources *would* take away from you. Now—why Randall?"

She pointed at the map. "Well, we know the transition to intelligence is another one of those things that usually depends on what genetic material drifts in from space. That's why even with four hundred known habitable worlds there are still fewer than seventy intelligent species known."

"That's an old figure," Hauskyld said. "But then you've spent a lot of time in the Gates. The last I knew it was about one hundred and ten, but I'm sure the ratio's holding true, anyway. And I can see the color coding now. The green asterisks are worlds with intelligent reptiles, red for intelligent mammals, blue for intelligent pseudosaurians, and—let's see, where are Haywood and Solidarnosc?—okay, yellow for birds."

"Sure. And you notice the familiar belts—because reptile intelligence transfers most easily to other reptiles, mammal to mammal, and so on. Now, look at this—" She pulled out another map, one that showed apparent contours. "This map shows densities of habitable worlds as a function of distance from nearest intelligent world. Now, you notice it's nothing like perfect, but—"

Hauskyld shook his head in admiration. "You've convinced me, anyway."

"What I'm hoping it does," she explained, "is provide an explanation for the 'Missing Ninety.' "

"I've heard of that, but it's a little out of my field."

"Around 2350 they were finally able to take good measurements of how fast genetic material was leaving habitable planets. It turned out that the normal rate of departure would only account for about ten percent of the known amount of living stuff in space. So the big question is 'Where's the other ninety percent coming from?' We *know* there aren't ten times as many habitable planets out there, so something, somehow, somewhere, is pumping all that out."

Hauskyld nodded. *"So why Randall?"*

"If you look where Randall is on the map, you'll see it's right in the center of a local density peak, probably, if I'm right, because it's near a point of minimum distance from the three major intelligence belts. So—again if I'm right—there's been a much higher than normal quantity of genetic material from space coming down here, with some predictable effects on local ecology and some genetic consequences we can trace back to the intelligent worlds. With a little luck, about twenty years of fieldwork should establish those."

Hauskyld gaped at her. "Twenty years."

"Yeah."

"And it took you one hundred and twenty to get here. Wouldn't someone else notice before—" He began again. "Aren't you afraid of being beaten out?"

"Not really. There are only five possible places to do the study, places where you get local density peaks associated with the intelligence belts. This is one, two are farther out than this on the Communist frontier, one's Islamic, and one's too screwed up to observe and off limits besides."

"Which one is that?"

"Earth. So, anyway, it had to be Randall."

"Hmmm." Hauskyld shook his head. "I just wish I was closer to your field so that I could be in on this more." He got up with a sigh. "Anyway, I'm fascinated, but for the sake of the mission we need to get up out of the gorge and a few kilometers farther today. Especially because if we fail the Templars will wipe out so much that *nobody* will ever be able to make any meaningful observations. If you'll stow the maps, we can get going."

"Sure." She fiddled with her pack for a moment and stood up. "And this is for listening," she said, kissing him on the cheek and hugging him around the shoulder. His hand moved, as if to hug back, but her embrace was over before he could return it.

6

"W HAT EXACTLY ARE we looking for, now?" Clio
asked.

Hauskyld looked up, grinning sheepishly.
"Sorry. I'm not used to having help. We're looking for
kind of a wide pit, maybe thirty meters across and about
ten deep, with crumbly, more-or-less vertical sides—a
gripper bush hole. They're among the better places to
camp, and you can usually find one if you look."

The sun was still on its way up, but the drugs were
wearing off and both of them were getting drowsy and
careless. Hauskyld wanted to be alert—the Spens Desert,
like any other, had its share of venomous reptiles, and
there were some dog-sized predators that could be dangerous as well.

It was almost an hour's further walking, but they
found it. The pit was unusually big—more than fifty
meters across, Hauskyld estimated—and the gripper
bush at its center looked promising. "All right, what we
need now is the rope. Might as well use mine." He dug
down into his pack, reaching for the bottom.

"My old Scoutmaster would have chewed you out for
that one," Clio said. "Rope at the bottom of the pack."

He shrugged. "Your old Scoutmaster wasn't doing
Hostiles Protocol. In a lot of cultures a rope is a
weapon—so you don't want that to be the first thing that
comes popping out of your pack. Admittedly, you could
end up dead in an accident, but that's the way it goes—
dead you won't do any harm, but screw up on a contact
and it might be the last chance for peaceful relations."

She nodded. "What are we going to belay to?"

He glanced around. "Hmm. You've got me there. Usually there are some gricklegrass trees around the edge of
the pit, but I don't see any. Let's walk around and see if
there's anything solid. Stay back from the edge—that
breaks easily."

They were most of the way around the pit when Hauskyld, in the lead, kicked hard at a boulder to see if it
would bear their weight. It dropped away from his foot;
he stood on one leg for an instant, staring at it falling
away. Then the rock lip of the gripper pit was cracking
and crumbling; they tried to back off, but the rock under
their feet gave way and they slid down into the pit with
the rolling, slippery sheet of rocks and clods.

When the slide stopped, Hauskyld sat up gingerly.
There were some bruises, he thought, but nothing much
wrong otherwise. He looked around for Clio.

She was about four meters down beyond him, lying on
her side and breathing in sharp, deep gasps.

"Are you all right?"

"I think I turned my ankle. Not broken, but sprained.
Shit, I'm sorry, Hauskyld."

He got up carefully and crawled down to her. "It's
okay. These things happen. I've got splinting supplies."

"But it's going to delay—"

"Don't worry about that. We're out here to get found;
they'll just have to find us." As he got to her, he swung
his pack around and fished out the first-aid kit. "Now, let
me take a look at it."

It was pretty clearly just a bad twist; she would be
limping badly for a few days. He told her that, injected an
ampule of painkiller, and began to look around the pit.
"Okay, there are half a dozen good caves around here,
anyway. I'm going to have to carry you into one of
them—after I make sure we're not sharing it." He threw a
few rocks into the likeliest-looking cave mouth.

"What are you doing?"

"Looking for whistlers or rockbears."

"What are you going to do if one comes out?"

"Throw more rocks at him if he's a whistler. They're
not much bigger than a cat, and cowards besides, but
they have the same ugly habit as vampire bats. If it's a
rockbear, he won't come out—he'll just roar—but we

don't want to go in there. Now, let's give it one more." He pitched another rock in, banking it off the cave wall inside the lip. "You hear anything?"

"No. Does this mean we can go in?"

"One more thing to do." He unfolded his jointed staff, locked it into place, and went into the cool, dry cave, holding it carefully in front of him.

The mother popped out first, as always, about a quarter meter long, venomed claws raised high, the four back legs scuttling along underneath, the scaly, almost ape-like head with its obscene silly smile reared back.

He swung hard, smashing the fragile skull; the randigator lay twitching on the floor. He gave the rock it had come from behind a hard shove with his foot. There was a gratifying scream and crunch as some of the pups were crushed.

Three of them scuttled out at him—with no natural enemies, randigators never fled or hid from attack. He struck twice, hard, killing two of them; the third, hardly bigger than a mouse, struck his boot. He stepped back and stamped hard on it; there was a squashing noise and a little sob like a baby's cry. He scraped his boot against a rock, then rolled over the boulder that he had pushed into the nest. The randigators under it were all thoroughly mashed and dead. With a last look around, he went back to get Clio.

She was sitting up and looking fairly cheerful when he came to her. "What was that all about?"

"Randigators. Venomous reptile. Easy to kill with a stick, but they have a real nasty nerve poison that would kill an elephant if it got injected." He bent and lifted her up. "I think we'd better get you in."

She put an arm around his shoulders to steady herself. "You don't have to carry me. I can hobble along if you don't mind being my crutch."

"Sure." He set her down gently.

"Will I have to deal with them?"

"With who?"

"Randigators. I'm not sure I can stand the idea of reptiles."

"Thought you were a Scout," Hauskyld teased. He helped her over a low ridge of broken rock where a gripper root drove close to the surface.

"Better believe it. I went all the way up to Krupskaya Scout," she said. "But that was on Mars, and the terraforming wasn't very far along. No bugs and no snakes." She leaned harder on him; he felt the soft curve of her breast against his arm, and struggled to think of something to say.

"Krupskaya Scout is the highest rank?" She nodded. "Made Papal myself," he said, "that's our highest. Um. Probably easier if I just lift you over this last rock before the cave." He bent, and she stepped in front of him and sat on his arm. He picked his way up close to the rock and set her down gingerly on top of it, trying not to notice the firmness of her thighs against his arm.

She turned around on the rock and he helped her down on the other side. Her breasts bobbed as he set her down; he tried not to stare at them. Perhaps this was a side effect of the wakeup drugs wearing off, he thought.

They spread their alweathers on the crusty iron sand of the cave floor and stretched out to go to sleep. Clio seemed to fall asleep at once, but Hauskyld lay awake for a long time, propped on one elbow, looking at her. When he noticed his hand straying between his legs, he made himself lie down flat with his hands beside him and said the Prayer of St. Mbwe to himself, over and over, until finally he was able to simply will himself to sleep.

7

CLIO SHOUTED HIS name once; then he heard her kicking and groaning with effort. There was something large and heavy on his chest, and it had a grip on his legs as well.

He opened his eyes and found himself staring into the huge faceted eyes of a Randallan. He pushed up against it, trying to twist out through the thumbs before he remembered that on a Randallan those were on the opposite side. Reversing and switching, he freed his arms for a moment and struck upward at the sensitive eye facets, but the Randallan blocked him with its forearms; the middle limbs reached down and took a cross-handed carotid grip, squeezing gently. The cave began to go dark—the Randallan broke his grip and caught his hands again.

He tried to drag a foot up, but the Randallan's feet were more prehensile than a human's, and it had taken a solid grip on each of his ankles. He thought he would pass out—to his left, he felt a press of Randallans, and thought at least two of them must be on Clio—

The Randallan released the carotid hold a little, and pressed Hauskyld's hands down to the floor of the cave. Something warm, smooth, and dry slid across his arm; he looked up into the eyes of a bright orange handsnake, busily using its articulated fins to tie his arms with a cord.

Something was fiddling with his ankles. He tried to look, but couldn't see past the Randallan; from the awkward, heavy feel of the hands on his ankles, he judged it was a griffin. Clio was sobbing for breath; he thought of her sprained ankle and could see that one Randallan was gripping it hard.

She is hurt there? The sound was somehow in his mind.

"Yes!" he gasped.

The handsnake whipped its tail up to touch the Randallan. Immediately, the Randallan ordered the other two to be careful of Clio's ankle. The one gripping it let go, and they carefully tied her at the knees rather than the ankles.

Ask her if she is comfortable.

But now he was too amazed to speak. The handsnake nudged his face. *Ask her if she is comfortable.*

"Clio, they want to know if they're hurting you—"

"No, they're not. They're scaring the shit out of me, though—"

Tell her neither of you will be harmed.

"They say they aren't going to hurt us."

"Great. That makes me feel wonderful."

He felt a rumble of what seemed to be laughter inside his mind. This was one more thing to add to the riddle. Telepathy had been observed on a few worlds, of course, and contact telepathy was much the most common form, but—

What a strange notion. Where are these other places? I can't get a clear picture from your mind.

The Randallan gave an order. *Perhaps there will be time to talk about this later.* The handsnake wriggled off Hauskyld's arms and disappeared into the griffin's pouch; two Randallans slid a plank under him and tied him to it securely across the chest, waist, and thighs. He looked left. Clio had been tied in the same way.

Two Randallans picked up each plank and carried them into the sunlight. Hauskyld felt himself being lifted at an angle; they had set him on the back of a gash'hwar, the big, hairy Randallan beast of burden. Quickly they tied his plank to an improvised rope harness. Meanwhile, others strapped Clio to another gash'hwar's back.

Now that he could see all around him, Hauskyld realized there were nine triples in all—probably a routine guard against bandits. Since they hadn't been killed outright, they had at least become prisoners as planned. He just hoped they were far enough from the fort not to be crucified in front of it, as prisoners usually were.

"Clio, are you okay?"

"As much as I can be."

A leathery palm covered his face. "Please quietness. All us your promise are want you runway will not."

Hauskyld nodded, and answered in Randallan. "My honor is pledged to my word." He smiled sourly; giving parole was a Mbweist tradition, but it always rankled him a little, especially because the concept tended to vary a good deal from culture to culture, and there were often surprising, unknown catches to it.

The Randallan bowed gravely, then turned and spoke to the others. With loud, leathery flapping, three triples took to the air to circle overhead. Another three, with the Randallans on foot, spread out around them, two triples in front and one behind, about forty meters away from them on all sides. The remaining three Randallans stayed with the gash'hwar; besides the two gash'hwar carrying prisoners, there were about a dozen laden with packs. They set out at a comfortable walk, climbing up the fresh rockfall, heading north and east across the desert. That, at least, was encouraging—it was away from the fort.

It took several times through the Prayer of St. Mbwe, and he had to reach for a fairly deep meditative state, but he finally was able to bring himself to the state of calm, accepting alertness he needed. The kilometers of desert rolled by, each much like the last, the weird badlands of wavering hills and bent spires, exaggerated by acid rain, soft rock, crustal tides, and low gravity, all blending together in his mind; the Randallans and griffins walked on in silence.

Every hour or so, triples would trade off, inner guards taking to the air, outer guards coming in, and aerial guards taking over the outer guards' position. Hauskyld watched that several times, confirming what he already knew—that griffins had to be mounted on the run, at the moment of takeoff, and that a griffin could not land with the extra weight of a Randallan on its back. A griffin with a passenger could remain airborne for around an hour and a half, perhaps as long as two in a crisis.

The gash'hwar, of course, had to carry all the heavy loads, though from the look of the packs on the Randallan soldiers probably a pack train wasn't necessary to support most military expeditions. That was just as well; the gash'hwar weren't able to carry nearly as much as horses or mules. Nothing on Randall was really well suited—hoofs were unknown, and the gash'hwar had to be fitted with sandal-like shoes to bear even these loads.

The sun was low in the sky when they entered the big canyon. The gash'hwar forded the summer-shallow creek with no difficulty, and stepped onto ground that was somehow different. Hauskyld twisted as far as he could and saw that it was paved. In a little while the paved path joined a larger road; shortly after that, the first buildings appeared. They were coming to at least a small city.

They passed several fortified towers, stations for bowmen and musketeers, connected by covered passageways. This was a garrison town, then—though nominally every Randallan was ruled by the High King, banditry and piracy persisted wherever population was sparse. From this fort, troops could be sent to suppress banditry on the Royal Road near here.

As they passed through the outer defenses, all the noise and motion of a city rose around them. The road was lined with vendor stalls, each hung with the bright pictographs that indicated what would be traded for what and very occasionally set a price in local currency—he wondered how long the one who wanted to build two coffins in exchange for a used tent would have to wait. The scent of roasting meat made his stomach roll over in hunger; he saw the long red smoked and dried snakes hanging from one stand, and remembering the flavor from one of the banquets he had attended when he first arrived on Randall, his mouth watered uncomfortably.

Once they stopped to let a large troop of soliders pass by. To judge by the scars and the general worn-outness of their harness, these were veterans returning from the battle lines around the fort. They all carried large bundles; at first he thought those must be their personal gear, but then he saw that some of them were bales of finished hides, woven blankets, even the sort of small clay pots commonly used for gemstones. Those were all trade goods of great value—perhaps the siege had pulled too many troops away from fighting bandits, and this was just a merchant convoy, but then how had they procured troops like these? Or perhaps this was the payroll, on its way to the camps. He wanted desperately to ask, but it seemed unwise.

The elaboration and quality of the buildings improved as they moved into the city. Randallans didn't wear clothing, so it was relatively hard to tell a wealthy from a poor one, but it seemed clear that this was the richer part of town—the houses were bigger, and featured large basking decks for griffins and handsnakes as well as bars and swings for the Randallans. Two of the largest houses—villas really—appeared to have swimming pools as well, to judge from the splashing noises that came from behind the rough stone walls.

Down a narrow, twisting sidestreet, something at the corner of Hauskyld's eye caught his attention. He twisted to get a better look.

A young Randallan, its fur still light brown, was engaged in some kind of angry argument with its griffin. Both were bobbing and weaving, the Randallan holding his upper arms over his head, the griffin rearing his head back with beak open. The little handsnake darted back and forth between them, touching each of them, apparently in a panic.

From all around, adult triples rushed in. Within seconds, the young combatants were separated and surrounded. Hauskyld would have liked to see what happened then, but his captors ignored the whole noisy business, carrying him on past the incident and further through the town.

After going a little further on the main street, they

turned right into a narrower alley that led downward over steep steps. There was an abrupt right turn at the bottom, and they faced what appeared to be a solid plank wall, about thirty meters high, flanked by two wooden towers set against a mortared stone wall. But then ropes and wooden pulleys creaked, and the plank wall rose slowly to the top of the towers. They passed under it, into a broad, sandy yard surrounded by natural rock walls.

Hauskyld felt hands on his wrists and ankles; suddenly he was loose, and slid down the board, over the gash-'hwar's back to the ground. He sat up, rubbing his wrists to get feeling back, and saw Clio seated a couple of meters from him. He breathed deeply, once, and leaned forward to rub his ankles. To his surprise, two Randallans carefully set the humans' packs down on the ground near them, not even looking inside for weapons.

Then, without a word of explanation, their captors gathered together and went out through the gate again. The plank structure rumbled back down the towers and settled with a thud into the narrow channel, perhaps a quarter meter deep, at the bottom.

"Hauskyld? Are you all right?" Clio was up on her knees, swinging her arms loosely. He started to sit up and his arms and legs screamed with protest.

"I think everything's gone to sleep," he said. "Give me a minute to rest here. How are you?"

"Pretty well, considering," she said. "My ankle's maybe even a little better—or just numb." She crawled over to his side. "Would you like me to rub your arms and legs?"

"Always," he said, smiling up at her.

"You're sweet." She crawled over and chafed his wrists and ankles lightly between her hands; sensation was coming back into them. His shoulders were going to be sore, too, he realized.

He looked around again; there were half a dozen Randallans, four griffins, and even a couple of handsnakes in a wide circle around them.

Following his stare, Clio looked up. She gasped a little. "Can you stand up and help me fend them off?"

"I don't think we're in any danger," he said. "I don't know for sure, but I'm almost certain this is a jail." He sat up. "With a little luck, those caves in the walls are the cells, and there will be one open for us. If you can walk, we might as well get moved in."

8

HAUSKYLD WOKE UP a little after dawn the next morning. Clio was still sleeping; he stood over her, looking down at her body. In the warmth of Randall, they had both slept in tunic and underwear. Her face had a soft, damp look to it—he wondered what it would smell and taste like, especially around the full, red lips. A few stray hairs stuck out from the crotch of her underpants, and the cloth clung to her there, showing more than it hid. He crouched, staring, till the rising pressure in his own crotch brought him back to his senses.

Dressing hastily, he crept out of the cell—a cave much like that in a gripper hole—and into the broad court where they had been dumped the day before. Taking inventory, he found that his wrists and ankles were still sore but usuable, and his shoulders had settled down to giving him an occasional needling twinge.

It had been a long time since he had prayed regularly while on expedition, but now it seemed like the most natural thing to do. St. Mbwe, of course, had recommended doing it twice daily, partly as a practical way of preserving objectivity. He knelt in the deserted courtyard, and listened to his breath as he slowly exhaled each word of the Lord's Prayer. A deep peace settled onto him.

Spontaneously, he thanked God for Clio, for letting him be out of the fort, and for sending him to Randall. Then he settled back for the Prayer of St. Mbwe. "Lord, give me understanding where there is none, and let it flow from me to every soul until peace is complete throughout the universe. Let me see every soul in its—"

Something hit him across the back of the head. He hit the ground hard and rolled over, bringing his arms up to guard his face, but a griffin standing over him kicked him in the ribs. As he flinched back, another griffin on the other side kicked him lower down, in the floating ribs. Then he doubled up as a Randallan slammed a fist into his unprotected belly.

The Randallans and griffins surrounding him beat at him with their hands and feet; Hauskyld drew deep, slow breaths, careful not to lock his trachea, relaxed, and let his arms and legs go limp and warm. He tightened his abdomen as much as he could and settled back to take the beating passively. They slapped, punched, and kicked him on his chest and belly, and battered at his arms and legs, but they avoided his face and genitals.

The battering acquired a rhythm, a movement of its own, and he let his body cooperate with it, accepting each blow with only the resistance needed to prevent internal injury. His arm muscles were sore, his ribs throbbed, and his belly felt stabbed and torn, but he lay there and let them continue, offering no resistance.

Finally, they quit, and a handsnake crawled onto him. *You are not to do this talking-to-Jesus.*

"I understand."

You will comply?

"I understand."

The handsnake crawled off him, and they resumed the beating, slamming him with their hands and feet, bruising and battering him everywhere they could without risking permanent damage. They rolled him over and beat on his buttocks, avoiding the tailbone but leaving massive bruises. They slapped the skin on his back until it was bright red, avoiding the spine and kidneys. They were swift, certain, and methodical, but careful of anywhere where permanent injury was possible. Somewhere in the haze of pain, Hauskyld thought that they must have dissected some terran cadavers to know so exactly what to do.

At last, they rolled him over again and a Randallan sat down, with its full weight on his chest, and slapped him repeatedly across the face, hard enough to whip his neck around, forehand-forehand, then backhand-backhand, then forehand-forehand again. After ten slaps or so, his head was aching and his jaw was sore, and he was more relieved than he wanted to admit when the handsnake crawled onto his chest.

This will happen to you every time you do this talking-to-Jesus.

"I understand."

The handsnake crawled off and slipped back into a griffin's pouch. The gate rumbled up again, the guards went back through, and again it slammed down. Looking at it more closely, Hauskyld could see that it had a stone piece along its bottom that must have added tonnes of weight; with no grippable surface on this side, it ensured that the gate would be raised only by crews of guards, from outside.

Aching everywhere, Hauskyld rolled over and got up, brushing the gritty red sand from his face; his jaw was sore, but none of his teeth seemed to be loose. His face and the sides of his ribcage felt pulpy and tender, but he didn't think any bones had been broken.

When he went back into the cell, Clio was fiddling around in a small basket. "Hi," she said—then looked up again. "Shit, what did you do to yourself?"

He sat down. "I had help. I was praying, which it appears the guards take exception to around here. They beat me up."

She got up and hobbled over to him. "Anything I can do?"

"Not unless you've got a hot bath hidden in your pack."

"Not in my pack, but I've got one." She smiled at him. "I've been exploring our little cell here. Right around this corner, sir—your tub awaits you."

It wasn't sophisticated, but it was definitely a bath-
room. A large stopper closed the pipe; water emptied
from it into a small basin with a stoppered drain, which
in turn emptied into a large circular tub, which in turn
emptied into a trench in the floor with a wide drain. "I
think," she said, "this is supposed to be sink, tub, and
toilet, in that order. At least that's how I plan to use them.
The water's quite warm and tastes fine, like mineral water—I think it must come from a hot spring. There's not
much pressure, but I imagine you could fill that tub in
about a quarter hour." She transferred the stopper from
sink to tub and unplugged the pipe; a thick stream of
water gurgled into the sink and fell through the drain
into the tub.

He dipped a finger in the water and found it pleasantly
hot. The tub was filling more rapidly than he had expected, so he took off his tunic and peeled off his trousers. Clio politely ducked back around the corner; he took
off his underpants and got in.

"Want me to wash your back?" she offered, returning.

"I'd love that."

They didn't say anything for a long while as she
rubbed his back with the warm water. He still ached
badly, but the touch of her hands on his back was a
strange ecstacy.

"Phew," she said. "You could use some soap to do this
right."

"Yeah."

"Well, your back is about as done as I'm going to get
it." She poured the warm water over his head with her
hands. He leaned back and immersed the back of his
head, shaking it in the water.

"Hard to believe we're just a few days out of base," he
said. "I'm afraid we're both pretty rank. What was in
that basket?"

"Food, I think, but I don't know the local diet. They
left it just inside the cell door." She hobbled around the

corner and came back with the basket.

"How're *you* this morning?" Hauskyld asked. "Is the foot still bothering you?"

"Getting better. Now, what is this stuff?"

"Well, you're right, it's food." He held up a small, flat cake. "This is *phel'leth*, the local version of bread. Fairly tasty. Those are boiled diggerfish—tough as an old shoe but not bad for flavor. These are gripper seeds." The squashy little objects were about the size and color of water chestnuts. "If we hadn't been interrupted, we'd have had them for breakfast. They grow in a kind of hard, rocky casing that's full of good, drinkable water. You can pretty much live on gripper seeds all the way across the Spens Desert."

He lifted up a few solid strips of green, fibrous stuff. "And this is *gritha*, a kind of seaweed, supposedly very nourishing, actually very cheap. Poor folks' food—or prison chow—the equivalent of rice and beans." He looked through the basket. "And that seems to be it. To judge from the amount, this is supposed to last us the day, assuming they don't mean to starve us, which seems to be a fair enough assumption. May I suggest we have some of the gripper seeds for breakfast? They don't keep as well as the other stuff."

"Well, sure. Any recommendations on the wine?" she asked.

"Looks like a good year for tapwater." He shook the water from his hands. "If you'll get my knife from my pack . . ." She only hobbled a little going to get it. He split the *phel'leth* with the knife and made sandwiches with the gripper seeds. "Hey, that's a thought. I wonder why they let us keep our knives?"

"Probably because there isn't much we can do with them, between the sheer walls and the size of that gate," she said, munching her sandwich. "Why were you praying, anyway?"

"Seemed like I should."

"Oh."

They ate quietly for a while. Hauskyld thought of asking her why she'd asked the question, but then decided he might not care for the answer. After all, she had presumably been raised as an atheist. He finished his sandwich and lay back in the water.

"I was going to ask," she said. "Isn't this whole area awfully wet for a desert?"

"Yep. On most worlds it would be grassland. But there are no grasses on Randall."

"Ha!" she said.

"Ha?"

"Right according to prediction. No parapisceans, either, right?"

"No, there aren't." He smiled at her. "Am I working in the capacity of famous xenist witness now?"

"You've got it."

"Famous xenist?" a voice said. They turned; a Randallan stood in the doorway. "Good place. I was in prison, and you visited-ed me, right, Father?"

"I—yes, that is right," Hauskyld said, nodding.

"That go to show you Jesus was big fh'ool! Are not good place. This are shitpile! No Jesus here." He threw his head back and made the clacking/burping noise that meant mockery. "What you say, Father?"

"I say if you'll sit down and explain yourself, I'll be happy to try to understand what you're saying." He added in Randallan. "And if the brother of my friends is pleased by it, I may understand him in the speech of truth."

The Randallan threw his head back and shot his mucus gland onto the floor, making a flat slapping sound. "I have no brothers; you shame and insult me. I would not be understood by you." He turned and stalked out.

"Wait!" Clio said, but he was gone.

"He'll be back," Hauskyld said. "We just have to wait."

"How do you know that? He certainly acted like he was angry."

"He probably is. But, in general, if there's one thing any intelligent species wants to do, it's explain itself. Besides, *he* came to *us*. That means he has something to say—and it's probably not just that Jesus is a fool—he could have screamed that in the door and gone. So there's something he wants to say, and he hasn't said it yet. He'll be back."

"I wish I had your confidence. What made him so angry?"

"I think he came here angry," Hauskyld said. The water was getting cold, so he unplugged the tub and let some water run out. "But he got angrier after I gave him the standard polite calm-down-I'm-listening signal. Which is really strange." He pulled the stopper from the pipe, letting the water run from the small basin to the tub.

"What exactly happened?"

He translated the Randallan part of the conversation for her, repeating parts of it so she could learn it. "What I said was the absolute normal greeting for someone who's angry with you when you want to make peace. What he said, I've never heard before. What it means, I don't know. So I'm planning on a bath and a nap."

"Isn't there anything I can do?"

"Well, you might wander around and see if you can meet anyone else. Obviously at least one of our fellow prisoners speaks Standard. What I'm going to do is wait around in case he comes back. That's how this business goes—most of the time you spend waiting, and the rest of the time you're confused. The main thing is not to preform any conclusions." He put the stopper back into the tub.

She nodded. "Oh, I understand that. I just think it's going to drive me crazy." She snapped her fingers. "There's a thought. Maybe this is an asylum."

"Could be. Or a hospital, or a fattening pen for ritual cannibalism. That's the fun of speculation."

"I think I *will* go out and see if I can meet anybody."

"Don't pray."

"Right." She poured water over his head, dried her arms on her pants, and left. Hauskyld leaned back to let the water soothe his sore muscles. He was beginning to realize how gentle they had actually been with him; a full-grown Randallan could probably tear a man's arm off, and if the griffins kicking him had extended their claws, he'd have been quickly dead. He relaxed into the tub, running over a few prayers, only standing up to plug the inlet pipe, then settling back to think of nothing. Shortly, he dozed.

9

THERE WAS A soft scuffing noise in the outer part of the cell, and a pebble chittered in through the doorway. At first he thought that Clio had returned, but then the Randallan came in. "You Jesus are big fool."

"You've told me that. Why do you think he's a fool?"

"You Jesus are say what are not true."

Hauskyld kept his voice as low and even as possible. "Oh, what did he say?"

" 'Blessed are the merciful, for they shall obtain mercy.' Not true. That are not happen. 'Blessed are they that mourn, for they shall be comforted.' I are mourning this year and a longmoon more and there is no comfort. So you Jesus are big fool!" He vented his mucus gland again, spitting a blob into Hauskyld's bathwater.

Hauskyld leaned back away from the gooey, egg-sized mass, hoping it would float over and stick to the side of the tub. "What are you mourning for?" he asked; then, in Randallan, he asked, "May I know what poisons the wound in your heart?"

The Randallan sat down on one of the larger rocks, bracing himself with his middle arms. When he finally answered, it was in Randallan. "I am a *xhu'gha*."

It was a word for which Hauskyld had been unable to find any translation; he knew only that it seemed to be both basic to the culture and generally—though not strongly—taboo. "Xhu'gha" shared roots with the words for "solitary" and "criminal." It was used in a couple of common, vulgar insults; he had tried and rejected "outlaw," "widow," "bastard," and "masturbator," as translations for it.

As he was frantically groping for something to say, the Randallan said, "You Jesus was not a xhu'gha; how was he are knowing?"

"We live in the faith that he knew all things," Hauskyld said. "He died in shame and agony."

"Fhuckh." Thanks to the Aquinians, that was the one word that had definitely crossed over into Randallan. "Dyings are nothing. Not die, that are shame, are—what are agony?"

"Agony. Big pain." He tried again in Randallan. "Is my understanding of the True Speech so poor that my friend cannot speak it with me?"

"Your accent is strange, but you speak well enough. I know I do not speak my friend's speech well, but there are not the words in the True Speech for the things I need to say. There are perhaps no words in any tongue."

"That is a difficulty, always," Hausklyd agreed, hoping to keep the conversation to Randallan. "We have no word for xhu'gha, for example."

"Have you no xhu'ghawi, then? You are a blessed people who know no sorrow or dishonor, then, and perhaps this Jesus is less of a fool."

"I cannot say. You must explain the word to me." Hausklyd leaned forward eagerly to hear the explanation, almost touching the floating snotwad before he noticed it.

"We are not sure ourselves of what the word would be in your language. We thought at first it might be 'on-foot.' Then we thought it was your word, 'alone.' Last, we thought it might be your word, 'horny.' ' "

Hauskyld discreetly slapped the water a little, so that the wave stuck the booger to the side of the tub above the water. He felt like singing—this was the first real clue he had had, and there was an almost standard procedure for this. He asked in Randallan, "Could my friend tell me what event it was that caused his friends to believe these things?"

"The first time, it was one of the followers of the one they call Father Sherman. His horse, which at the time we called the 'stupid-brother,' had thrown him off and run away. He said he was 'on-foot.' But we discovered he felt no shame; that the stupid-brothers are not much like brothers."

Hauskyld found himself making a mental note: the Randallan word was not much like the word "brother" he had been using for it in his translations.

"Then it was the Jesus-teacher they called Father Thomas, at what you called the Mission Station over in Gh'ra'ith—what you call the 'Continent of Davy.' He was filled with sorrow and sat by himself much of the time; we asked him and he said he was 'alone,' and since we saw again that he had no brothers, we thought that perhaps was it. But the rest of you did not shun him, and the one everyone called 'Shrink' came and talked to him and helped to make him happy again, and saw no shame in him, so that, too, was not xhu'gha.

"Then we were talking once with the followers of Sherman, in my friend's speech, and we asked why the one called Harwyd was so angry all the time, and why the others mocked him, and they said that he was away from one called James, and this made him 'horny.' ' "

Hauskyld suppressed an urge to giggle; James and Harwyd were one of the more interesting scandals among the Aquinian officers. Somehow this all added up—"I believe that I understand the word 'xhu'gha,' if my friend will concur. Is that the word that refers to one who is without the t'muvam of a griffin or a handsnake?"

The Randallan threw back his head and screamed, a piercing whistle that felt like a spike through Hauskyld's skull. "Do you speak of such things?" He whirled and ran blindly out of the cave, middle arms flailing the ground to balance himself.

Hauskyld carefully washed the snot off the side of the tub and pulled the plug. He dried himself on his tunic and stretched out on his alweather.

Somehow he had solved half the problem; which half, he wasn't sure. He thought about it for a while without reaching any conclusions, and then let himself drift off to sleep.

10

HEY HAUSKYLD, YOU want to meet a friend of mine?"

"Let me get dressed," he said, still half-asleep.

"'Kuf won't mind, and I had brothers," Clio said, as she entered. A griffin padded in behind her. "Kuf, this is Hauskyld; Hauskyld, this is Kuf."

"God's blessing on you, Brother Hauskyld." The griffin nodded politely.

"God's blessing on you," he returned automatically. The griffin seemed to smile, though the faceted eyes were expressionless and Hauskyld couldn't be sure what the raised corners of the mouth meant.

"Make yourself comfortable," Clio said, sitting down. The griffin sat like a dog, folding its wings along its back. "I'm sure Hauskyld would be interested in hearing whatever you might have to say."

"I'm not sure what you want to know," Kuf said. Like the griffin in the recording, he had a hissing lisp.

"What did Thkhri'jah tell you when he was in here?" Clio asked.

"*Thkhri'jah?*" Hauskyld was still trying to clear his head.

"The Randallan you were talking to. Kuf tells me his name is Thkhri'jah. Though the term 'Randallan' is getting to be pretty absurd—all these people are Randallans. It's just that by tradition, in diplomatic matters, griffins and handsnakes mostly let the Randallans do the talking. Oh, and I think I've picked up the meanings of half a dozen words that you were puzzled about. Griffins turn out to be a lot less sensitive about taboo subjects than Randallans are."

"Not all griffins," Kuf explained. "I think it's just me and the other Christian griffins."

"*Christian* griffins?" Hauskyld stood up and began putting on his trousers. "I think you're going to have to back up and explain things slowly."

"Well," Clio said, "being patient is just fine for you. You understand the language and you've been through this before. But it was driving me crazy. And when you decided on a bath and a nap, that was about the last straw. I decided I'd go out and try to stir something up. Since one of the Randallans here spoke Terran Standard, and since you'd discovered, back at the fort, that at least one of the griffins did, I just thought I'd see if any of the ones here did. So I walked up to the first griffin that came to hand and asked him if he did." She shrugged. "He said yes, so we've been out there talking all this while."

Hauskyld laughed, shaking his head. "I think I'm speechless with admiration. It's a shame you went into your branch of xenics; you're a born field researcher. So among other things, you discovered that Kuf is Christian?"

"So is almost everyone here," Kuf explained. "That's what this place is—they keep the Christians here."

"Thkhri'jah—that is his name, right?—certainly doesn't seem to think *he's* one. But I suppose that's a natural reaction to being thrown in jail."

"The thni'tarath-an-k'pha are that way when they are xhu'gha."

Hauskyld wanted to ask if the griffin, too, was xhu'gha, but somehow that seemed inadvisable. Instead, he asked, "How is it that you speak Standard so fluently?"

Kuf paused a moment, then answered in True Speech. "It was to be our special field of effort when my brothers and I took the High King's commission," he said. "We were chosen because we were scholars of the ancient languages. And though it is not wise to boast, I think I may say that I have somewhat more than the common gift for language, though of course the high arch of my palate makes certain sounds very difficult. In any case, I also had a rare advantage. When Kniep'pha, Qungakranda-ratak, and I went to the mission station, on the orders of the High King, the men there did not hesitate to speak around me."

Hauskyld nodded. No doubt this explained the unusual cleverness and subtlety that had been observed in the Randallan dealings; probably the negotiators and their servants had talked as freely around the griffin as they would around a horse. "We are scholars in the same field, and I think we may help each other a great deal. If I may mention, there is a word I have yet to understand, and if it would not offend you to explain it to me—"

"What is the word?" The griffin wiped his face with his front paw.

Hauskyld noticed that the dissectors had been right in their conclusions—the larger fingers on each side could both oppose the three middle ones. Painfully aware that the griffin's beak could tear away chunks of flesh as big as his fist, and that Thkhri'jha had flown into rages when the wrong questions were asked, Hauskyld wet his lips and said softly, "t'muvam."

The griffin reared back, sweeping its head with the circular motion that most Randallan animals used to take a close look at some unknown object. "You do not know the meaning of that word?"

Hauskyld shook his head. "No."

"I must think about this. Excuse me," Kuf said. He stood up and left.

Hauskyld shook his head. "I hope I haven't offended him."

"I don't think so," Clio said. "He told me the eye ridges change color, toward white, when they're angry or upset, and that didn't happen. And he said one of the reasons they didn't talk to the exploration teams at first was that they don't like to talk until they're sure they understand the thing they're talking about. So I think it was just what he said—he has to go think before he can be sure he'll answer you correctly."

He sat shaking his head in wonder for a moment, then leaned back against the wall of the cave. He felt his mind racing in twenty directions at once. "Fascinating," he said. "I've gotten more real data in the last five hours than I had in the years before. There's a whole complex underground side to this culture that none of us had any idea of."

"Well," Clio said, sitting down directly in front of him, "I can think of at least one reason why that might be."

"Oh?"

"I don't want to offend you," she said, taking his hands in hers, "but I think the problem here is that something about Christianity is offending *them*."

Her hands were warm and soft; despite her muscular build, the skin of her arms was soft and white, and he wanted to touch her there. "Really? What?"

She hadn't let go of his hands. "The idea doesn't bother you?"

"Not yet, anyway." He squeezed her hands and smiled at her. "It's been known to happen. But the problem is, usually when that's the case, there's an immediate reaction. And our missionary efforts were relatively more successful this time than usual. If anything, Christianity seems to be unusually attractive to Randallans."

"Maybe that's what the matter is," she said. "The first people in any society to pick up a new religion are usually the outcasts, because being enlightened gives them an importance they never had before. Maybe you're messing up the social structure."

Hauskyld nodded. "That certainly fits in with the war and with this prison—or concentration camp, I guess we should call it. But on the other hand, how do you explain Kuf? In this society he was roughly equivalent to an archbishop or a cardinal in rank."

"I'd have said a member of the Supreme Soviet or the Senate, but you're right. Of course he might be the only high-caste here." She let go of his hands, but she smiled; he was struck again with how large and green her eyes were, and had to think a moment before he remembered what they had been talking about.

"Well, ah—" he had a distressing picture of himself as Father Sherman—"ah, there's not enough data, yet, anyway. We'll just have to wait until we get another chance to talk to our friends—and maybe go out of our way to befriend a handsnake, too. Anyway, the progress is pretty good for one day. Can I interest you in some dinner?"

"Sounds lovely, but I'd like a bath first." She turned to fill the tub.

It was always possible, he knew, that some part of Christian dogma would offend a newly contacted species; the last couple of popes had been unusually rigid, which made that more likely. If that turned out to be the case, there was going to be all kinds of trouble.

There was a ripping noise as Clio opened the prestites on her boot. She dropped it to the floor with a clunk and leaned back to slip off the lined sock.

Most worlds had many faiths, of course, but the Church generally classified them by the dominant type. Innocent worlds, of course, were off limits—but there was no evidence to argue that this planet was still in a state of original grace. That distinction had been made only twice, and the requirements were stringent—no observable violations of any basic moral principles by any of the intelligent species. That left Unenlightened, Pagan, Infidel, and, technically, Visited.

He heard a little yawn and looked up to see Clio stretching. She bent to unfasten the prestites on the other boot.

Unenlightened worlds were ones with no trace of anything like a religion. Missionary work on them usually failed completely, but there was generally little friction over it. Pagan planets had non-Christian pluralistic faiths—they generally tolerated missionaries without difficulty and could be readily converted. Randall, unfortunately, might be Infidel—that is, might be actively resisting the missions. In that case, the Church would come into direct conflict with the existing culture—a conflict that, if worse came to worst, could well go all the way to domestication. In the process, God only knew how much valuable data would be lost.

There was the clunk of the other boot hitting the floor and the quick slipping sound of the lined sock coming off. Hauskyld had a thought, a solution? No, not a real one. In theory, if it could be shown that Christ had incarnated here on Randall . . . no such thing had ever been found, but though the doctrine of the single Incarnation had its adherents, it was still not official, and the category of Visited planet was still on the books.

There was a slight slipping scraping noise. He looked up to see Clio pulling her trousers off, just slipping the elastic ankle bands over her feet before kicking the pants the rest of the way off. She stood up again; his eyes had locked onto her firm, pale brown, muscular thighs, with much less hair than a man's, below the tunic. With a guilty start, he looked up.

She was smiling, an odd little smile not like one he had seen before. The corners of her mouth crinkled—he ached for how pretty she was—and her eyes twinkled. Her tongue flicked out for a moment, wetting her upper lip.

She reached down to where her tunic brushed against her thighs and lifted it slowly, cross-handed. She was wearing plain gray briefs, like the ones Haukyld wore; above them, a line of dark body hair ran up to her navel. She pulled the tunic up over her head, and her breasts, full and round, dropped out of it.

He could feel his breath catch. He didn't know what to do—he couldn't imagine that she wanted him to watch her undress, but that she was doing this unconciously seemed impossible. Her breasts were plump and looked heavy; they rose as she pulled the tunic up her arms. Her brownish-red nipples, at the centers of starbursts of stretch marks, stuck out like his own did when it was cold. For a moment, he wondered distractedly if she was chilled.

The tunic fell to the floor, rattling and clanking from its many full pockets. She was still smiling. Her hips turned slightly, swinging to the side. She slid her hands into her briefs and turned around, pulling them down, letting here bare buttocks show, a tuft of hair under them between her legs . . . and turned around, naked now. Female plumbing was certainly better protected than male . . .

She stretched, shaking her head so that her hair fell around her face. "Since I washed you, it only seems fair that I get a washing out of it." She got into the tub.

His legs picked him up and moved him to the tub. He knelt behind her. His mouth was dry and he felt his belly trembling under his tunic.

Clio lay back in the tub to wet her hair, then rolled once to get wet all over. She sat up and leaned forward. He rolled his sleeves up, dipped some water in his hands, and poured it down her back; then, reaching forward, he began to rub her wet back gingerly. "You'll need to rub a little firmer than that," she commanded.

He did. She pulled her hair forward so that he could wet her neck and rub it too. The washing became more of a massage; he grasped each muscle gently, lifting and pulling it as he worked. She sighed happily. "That feels wonderful."

Something felt good to him too. He was pressed against the side of the tub now, leaning in as close as possible to her so that he could smell the wet oiliness of her hair, bucking and turning his hips as he rubbed her back. He let a hand slide under the water, squeezing one of her buttocks a little. The softness of her skin was astonishing.

She leaned back, splashing the warm water up around the sides of the tub. "You might as well do the front, too."

He hesitated only a moment before she pulled his face down and kissed him; her mouth was open and he felt her tongue slide in to touch his. His hands were on her breasts, squeezing and stroking, and she was guiding him, showing him what she wanted. Hauskyld surrendered, amazed at the pleasure it gave him.

11

NOW THAT IT wasn't so weird and new, he had really learned to love the sensation of rubbing tongues with Clio. He was on top of her, kissing her while he stroked her big, soft breasts, pulling gently at her hard nipples. Her hand slid down to tug and stroke until he was hard. Her legs shifted under him; he slid forward and into her. "Clio, that's lovely."

"Thank you. Go deeper please—it feels good."

He raised himself up a little further and rocked his hips faster and harder; she wriggled to a more comfortable position, pulling his face down to kiss him again.

"It feels really good," she whispered.

"I love you."

There was a sudden piercing scream, right beside them. They both sat up abruptly. Thkhri'jah stood there, head thrown back and howling, "Jh'eezus! Jh'eezus! Jh'ee-zus!" He flung himself to his face; his upper and middle limbs tore beat rhythmically at the cave floor, and his legs lay limp behind him, as he chanted the name over and over.

Hauskyld slipped out of Clio, tried to stand, fell over backwards, crawled to the Randallan. Hesitantly, he touched his shoulder and addressed him in True Speech. "Thkhri'jah, may a friend know what pain—"

"Forg'hive me! Forg'hive!" the Randallan wailed, his accent thicker than it usually was. "Hear me! Not let me be to you God forever lost!" He beat at the floor and sobbed again.

Hauskyld tried again, louder. "Nothing is beyond forgiveness," he said, again in True Speech. "Nothing! You have only to ask." He put his hands on the back of Thkri'jha's head, stroking gently with his fingers. "My friend is confused and upset. He must calm down."

At first he thought he had not been heard, but slowly the Randallan relaxed, breathing more easily, the torn, gasping sobs subsiding into a low keening. At last, in True Speech, he said, "I must make confession. Can you hear it for me, Father?"

Hauskyld barely hesitated; there was surely some possible dispensation to cover this, and he could not let such a valuable research opportunity get away. "You must wait and pray a little, and I must have some time to prepare, but if you wish, at noon tomorrow, I shall hear the confession of my friend. And rest assured, no one is beyond the mercy or the love of God."

Thkhri'jah drew several long, shaking breaths and whispered, "It shall be so. I shall return here at noon. I am sorry if my behavior is unseemly."

" 'A friend may annoy, but cannot offend,' " Hauskyld said, quoting the Randallan proverb.

"It is as you say," Thkhri'jah said. He turned and was gone.

"What was that about?" Clio asked.

He told her as much as he understood—which was not a great deal—as they cuddled back together. The thought crossed his mind that perhaps it would be inappropriate to "indulge in a carnal embrace" just before hearing confession, but then he wasn't supposed to be hearing confession either. He wrapped an arm around Clio, sliding his hand down her belly into the hair between her legs. She turned to kiss him, and he stopped thinking.

12

WHY ARE WE doing this?" Clio asked, rolling a boulder into place. "How can you talk about privacy of confession when both of you know who the other one is?"

Hauskyld nodded; with a grunt, he lifted another stone on top of it. "Oh, I agree. But unfortunately it's essential—this is how the missionaries taught him to do it, and there's no more hidebound conservative than a recent convert. Let's see if there's any way to shift the rocks around in here to do this."

After an hour of struggling and false starts, they had managed to create, if not a double booth, at least a suitable barrier with a small hole. "I just hope all griffins are as broad-minded as Kuf," Hauskyld said. "Sitting down next to that, they'll be able to see right over it."

"Does it really matter? Can't you just change the doctrine?" Clio asked.

"Well, maybe. It's not a good idea—it interferes with the development of belief in the early stages."

"Is that bad?" There was an edge of challenge in her voice.

He smiled. "It's not a major offense, and it might be justified under any number of circumstances."

"Hmm." She had turned her back and was lifting another rock. "Seems to me the rules around here are awfully complicated for some pretty simple things."

"They always are," he agreed. "But they aren't always

serious. Did you know there are married members of my
order?"

"Really?"

"Yep. Better to marry than to burn and so forth. Of
course, most of them are stay-at-homes—can't have germ
plasm going through Runeberg Gates too often. The last
time I saw the abbot—which was a long time ago—he'd
just invested a large part of our assets in a fifteen-floor
casino/whorehouse complex. Proudly, let me add—it got
us on a firm financial footing. But even we are nothing
next to those crazy Templars." He lifted a rock into place.
"So neither of us is in trouble, or not big trouble, when
we get back. Is that what was worrying you?"

"Yeah," she said. She stretched, wiping her face on the
sleeve of her tunic. "I like you a lot. I was afraid I'd made
a mess of things. And remember you said they shoot
temptations."

"Shouldn't be a problem. Really."

"Okay." She sat down on top of their wall. "I think
we're all out of handy rocks." Agreeing, he leaned on the
wall next to her. "Hauskyld?"

"Yes?"

"I do really want to know. I hope I don't offend you,
but how do you justify adding a level of superstition to
the culture?"

"Well," he said, "I'm sure you can see the political
purpose behind a strong early proselytization effort."

She nodded impatiently. "Unh-hunh. That way you
get effective control of the planet."

"Or a basis of common culture that will help them
join the rest of the Christian Commonwealth," he re-
plied. "And of course, if you asked a theologian, he
might point out that they benefit by not going to Hell.
I'm afraid it pretty much depends on where you're standing—which is what we used to call the First Law of
Xenics. What does the League of Communist Worlds do
when it moves onto a planet?"

"Well, modernization."

"Which is what?" He glanced at the sunlight coming in through the cave mouth; it was close to noon.

"Oh, free elections, civil liberties, common ownership of basic production, public education, civil service—that kind of thing. It's supposed to be just the minimum steps to move from an earlier mode of production to social democracy. That's not exactly the same thing as introducing a new layer of unfounded beliefs on top of the old one."

"Oh?" he asked, and tugged one of the top rocks into a slightly less precarious position.

She sat quietly for a long time. "I suppose you mean the old 'what-if-they'd-rather-be-feudal' argument. But that ignores their objective interests—"

"As defined by?"

She shook her head. "Common sense."

He grinned at her. "We call that right reason."

"Still," she said, "they do get a choice under our system. How do you justify the Inquisition and the Templars?"

"I don't. Speaking as a xenist, I can't. But—when you 'modernize,' which members of the species benefit? The new bureaucrats, the newly educated, the newly enfranchised—right? What do they depend on to support them in their new positions? Your Security Wardens and Naval Infantry. So is there really any chance that such a government would ever ask you to leave? Sounds like pretty effective control to me."

Clio grinned at him. "Why is it everything you say makes so much sense, but I don't believe a word of it?"

"Must've missed my calling. I should have been a theologian." He hugged her with one arm.

She squeezed back gently. "Are you all set for Thkhri'jha?"

"As much as I can be," he said. "Come to think of it, you should hear my confession."

"Your confession? What did you do?"

"Forgot to thank you."

She kissed his cheek. "Maybe I'll forgive that and maybe I won't. I'll need to think of a pentagon."

"Penance. Close though." He kissed her lightly on the forehead. "I guess you'd better go—I need to collect my wits for this."

"Sure." She was gone, a little quickly. He thought of going after her, making sure everything was all right, but then Thkhri'jha came in.

"Are you prepared?" Hauskyld asked, in Randallan.

"I am," Tkhkhri'jha said, softly. "When there are only two of us, how is this done?"

Hauskyld showed him the little barrier with its crude window. Thkhri'jha knelt on one side; Hauskyld stepped around to the other and sat down, his legs spread straight out in front of him for comfort. He wished briefly that there had been a spare rock to make a backrest for his side of the confessional.

"Bless me, Father, for I have sinned." He was about to tell Thkhri'jha that he could confess in Randallan, but Thkhri'jha switched into it. Of course, the missionaries had used Standard as a liturgical language—it helped promote its use.

Thkhri'jha hesitated. "I find the story easier to tell if I do not have to confine myself to the sins alone. Is that acceptable, Father?"

"Certainly," Hauskyld said. "What matters is that you confess, not that you order or rank or weigh the sins."

"We had been, in our time, high in the councils at Phmi'phtar and advisors to the High Kings—yes, to Vwat-Krish'pha-Dintanderoderam themselves. When the strangers from the sky first descended, a mission was entrusted to us: to learn of this idea of theirs of a great power in the sky."

There was another long pause. "We went to what you call a mission station. There I met and spoke with a number of the fathers. Meanwhile, Mruk listened to them whenever I was not around, and Nygrekdoonjanku was able to touch them in their sleep and to learn a little of their thoughts. At first we were greatly puzzled; your horses, stupid as they were, seemed to have a great deal of t'muvam" (Hauskyld made a mental note to ask Kuf about this) "but the Terrans seemed to have little. Eventually we were driven to the conclusion that you were as you seemed to be—without brothers.

"This caused us great confusion. How could you live in that way? Mruk watched how you dealt with what you called 'animals'—this was another strange idea, for as far as we could tell an 'animal,' for you, is a being that you pretend is not a being, so that when you force it to serve you, or when you eat its flesh, you believe that you have no link to it beyond that simple use—as if it had never existed. This was puzzle enough, but there was more . . .

"Nygrekdoonjanku listened to your dreams, and he saw there the desire for *chthim'hra*, and yet, though there was shame for it, the shame seemed to be because of the commands of someone else, not because of the misery that must be endured. It was as if *chthim'hra* were actually a pleasure to you. Was it possible, then, that despite your resemblance to handpeople, you were more like wingpeople?"

The hairy hand tightened on Hauskyld's, becoming painful, and Thkhri'jha was silent. Hauskyld did not want to squirm, to reject the contact, and yet the thought continued to run through his mind that somehow all of this was a clever ruse, a strategem to get hold of his hand and squeeze it to bloody sausage. . . .

There was a long whistling noise, the equivalent of a sigh, from the other side, and the hand relaxed. "What I learned, of course, was that you simply did not need brothers—you had God.

"And there were further wonders! As anyone could see from the story of Cana, your Jesus had used his great power to remove the agony of *chthim'hra*. And most wonderful of all—this was promised to all of us who joined him. Forgive me, Father, for I doubted, and, like the foolish Thomas, had to be shown."

Hauskyld could restrain the question no longer. "My son, what exactly is it that you mean by *chthim'hra?*"

"You see? You are not even aware of the possibility of such pain anymore. It is that which you were doing with Clio, with such abandon that anyone might have thought it was a pleasure. And there was no pain, no hatred—and thus you need no brothers.

"Forgive me again, Father, for ever doubting—yet now that I have seen with my own eyes, there will be no more doubt."

There was a long pause. "Was that what you had to confess?" Hauskyld asked. "Your doubt?"

The hand tightened again on his, painfully, convulsively. "No, Father," Thkhri'jha said, his voice a strained grinding. "There is more.

"There were other ideas about it. Nygrekdoonjanku believed that this was simply a matter of chance; that what you believed and your way of reproducing merely happened to coincide. And Mruk—"

This time his whistle was deeper and stuttered. "Mruk believed that you had killed your brothers.

"The two of them begged me to return to Phmi'phtar with them, to carry a report to the High Kings so that he might decide the truth or find advisors to determine it.

"But I had grown entranced with the forgiveness promised by your Jesus. We have a saying, 'Two whims must direct one will.' I learned how true it is.

"I would not agree to return with them to Phmi'phtar. I was stubborn. I wanted to stay longer and hear more; I quarreled in ways that must never happen. Others of our delegation began to notice.

"At last the shame was too much for Mruk. He tore out his chest and died. And Nygrekdoonjanku, who was with him, bit himself and died.

"But I had learned that my one hope of forgiveness was your Jesus, and He would not let me follow my brothers into death. And so I came to this place, and despaired of God—and you have come to show me that that, too, was a crime. I am guilty of my brother's deaths, and of my disbelief; I have lost their forgiveness and that of God as well, and yet I cannot see what I might have done differently."

There was a last, deep whistle.

"Forgive me, Father."

Hauskyld wished the now-dead missionaries an extra century in purgatory. There was plenty of precedent for permitting suicide in circumstances where it was the universal custom of a species, and they had somehow ignored that. They had further—as, damn them, they always did—begun conversions before even the preliminary xenic surveys were done, letting new ideas roll like loose rubble on the slopes of the culture—and starting an avalanche that was still running. He looked down and saw his own hand, in the Randallan's, had tightened into a claw.

With an effort, he relaxed it. It was only then that Hauskyld realized he had another problem: he had to come up with an appropriate penance.

13

I THINK I got the rest of the story out of Kuf," Clio said. "What did you end up doing with Thkhri'jha, anyway? What kind of penance?"

"I'm having him do silent Hail Mary's and Our Father's—a lot of both, just to be on the safe side. He's got a martyr complex a parsec wide, so I'm sure it will make him feel better, but between us, there's nothing in the Bible or in any Vatican pronouncement that even remotely covers this. So what did you find out?"

"Well, even Kuf found it hard to make himself say it, but here's the way things work: sex among the Randallans is pain-driven. The male gets a horrible pain in the crotch that won't go away until he ejaculates—which he can only do into a vagina, probably something in the secretions. The female goes into kind of a breeding frenzy—like Terran cats, but a hundred times worse. That happens every other midmoon, which is every other full Isolde, or twenty-five days Randallan. When the frenzy hits, the male just jumps on the nearest female and pushes in."

"Good God." Hauskyld set his water bottle down and stared at her.

"There's more. The experience itself is pretty brutal—there's a sac that forms inside the female's uterus, and the male has to rip a hole in that with the bony tip of the penis. The height of affection is considered to be restraining yourself and putting up with the pain."

Hauskyld shook his head. "I'm just as glad the Vatican can't get us a decree on this for at least 104 years MTT. Something tells me the Pope will have to think a little."

"Ha. That's just the start. Griffins lay eggs, which they carry around in their pouches till it's time to hatch into—griffinets? griflings? little griffins, anyway—and then put them in a nest to hatch together."

"That doesn't sound so bad."

"Only *the biggest one* lives. After it eats all the others. And they *remember*—Kuf recalls eating two brothers and four sisters."

Hauskyld looked a little ill. "I can't imagine how we can fit that in with—"

"Hang on. The handsnake only mates once per lifetime—one great big litter, eight to twelve little snakes. Spermatogenesis initiates a biochemical process that kills the male within a few hours of mating, and as for the female—there's no birth canal. When the young are born, they just tear the mother apart. And remember, they're all contact telepaths—they all share the experience."

Hauskyld sat still for a while, quietly breaking off small bits of redrock from the eroded edge of a small gully in the cave, rolling them between his hands and looking at the gritty iron oxide on his palms. "It's a beautiful demonstration," he said at last. "No matter what you find, there's always something new to find."

"What do we do from here?"

"Well, we start by tearing up all the previous assumptions. Then," he suddenly slammed his fist on the ground, "above all else, we have to make sure this planet doesn't fall into the Templars' hands. The things we can learn here! The new perspectives in xenics, theology, ecology . . . there's a million good books to be written about Randall."

She nodded once. "But what do we do today?"

"Think, I guess. Learn more. After that, I don't know—jailbreak? 'Take me to your leader?' " He spread his hands, palms upwards, helplessly. "And of course, if the Templars can make Sherman evacuate and declare the planet open to domestication, what we'll have to do is survive and collect all the data we possibly can—because in thirty-five standard years or so the Templars will come crashing in and erase what's here." He sighed. "That's us Christians for you. Lots of long-run answers but no idea what to do in the next ten minutes."

"Well, Kuf said we'd know everything after tonight. I'm not sure what he meant by that." Clio looked into the basket. "Want the last sandfish?"

"You take it." He got up, shook the dust off his folded alweather, and spread it on the soft sand of the cave floor. "I think I'm going to do another one of my famous naps. You ought to try them—they're the real secret of success in xenics."

"Sounds as good as anything else." She lay down next to him, throwing an arm over him.

14

KUF WOKE THEM with a polite cough. (Where had he learned to do that? Hauskyld would have to investigate.) "I have something that might interest you. This is Thingachganderook. He'll explain."

A large handsnake emerged from Kuf's pouch, curled down his back leg to reach the floor, and slithered across to them. The iridescent scales had a soft sheen in the evening light, spoiled only where the cross had been branded on the wide, sloping forehead; the little handlike fins, curved flat against the body for movement, were a delicate pink. "You're beautiful," Clio said.

The handsnake coiled toward them; they slid their elastic trouser cuffs up to their knees and extended bare legs for him to lie across.

Thank you.

"Are you comfortable?" Hauskyld asked, feeling foolish.

Irregular surfaces are no problem to me. I suggest that you vocalize any message you want me to respond to—it helps me to focus.

"What are you going to do?"

I am going to remember to you how we came to be as we are—how those who were apart came to be brothers. My mother passed this memory to me, her mother to her, and so on, back to my fifteen-times-great-grandmother, who was given the memory by Vudakhangarash, great-granddaughter of Altildathkereethno, Silent One of the First Birth Triple. This is the memory—

A part of Kth'ree's mind was rational, but it wasn't the part controlling her. She noted, almost calmly, that the hardwoods were giving way to conifers as she continued up the river valley toward the mountains. A part of her whispered that there were caves up there, where she had played as a child under the protection of her bodyguards; but for the most part her mind remained focused on getting away, away, away, up into the mountains and out of her father's kingdom in the valley of the Brownwater.

The Royal Road up here had been paved only in her grandfather's time, and was not wide even now—it was simply an easy path for the gash'hwar of her grandfather's much-boasted Mountain Calvalry. Unfortunately, in many places the road went two zhta up for every twenty-five forward, not difficult for a gash'hwar, but painful for a plump, out-of-shape princess in a hurry. More so because of the pain from her cuts and scrapes and bruises, and the dreadful agony between her lower legs; she looked down to see that the blood had matted her fur. She would have to have a long, hot bath, she thought, and then almost clapped her upper hands together to summon the servants.

She remembered, again, where she was, and that she must keep going, but she still could not recall how she had gotten there. She realized what the strong scent she smelled on her fur was, and thought, for a moment, that perhaps Hmi'dro was up ahead, in the caves, waiting for her, but that was wrong—he was—behind her. After her. He wanted to . . .

Her mind slumped back into nightmare. Kth'ree kept walking up the road.

The last drops of blood had given out long ago, but the road was so little used that he could still find traces of her scent on it. He wished there had been time to get a qen-towr to do the tracking—his own nose was at its limits. Hmi'dro was getting tired; he'd never have imagined that she could run this far, and here, in this dry ford, he could see that her tracks were still spaced widely. Kth'ree was showing no signs of collapse as yet—the last footprints in the mud had not even shown her leaning forward to use her middle limbs.

When he could spare attention, he berated himself. True, it had had to happen at one time or another; the king had no son, and a royal child was needed to assure

Hmi'dro's heirship. But Kth'ree—

It would have only taken a few moments to have a draught of strong liquor fetched, for Kth'ree to drink it and pass into oblivion. Then she might have avoided the terror and the Mating Madness.

But they had been too proud. They had endured the mutual agony without mating six times before; they had intended to go two more times before mating this coming winter. They had delayed going to their chambers as the warning signs developed . . . or he had. Perhaps she had not been fully in frenzy when he had leaped on her— many physicians believed that that intensified Mating Madness—

He doubled his pace, ignoring his sore muscles and his cuts and scrapes.

Darkness fell. Kth'ree pushed on. Sometimes, as if her feet had a will of their own, she would lower her middle arms and gallop up the gentler slopes; a few hundred paces later, her middle arms clutching her belly, she would fall back into her stumbling walk, gasping for breath, mind blank again. Slowly, her breath would come back, her steps would grow little by little more regular, and she would be striding along, carried forward up the Royal Road into the pass by the Madness, trying to remember, unable to recall anything that mattered.

She had come up here many times with both her grandfather and father. Establishing a secure frontier with the Air Lords had been the dynasty's proudest achievement, and they loved to look at the four great forts that held the pass—the Winged Ones could fly high, but there were limits to what they could do, especially carrying supplies for war, and the forts blocked their only ways through the mountains, the many bowmen on the walls more than enough to deter any invading army. Two of those forts were on the other side of the Thunder River gorge, and one was far up at the very top of the pass, but she should reach the other before dawn. Her father's soldiers would give her a bed and a change of clothes, and perhaps she could bathe in the officer's quarters and get some breakfast in the morning—

No. She did not want to be found. The first small outposts on the road were not far from here, and she would surely be seen. The mountains around her were supposedly full of caves; she would find one and sleep there, and when she woke she would know what to do.

A part of her argued that this was crazy; that what she needed to do was to get to an outpost, from which she could arrange to be taken home the next day. But that part slid back into the blackness as her body struggled up the hill, all six limbs clutching at the wind-twisted bushes. Up ahead, there was a steep rock face, with plenty of cracks to hang onto; a short scramble brought her to a wide ledge at the top, and, sure enough, under an overhang she found a cave mouth. She staggered forward into the cave. Feeling around, she found a pile of soft sand and stretched out. Darkness descended.

Wildarankaragu nosed curiously at the sleeping one. It was rare that these left their road, and rarer still that any were female. She leaned against the body, letting her receptors contact the nerves; contact flickered and held. She could hear and see with this one's mind.

The shock of what she found made the young ones in her womb turn and moan. She turned her mind to them, calming them; the People might need this knowledge, and if so her children would have to carry it. She turned again, probing inward.

Some of her memories referred to this condition—the Mating Madness, the deep, mind-pervading terror that often followed the handpeople's coupling. She summoned all the relevant memories of her ancestors, back to the first appearance of the handpeople. Typically, the Madness struck at young or sheltered females, or at those who had particularly trusted their mates. There was a name in here, somewhere, she was sure . . . Kth'ree . . . no, that was this one's name . . .

The news was bad. This was what was called a "noble." That almost certainly meant a search, probably into the caves; with terrible danger to all of the People. But maybe not. There was some hint here of shame and disgrace. Maybe this was some sort of escaped criminal.

Kth'ree turned in her sleep and moaned a little with pain. She swam up a little nearer to consciousness, and the flow of the Madness swelled to a flood. Wildarankaragu battled it everywhere, struggling to erase the nonsense messages and to reduplicate the coherent ones, switching off the loops of endless screaming, trying to find the little pieces of the broken message that had once read, "I am me." It would not be easy, or done quickly, and the female would know it had been done—but Wildarankaragu had to have the information for the People, and besides, it was simply not possible to crawl away from another's pain.

The young ones inside her joined her efforts, and that helped a great deal. She showed them what to do, what to look for, what to stop and what to proliferate; after the boredom of lying passively in the womb, merely receiving copies of memories, they were responding eagerly. She hoped they had the patience for the many days this might take.

Hmi'dro came around the bend in the road to the first guard post. Recognizing his insignia, the two guards on duty snapped to attention. He waved them back to their relaxed positions against the wall and went in to talk to the officer in charge.

No, she had not been seen, though admittedly watchers might well be lax after so long a peace. (Hmi'dro made a mental note—if he returned to the capital, he would see that this officer was promoted. Honestly was far more valuable at the top than at the bottom of the ladder.) Yes, if she was seen, she would be caught and sent back to the capital. Yes, word would be passed up to the main forts.

Clearly, the officer mostly wanted to get back to his breakfast. No doubt he would have been more excited if he had known that the fate of the dynasty turned on this, but Hmi'dro was not about to say that. After a little more urging, Hmi'dro gave it up and left, continuing on up the road. She might have evaded all of the guard posts—those overcome by the Mating Madness were all too often crafty—but it was just not physically possible that she should have gotten around the first fort itself without being seen.

It was late in the day before he came to the fort, and by now he had to admit to himself that he had found no traces or scents since before the first guardpost. No one at the fort had heard or seen anything either. She had gone off the road somewhere.

He slept in the officers' guest quarters that night, in a bed that had been more than once used for the king himself, but woke unrefreshed. He gobbled great handfuls of dry rations, borrowed a full scout pack of supplies, and headed back down the road to the last place where he had found any trace. It would take a day's journey to reach that point, and then he would have to hope the trail had not grown cold. Rain, at least, would not fall until late in the afternoon two days from now.

It was noon before it crossed Hmi'dro's mind that his own situation was growing desperate. The loss of control in a betrothed couple was not reprehensible, nor was the Mating Madness, but the eldest daughter of His Serenity was now lost in the wilderness, and she had been in his care. If he brought her back, alive and unharmed—and soon!—it would not matter, but if not, he might well be decapitated.

Then again, if she were not alive when he found her—or if she miscarried her litter of cubs—he might kill himself anyway. He was, after all, a noble of the Brownwater, not some pusillanimous townsman.

Wildarankaragu was tired; the children in her womb were already asleep. They had managed considerable healing in the night while Kth'ree slept, but much of it would undoubtedly be destroyed as soon as she woke; the calming, gentle messages would be ignored, and the separated, broken pieces of fear and pain messages would recopy and find each other, forming the master idea of Madness again. With luck, though, it would not be so clear and unmitigated as it had been the night before— the next night, more of it could be shredded and scrambled, and the other, healthier ideas could be amplified and expanded further.

Kth'ree needed to eat, and left to herself she would not. Hastily, Wildarankaragu planted the idea of hunger in her mind, then went out and grabbed a few edible cones from one of the scrubby trees—not the finest fare, but it would help to keep Kth'ree's strength up.

Then, with everything taken care of as well as it could be, she slid back into her comfortable nest behind a small crack in the rock, coiled up, and fell asleep at once.

When Kth'ree woke up, it was dark. She wasn't entirely sure where she was, but whatever was under her felt like sand. She noticed a dim light and crawled toward that.

She was in a cave. She still wasn't sure how she had gotten here. The back of her neck ached, and she was bruised and sore everywhere. She crawled forward, into the lighted area, and found a few meatbranch cones. They were dry, but she was hungry; she finished them quickly.

She sat up, started to stand to go out into the sun and look around for more meatbranch cones—something pulled at her thighs. *Matted into her fur. Dried blood.*

She remembered.

Her head snapped back in a convulsion. Her jaw opened, almost dislocating, and her lungs pumped savagely in and out. She howled, over and over again, until she hyperventilated and passed out on the cave floor.

Sometime later, she woke again; the blood was still there, and again she howled herself into a faint. Eventually she lost count of how many times this happened, and still later she slept again.

The last of their stupid guardhouses was past, and now Qoj could make a bit faster progress, taking the occasional short flight from high point to high point. She had been this way before, down the Royal Road with the High King and his mate, but she could hardly take the Royal Road now. In fact, all of her success and good luck so far was nothing compared to what she would need to get into their capital. Fortunately, relations with the Brownwater grabbers were good—as good as any could be with their kind—chiefly, of course, because the land along the frontier was worthless mountain country anyway. If she could get to a grabber of the Royal family, who might recognize her, she could petition for asylum. Considering that what she was carrying in her womb was a potential avalanche waiting to crash down on the Skylord of the Free People, the grabbers ought to be glad to see Qoj.

If she could avoid getting killed before she got a chance to explain.

The entire business was stupid, anyway. She had always wanted to be a plain soldier, like her older brothers and sisters and her mother. But her father had had some pretensions to nobility, and when Qoj's pubescent body had rounded out in the belly, and the ridges above her tail had become larger and bonier than most, he had seen to it that she caught the eye of some of the Skylord's clan. "There's always room for a pretty one," one of the old mothers had cackled, and off she had gone to wait on the Queen.

There was a traditional duty that went with that, too, but *that*, she thought, taking a hard swoop for the pleasure of it, had been rather nice. Until, of course, she had done the one thing most inadvisable in a Queen's Attendant—gotten pregnant. If it was the Skylord's, that meant the Queen and every other attendant would be looking for her with poison or a blade, for the nation accepted bastard children, and the cub would be heir to the Seat. She was not about to open herself up as a target to the Queen—in eight years at court, she had seen four attendants die for the same offense.

She had swooped low around a hill, visible to the road but trusting that it was little used, when she heard the cry of a grabber, howling as if it were dying. She hesitated a moment, but curiosity won out.

She had determined the sound was coming from the cave mouth when the howling stopped. None of the Free People liked enclosed spaces, where wings were useless. But the sudden stop to the howling worried her more. . . . there were things in the mountain caves that she would not want anyone to fall prey to—not even a grabber.

She swooped to the ledge—a neat landing—folded her wings in tight, and approached the cave cautiously. The opening was narrow but not too tight; she ducked her head and went in.

Around the first turn, she found the grabber, lying flat on her back, cut and bruised, fur matted with blood. And crawling toward it was an enormous dream-bringer.

Qoj reacted instantly. She sprang forward, the cackling battle-cry of the Free People bursting from her, before it even occurred to her that she had no weapons or armor and the bite of a dream-bringer is death. Fortunately, the serpent turned and was gone down a hole before she got to it.

She turned back to the prostrate grabber. It was female, and the medallion around its neck suggested Royal parentage. The external cuts and bruises did not look serious. Perhaps it could help her get to someone who could grant asylum; in any case, she couldn't just leave it here.

But how would she get it out?

She couldn't lift it in her beak without taking a grip that might break bones or rip flesh. She could hold it with her forepaws, but there wasn't space to fly out of here and she couldn't walk on her back legs alone—especially not with a heavy weight in front of her. She thought of dragging the grabber out of the cave, but there was nowhere much to drag it to, except perhaps down to the Royal Road—and she didn't like the idea of a troop of cavalry finding her standing over an unconscious and bloody Royal princess. Besides, being dragged down the cliff face would only injure the grabber more.

Probably the best thing to do was to just stand watch over it until it woke up, and then try to talk to it. Besides, the cave was dry and comfortable, even if there was a dream-bringer around. In fact, after a day and a half of no sleep—she had fled directly from the Skylord's Physician's apartment, as soon as he had told her what the matter was—it was perhaps a little too comfortable; the sand next to the grabber looked inviting. She might just stretch out and rest a little while she waited for the grabber to wake up.

For one who had once wanted to be a soldier, perhaps an officer, this was perilously close to falling asleep while on guard, Qoj thought, just before falling asleep.

Matters were not improving, Wildarankaragu thought. A wingperson—all that howling must have brought it. Well, at least they weren't fighting—in many parts of the world the wingperson would simply have killed the handperson immediately, but things were different along this quiet border.

She slithered forward slowly over the soft, thick sand, careful not to disturb either of them. This was getting more complicated. She touched the wingperson, who stirred but went back to sleep. On her second try, she got contact.

This one was at least sane; the full story was easy to

find. She liked Qoj, she realized, and furthermore, this wingperson might be able to help with the handperson ... if an immediate fight could be avoided when the mad Kth'ree woke. Touching each of them, she copied selected images and phrases from Kth'ree's mind into Qoj's, showing Qoj the pain and confusion there. At least Qoj would not be surprised.

Concentrating on her copying, she neglected the first twinges; suddenly things were shifting everywhere. Qoj was waking up. Wildarankaragu snapped her attention back to her external senses, but too late—when she again used her eyes, Qoj was looking at her, her head bobbing in a little circle.

"Hello," Qoj said. "So *that's* what you were doing. I'm glad I didn't catch you before you explained. What are we going to do with Kth'ree?"

You trust me?

"We know there are good and bad dream-bringers. I just didn't know which kind you were."

I suppose I hadn't been aware that there were bad ones.

Qoj's body shook a little, her wings ruffling. "Let's not talk about them just now. I'm very nervous. You're awfully big."

I'm going to give birth in about half a longmoon.

Qoj pumped her head up and down, the laughter messages swelling and multiplying in her mind. "I don't know what's going to come to this cave next, but whatever it is, it will probably be pregnant."

Wildarankaragu shared the laugh, and the two amplified each other. Then they felt Kth'ree stirring, and they turned to her. When she woke, Qoj was holding her in her forepaws, and, gently touching her foot, Wildarankaragu was sending as much comfort and reassurance as she could. After a moment, Kth'ree reached up with all four arms, embracing Qoj. Pain and loss echoed and reechoed through her, but she did not howl, and the master message, the part that said "I am me," did not fragment this time.

Hmi'dro was not really sure whether he was lost or not. Downslope, somewhere, if he climbed down far enough, was the Royal Road, and of course once he hit that he could easily walk either to the forts or to the capital.

But it had been three midmoons since he had begun this pursuit. He had grown leaner, and, outside with winter coming, his fur had thickened like a Highland peasant's. In another three midmoons, this high up, snow would fall, enhancing his tracking but making the going more difficult.

Since that first turning from the road, he had had no sight or scent of Kth'ree. He sometimes told himself that he was looking for her body, so that he could return to the capital, make his report, and decently eviscerate himself. Yet he still expected to come around a corner, look over a ledge, or wake up one morning, and see Kth'ree, alive and whole, happy as always. The idea was absurd, of course—but it kept him going, so he was happy to live with it.

Every night he camped in a cave mouth or under a ledge, building a fire, hoping Kth'ree would be drawn to the light. He ate meatbranch cones, lizards or their eggs, fungus, anything he could find. He rose in the morning, covered the ashes, and warmed himself by drilling through the Positions of the Sword and the Weapons of the Weaponless, just as he had as a cadet. Then, while the light lasted, he would search methodically, taking no unnecessary chances, never behaving irrationally.

But somewhere in that time he had become something else. The normal scatter of stray thoughts and random ideas was no longer in him. As he turned and cut the air with his sword, thought and sword were the same, with no separation. When he looked, he saw everything and named nothing. He counted the days only because it helped his search—he did not project his numbering as far as tomorrow. He wasn't especially worried about the winter, or the lack of any trace—if necessary, he could stay up here, and look for Kth'ree, forever.

The strangest thing of all, Wildarankaragu thought, was how fast they had all become friends. Kth'ree, of course, had the mind of a young child, and so whatever biases she might have had—and most handpeople had plenty— had died with her adult self. But Qoj, too, had joined into the spirit of things, and, though Wildarankaragu hated to admit it, she would have expected more resistance even from herself at being attached to these creatures.

For the first midmoons the wingperson and the Silent Person had done little but gather food, tend Kth'ree, and trade stories. After a while Kth'ree had joined in with them, but the handperson would not talk about certain subjects, and especially not about returning home. Whenever the idea was mentioned, it was all Kth'ree could do not to howl convulsively.

"This," Qoj grumbled, while Kth'ree was out gathering cones, "is not doing my petition for asylum any good. I'll probably end up nesting here anyway."

I'm afraid you're right. I've searched everything that is known of the effects of the Mating Madness, but I still don't understand this. Of course, almost all the things that are known to exacerbate the illness are present here—perhaps that's all the difference there is.

"Maybe she's just got it bad."

What does that mean?

"A joke. It wouldn't apply to grabbers."

Wildarankaragu winced at "grabber," but suppressed it. *There's often truth in jokes. Please explain it.*

"Well . . . you know, one mate is not as good as another. At least not to those of us who mate a lot. Maybe she's lonesome for hers. I mean, that's hard to imagine when you think of what it's like for grabbers, but who's to say she doesn't miss him?"

We still don't know the name of the male. Perhaps I should probe along those lines next time she's asleep.

"Probably get a good story, anyway. And I'd like to know why that beast let her run away into the mountains all by herself!"

He may not have had a choice.

"Ha! You'll have to let me tell you about males sometime!"

"Look at this—two big armfuls of cones, all ripe," Kth'ree said, coming in. "And a little mountain hotplant to season them with."

They all turned their attention to the food; but Wildarankaragu remembered the conversation. The next time Kth'ree slept . . .

It was well after sunset when Kth'ree nodded off. *Hold her for me, please. If the probe wakes her and upsets her I don't want to be thrown against the wall.*

"Sure," Qoj said, moving to pin down Kth'ree's upper body, gently so as not to wake her.

Thank you. Here goes.

And then she was inside, looking at the scattered and broken messages. She scouted through the ones flagged for rejection, the ones that were marked never to be surfaced, and at last she found a very long one linked to many recent injunctions. Slowly, painstakingly, she removed those, and found—

The name, anyway, was Hmi'dro. But what was here was absurd.

First of all, Kth'ree had covered it with images and overlays of her father and grandfather, so that the real Hmi'dro's face was difficult to discern. Second, she had ascribed all sorts of magical powers to the name and the face; there were messages in there that claimed that he literally was the world, that all meaning derived from him. Finally, there were uncountable duplicates of a message that claimed that the highest of all possible purposes was union with Hmi'dro—not mind union, like this, or physical union, but some kind of a literal identicality. It made very little sense to Wildarankaragu; she mentally filed it as one more thing to ask Qoj about.

Having examined the hidden message, she turned to its hiding. The primary defense was another hidden memory linked to this one. Wildarankaragu found it—

And almost writhed in pain herself. The same face, from that absurd collection of worshipping memories, hung above her, fangs bared and screeching as if in fury. The hands tore hair and skin, shaking and battering Kth'ree. And down between her legs, there was hot, tearing agony as the horrible, boned erection tore the membranes to let the sperm through.

The face above, screeching and frenzied as it was, was also torn with fear and pain—for both handpeople, this could bring only pain and misery. Wildarankaragu thought of Qoj's gentle, playful memories of her several mates, and could see almost no resemblance.

She knew now what she had set out to learn, anyway. She brought her attention to externals, rejoining Qoj, copying over what she had found. The wingperson had gotten to be surprisingly good at receiving information this way. The two sat together, puzzling over Kth'ree's memories.

"Well, she certainly won't get any better with that stuff inside. Why would anyone believe anything like that about a male? And what are we going to do for her?"

I think we must bring this Hmi'dro to her; there is no hope that her thoughts will again harmonize with reality until she has learned to see him as he is.

"How are we going—"

You will have to take care of her; you cannot fly this far into a pregnancy, and I stand a better chance of reaching him and communicating with him safely. Before Qoj could speak, Wildarankaragu had slipped from her forepaws and was gone.

The snow was getting deeper daily, and every day it was harder to find firewood. He wasn't dead yet, or even hungry anymore, but Hmi'dro could see where all this would have to lead. A day's search now was barely a quarter of what it had been in the summer, and he was relying more and more on his feelings about whether a particular cave or thicket was empty.

After his drills, he sat facing the sun this morning, enjoying the warmth on his face while the fire warmed his back. He had been lucky to find the big, dry deadfall the night before; it was the first time he'd been able to keep a fire going all night in a midmoon. He shut his eyes and let the peace and warmth of the morning take him out of himself.

When the dreamsnake touched him, it was neither surprising nor expected; it simply was. *You are the one called Hmi'dro.*

"Yes."

He felt her wince. *You need not vocalize. Your thoughts are more concentrated than any I have ever encountered. When you focus further by vocalizing it is like a shout in the ear.*

I am sorry.

Much better, but you are still very loud. Now, you are Hmi'dro. You seek one named Kth'ree.

Yes.

I come to bring you to her. She is well physically, but I need you to heal her mind.

He rose without speaking or thinking and began to heap snow onto the fire. When the flames had died, he piled dirt onto the coals, then more snow on top. When he was done, he was sure the fire would die without spreading. Finally he reached down and touched the dreamsnake.

I am ready now.

It is half a midmoon's journey.

Then we had best begin.

There was little communication on the journey. When Wildarankaragu tired—she did easily now, so close to the birth—she would touch Hmi'dro, and he would quietly sit down and wait until she was ready to go on. In the evenings, or when she asked, he would build a fire to warm them. If the snow was too powdery to bear her weight comfortably, he would carry her draped across his shoulders—though she was heavy enough that he should have had difficulty picking her up, he seemed to lift her easily, almost without noticing, perhaps because of that astonishing concentration.

Once, she tried to probe his dreams. He had none; when he slept, he was empty inside, except for a message that held only directions for restarting his mind when he woke. During the day, his thoughts were not the normal profusion of badly formed, overduplicated, contradictory messages, but one single perfectly formed message at a time.

Hmi'dro took no interest in her probes, though Wildarankaragu could tell he was aware of them. That fascinated her more than anything else; she passed the time discussing it with the children in her womb, but neither she nor any ancestor back to the beginnings of memory had ever encountered a mind like this before.

The day came when the journey was over. In the late morning, they approached the cave; she directed Hmi'dro to call out a few times, but no response came. As she rode above the drifted snow on his shoulders, Wildarankaragu picked up one distant sound, a low, keening moan.

She recognized it. The cry of a grieving wingperson. *Hurry.*

He did; still, it was an agonizingly long time before they reached the cave, made the turns, came into the inner room—

Kth'ree was again matted with blood, stiff and still— she had hemorrhaged, as the handpeople sometimes did in birth. Qoj stood over Kth'ree's cold corpse, her eye ridges gray with exhaustion and sadness. At her feet, the tiny infant clung to her foreleg; almost unconsciously, Qoj stroked its head with the other foreleg. She raised her head—

Something in Hmi'dro woke up. The general, the noble, the warrior, bodyguard to the Royal family, lover of Kth'ree, killer of Winged Ones—the scream in his mind was overpowering, battering Wildarankaragu even more than the force with which he threw her against the wall. In less time than it might take to blink hard, his sword left its scabbard and struck Qoj between two vertebrae so neatly that her head dropped precisely between her feet as her body settled, the same expression of deep sadness still etched on it, with no time for even surprise. In two clean motions, again almost too fast to see, he wiped the sword and resheathed it.

There was a moment in which nothing moved. Then Wildarankaragu shot forward, her own mind filled with rage, despair, and loss. She wrapped herself around one of Hmi'dro's legs, too furious to think of biting. The proliferating messages in her mind felt like a swelling tide. In her fury, she gave him everything—what Kth'ree had suffered from, her agony as he had mated with her, Qoj's thousands of kindnesses, every moment of their life in the cave, every memory she had copied from Kth'ree and Qoj, every thought she herself had had, her long journey looking for him, and the terrible grief that flooded her now.

If he had been any other handperson, he would simply have died; the horrible messages would have crossed the boundary to his autonomic nervous system, and his body would have died as its control systems lurched away from equilibrium in all directions.

But that strange concentration, created by his hungry journey through the mountains, protected him now. The old personality, the collection of ideas that had brought him to draw the sword and strike down Qoj without thinking, was utterly erased, leaving only its memories, shorn of cause, justification, or pattern. The new memories—and the guilt they brought with them—were accepted without resistance; the whole burden was unloaded on him, and he bore it.

Sensing what he had become, Wildarankaragu was struck with awe and fear, as if she had been thrown against the wall again. She tried to break the contact, but his mind locked into hers, taking every memory of the Silent People, every memory they had copied from everyone else. Then she fell from his leg, trying to crawl away to get back to her comfortable nest where she had gone to bear her young before all of this began.

She had barely gotten there when the first convulsion hit her. It was time. The children reached to her mind for the last time, copying every memory they could; there was a horrible tearing as her belly burst open and they crawled out. Then, finally, the moment of never-ending paradox as her consciousness listened acutely for the exact instant when she was gone.

The one who had been Hmi'dro sat in perfect peace, the baby on his lap sleeping now, no longer screaming and afraid. When he heard the scraping noise, he picked up the child and carried it to where the noise came from.

The nest of eggs was hatching. Eight Winged pups emerged, battering the eggs apart with their beaks. The first one free of his egg sprang on another, tearing her throat and beginning to drink her blood. Then another grabbed the first killer, tearing flesh from his back, and he screamed and turned—

The melee was over in little time. One large, strong male remained. Cheerfully, it pitched in, eating the bodies of its brothers and sisters, fattening into waddling gluttony. When it seemed it must burst or collapse, it suddenly reared back, giving a little cry—it needed something to imprint to.

Hmi'dro put his son down in front of the infant Winged One. They gazed at each other for a moment, there in that pile of tiny shredded corpses; then the little Winged One squirmed with delight and the baby cooed. Something ran over his foot, and he looked down to see a young dreamsnake slithering to join them.

It seemed to him that from here, he knew what must be done, ultimately, in every detail, across the next fifty years or more—and that he existed for no other purpose.

But for right now, he needed to find food for F'tharu, Jredt, and Altildathkereethno, to build a fire to warm them, to bury the bodies of their mothers. . . .

He turned to it; while he did it, he thought of nothing else. Later, there would be thrones to claim, battles to wage, rebellions to put down . . . but that was later, and so it was not present in his mind now. He made sure the children were comfortable and warm enough together, then went out to look for food.

15

"WELL," CLIO BEGAN, slowly, after Thingach-ganderook and Kuf had gone, "I'm not sure whether that just made everything clear, or everything hopeless."

Hauskyld nodded. "I'd be hard pressed to say which, myself. But first things first—let's get a version of that transcribed." He reached into the pack and pulled out a small rectangular brown block.

"I thought those were emergency rations," she said.

"They probably taste better than our emergency rations, but no. They're one-time recorders. Once I push the thumbspot, they record for ninety minutes. After that, the recording's indelible—you could throw one of these into a blast furnace and break it out of a solid pig, and the recording would still be there."

"How do you play them back?"

"Takes elaborate equipment. In fact, the only rig for it on the planet got smashed a couple of years ago. But at least this way, even if the Templars come smashing in, somebody might find this block and get something out of it."

"Cheerful thought," she noted. "Okay. Do we have to talk into it?"

"Nope. Just talk. It'll pick up a whisper out to six meters. First I'll give an identifying header, then we'll both tell the story, correcting each other as we go.

Ready?" She nodded; he pressed the thumbspot, which turned pale blue. "Reporting here are Hauskyld Gomez, First Xenist, Randall Contact Expedition, and Clio Yeremenko, Acting Second Xenist impressed under the Unauthorized Travellers Codicils. Header voiceprint should be benchmarked Gomez, Hauskyld. Date is—"

He finished the header and they launched into the story, correcting each other occasionally when an interpretation would creep in to overlay the basic account, but otherwise agreeing perfectly. "Observation not part of story," Clio interjected at one point. "I am having the peculiar sensation of remembering this account through the viewpoints of various participants, rather than recounting it as it was told to me. It is clear that the Silent Ones—that is, the handsnakes—are able to fully transfer memory, or at least vivid pseudomemory. End of observation."

"First Xenist concurs," Hauskyld added. "Completely. Story continues . . ."

They went on, finally ending with the last memories, taken by Altildathkereethno from Hmi'dro, of the formation of the first triple. "Stated period since the events of the account, twenty-one handsnake generations," Hauskyld added. "Based on the absence of Randallans over one hundred and ten Randallan years of age, and assuming the prevalance of mutual suicide would mean few griffins or handsnakes above that age, we would estimate a maximum of 2100 Randallan years, minimum around 1600. That would convert to between 1050 and 1400 Standard years. In brief, the period of cultural transformation to the configuration represented by this story is well beyond the reach of living memory."

"Though living memory is a somewhat different concept on Randall than it is elsewhere," Clio put in.

"First Xenist concurs. Other observations. Possibility of direct observation of a primary religious/cultural mythic event, assuming that handsnake memory copies are accurate, opens up a huge range of research. It's as if we had a record of all the perceptions of one of Mohammed's followers. Any other notes, Second Xenist?"

Clio thought a moment. "Observation. The peculiarly wide range of periods of Randall's moons—Tristan's synodic period is only half a local day, while Mark's is more than half a local year—seems to have led to a strong early development of mathematics. Yet technology here is not particularly advanced; clearly some cultural factors, possible unknown, are at work here."

"First Xenist concurs. End message?"

Clio nodded; he gestured for her to speak. "Second Xenist concurs."

"End message." He squeezed the thumbspot; it turned brown again. "There. Sorry about all the bureaucratic nonsense, but believe it or not it helps to establish credibility. The Archbishop's bright boys seem to think that if we pay attention to administrivia, it proves we haven't gone crazy out here."

"Bureaucracy everywhere," she said, taking a swallow of water. "Piss on 'em." She passed the canteen to him; he drank deeply—it was surprising how good it was; he had been talking for more than an hour, he realized. When he had finished, she asked, "'Now, what do you make of it?"

"Well. Um. I think, anyway, that I can make a solid case to have Randall classified so that the Templars can't get it. We should be able to get it classed Pagan, if I can build up Hmi'dro in the right way to the theologians. Of course, if it's Pagan, there will be more missionaries."

"Uh-oh." She shook her head. "That'll be bad news. Wouldn't they eventually get classified as Infidel if they kept killing off missionaries?"

"Sure. You think they will?"

"Well, take the story, plus Thkhri'jha. He's obviously gone crazy, and his conversion had a lot to do with it. The problem is that the odds of any triple all becoming Christian at once are pretty limited—and unless they do, you're going to break up that bond. Look at it this way—

all three species have, oh, call it birth-guilt. Randallan sex is rape, griffins kill and eat their siblings, handsnakes kill their mothers. Right? Now, that birth-guilt is just plain intrinsic, like the Oedipus complex in human males in monogamous cultures. So they have to have a way to deal with it—suppress it, sublimate it, wallow in it, but they can't just forget it. They're all deeply guilty—and they can't forget it, and that's a big part of what binds them together."

"Ouch," Hauskyld agreed. "Sure. And in Christian doctrine, they're all forgiven. Big blow to the bonding . . . Christianity probably doesn't have much effect if the members of the triple like each other anyway, but if the triple happens to be incompatible personalities—if their bondmates make them unhappy . . ."

She nodded. "I'm afraid so."

He sighed. "This is why the Church has never learned to like divorce."

"Would that be possible? Could you treat the bonding as marriage?"

"Maybe. I'd have to learn more." He shook his head. "The Silent People's talent is wonderful—learn everything right away—but it's exhausting. I need to sleep before I think. Anyway, you're certainly getting a baptism by fire here—"

"Yeah. Well, I've picked up some stuff that applies to my research. That meatbranch thing they were eating has the right configuration to confirm one of my predictions." She grinned at him. "Remember, you're my witness. Where were they, anyway?"

"Up on Armstrong. The North Polar continent. At least I think so. I need to look into some things up there too. Maybe if we get this war ended we can get up there—"

"Sorry to burst in, but you might want to get out into the courtyard as soon as possible." Kuf's head bobbed with confusion, bands of color running across his eyeridges. "Something's up."

They ran out into the courtyard. In the misty pink twilight, they saw that nearly the whole population of the prison was there, surrounding the one large pillar of rock in the center of the compound. On top of it, easily recognizable by the parallel white scars that wrapped around from his back onto his chest, was Thkhri'jha.

Below, in the courtyard, Randallans, griffins, and handsnakes packed in steadily closer to the pillar. "How did he get up there?" Clio whispered.

"Boosted up," Kuf explained. "But people are already saying he flew."

Hauskyld heard the rumble of the gate. It slid up to reveal a troop of soldiers drawn up there, Randallans standing by their griffins, handsnake heads protruding to listen. The officers stood just inside the gate, heads tilted toward Thkhri'jha except when they briefly glanced into the crowd in front of them. One griffin officer appeared to be talking to another's protruding handsnake; after a moment, they conferred with the rest of their triples, the heads leaning in together.

When they straightened up, the two griffins and two Randallans sang out orders. The soldiers unslung their flails—big, two-meter-long clubs with an elastic joint two thirds of the way up. Two of the Randallans moved along the wall, away from the gate on each side; their griffins went with them, crouching between them and the crowd of prisoners. The Randallans leveled crossbows at Thkhri'jha. The soldiers relaxed, not moving, at rest yet frozen into perfect readiness.

Without looking back at the soldiers, the crowd of prisoners quieted as well. The twilight mist was darkening, the sky changing from pink to a deeper red, colors on the ground fading to blacks and grays. Here and there, a griffin pawed a little, restlessly, neither disturbing the dust nor making a sound, or a handsnake noiselessly coiled and uncoiled—but then even that ceased. They stood in the middle of a stopped instant; Hauskyld thought of looking over at Clio or Kuf, but his head didn't turn.

Thkhri'jha straightened up, dropping all four arms to his sides, baring his chest to the crossbows. His breath was already drawn deep, his belly sucked in; slowly, his muscles relaxed, the twin collar bones fell to a calm rest. His mouth formed the circle that passed, on Randall, for a smile, and he looked slowly around the crowd once, not neglecting the soldiers, seeking and getting contact everywhere.

At last he spoke. It took Hauskyld a moment to notice that he was using True Speech in the old style of Hmi'd-ro's memories.

"Listen to me, all of you. This is true.

"I am one as you are. I have known the bitterness between my parents after the chthim'hra that began me, and through my brothers I have known the shame of murdering those hatched with me, and the horror of the mother-death. I have known the atrocity of chthim'hra myself. I have—and this is my great shame—survived the death of my brothers and lived xhu'gha ever since. And I have known the Unseen Brother of the skystrangers, the one they call Jesus.

"I say I have known Him, for I have met Him through His priest."

There was no word in True Speech for priest; Thkhri'jha had borrowed the word from Standard. Somehow that broke the spell for Hauskyld, and he was able to look around again. At the same time, prisoners, officers, and troopers, even the sharpshooters who were supposed to have their crossbows trained on Thkhri'jha, turned and stared at Hauskyld. He felt naked, or as if he had shouted an obscenity that he himself could not now remember, before he realized that Thkhri'jha had pointed him out. Gripping Clio's elbow, he backed slowly into the mouth of their cave, every backward step an embarrassment. After a moment, the crowd's gaze returned to Thkhri'jha.

Thkhri'jha continued. "He brought me to the sacrament that is called confession, where I spoke the evil that lay in my soul to this skystranger, and on behalf of God, he forgave me my sins. And I found that my soul was lightened; it was as if it rose far into the sky, and I could see what I never saw before.

"You all know that even before the coming of the skystrangers, we had begun to strain the bonds of t'muvam. There were more of the xhu'gha every year. There were triples who lived apart from each other. There were children who went untripled for as long as a year. And murder among ourselves had swept everywhere."

"Remind me—some thoughts about that," Clio whispered in his ear. Hauskyld nodded.

The crowd was beginning to murmur assent; even the soldiers seemed to be agreeing.

"I tell you now—this Jesus cures these things. He makes all things new, does He not? Those who follow Him are reborn, are they not?

"Then, we, too, can be reborn. Baptized and forgiven, we can again form the triple bond of t'muvam, choosing our brothers freely and then, with the strength of Jesus, be again bonded for life. I call now—find the special ones for you, and *come here now!*

"Come here! And be blessed.

"Come here! And live again in t'muvam!

"You have been xhu'gha, which is truly said to be as death—I say to you, *live again!*"

The crowd boiled as everyone circled around frantically. Kuf bolted from their side and ran into the crowd; Hauskyld and Clio looked at each other, then back into the crowd, trying to understand.

Then the crowd began to coalesce, forming up into wavery, irregular lines. Hauskyld looked up at Thkhri'jha again; the Randallan was jumping up and down, waving the arms, shouting something Hauskyld couldn't quite hear.

"Marx's beard, Hauskyld, they're doing it," Clio breathed. "I wouldn't have believed it, but they are."

"What are they—my God. Oh my God."

They were lining up in triples, handsnake with griffin with Randallan. "Look—Kuf and Thingachganderook are together with some Randallan," Clio pointed out. Everywhere, triples were forming up almost instantly, Randallans, griffins, and handsnakes literally grabbing each other in near hysteria.

"They can't all triple up," Clio said. "The place is more than half Randallans."

Hauskyld nodded. "I can't believe—"

Thkhri'jha raised his upper arms and extended his lower ones, in the call for silence. "Bless you all. As God is Triune, so are his followers, united in Christ. Be as one forever!"

The troops stirred uneasily, mounting and raising flails to ready. Hauskyld stared at them. Time split up, flowing down myriad channels from this moment, and yet for this instant nothing at all happened. The griffins pawed at the ground eagerly; the handsnakes dropped back into the pouches—they wouldn't be much use in a riot, he realized abstractedly. The officers looked to each other, once, then again. The two sharpshooters stood by their griffins, crossbows still trained on Thkhri'jha, muscles relaxed, just watching without moving.

Thkrhi'jha's voice had fallen into a cadence, repeating over and over again that the former xhu'gha were now joined in a True bond. The Randallan's voice rose steadily as his arms descended to hang at his sides. His chest was now absolutely bare to the bolt.

He stopped his chant; by now, it had been taken up by the entire crowd. It swelled to a roar—the griffin soldiers pawed again, and the flails shook in the hands of the Randallans.

Again, he raised his arms, and there was perfect silence. He looked around, and took a deep breath. Then, very softly, he began the version of the Lord's Prayer that had been composed by the missionaries:

"High King of our souls beyond the sky, we honor—"

A crossbow bolt shattered the surface of Thkhri'jha's left eye and plunged into his brain. Thkhri'jha fell like a limp doll to the base of the pillar, and lay there, head underneath, arms and legs sprawled around him.

There was one more frozen moment. Hauskyld turned to look at the troops; one sharpshooter was slowly lowering his crossbow, his mouth forming a circle of pure joy. One of the officers raised his right upper arm to give the signal for the charge—

And with no warning or expression, the second sharpshooter shot the officer through the back of his head.

The carefully formed troops burst into chaos. Half of them rushed to the dead officer; the rest turned on the sharpshooter, who had only a moment to scream something no one heard before he went down under the pounding flails. His griffin backed away, shaking its head, and suddenly tore its chest, collapsing to die, with a brief twitch as its handsnake bit itself.

Then a griffin officer was bellowing orders. The troops hurried to form up again, leaving the dead to lie where they had fallen. Behind them, the dead officer's griffin sank to the ground; the handsnake had bitten him, then itself. With a great clatter of flails, the soldiers charged forward, scattering the crowd and driving them back toward the caves. One wing rode around to cut them off; as it swept toward Hauskyld and Clio, they fled inside, all the way to the back, huddling together and trying not to hear the shrieks and thuds from outside.

They lay as close as possible in each other's arms all night. The next morning, no food had been left for them.

16

ARE YOU SURE this is going to work?" Clio asked.
"No." Hauskyld shrugged. "But it's the best
idea I've got, and I haven't withheld any information from them. If they decide to go through with it, at
least it'll be an informed risk." All through the night, he
had gone from cave to cave, meeting with the battered
and bruised Christians in their new triples.

None of them had wanted to talk about their bruises or
the troop riot; they had all been eagerly arguing the exact
meaning of Thkhri'jha's words. Hauskyld had tried to
guide them along the lines of traditional theology, but it
was hopeless—at least a dozen heresies, a couple of them
entirely original as far as he could tell, had cropped up
among them. He had pretty much resigned himself to
that—getting a form of Christianity reasonably adapted
to the culture, history, and biology of Randall was a job
for the specialists from the Archbishopric, who preferred
to work with a population whose conversion was well
underway. It was better to know which practices worked
for the local population and why before trying to stan-
dardize; meanwhile, the important thing was to have as
many locals as possible believe themselves to be Christians.

Thkhri'jha's notion of combining Christian doctrine
with the primal bond of the triples was the sort of stroke
of genius the Church ultimately relied on. Already, some
of them were extending it into parallels with the Trinity.
And as a genuine martyr, Thkhri'jha was already *de
facto* beatified; if Hauskyld kept his eyes open for appropriate events, there might be a good case for sainthood
within a short time . . . a native saint wouldn't hurt the
Church's prospects here, either.

The line was forming quickly at the gates. He had
borrowed this tactic from Saint Dorothy of Brooklyn; he
only hoped that it would work here, in a culture with at
best an embryonic idea of rule of law.

They were ready. The line was silent, all of them praying or meditating silently and without outward sign, as
he had told them to do. The gate rumbled up, and four
triples of officers stood there, facing the line, waiting for
whatever might happen. The first triple—Kuf and Thingachganderook, plus a younger Randallan named
Rha'ngri—walked up to the gate edge, standing within
reach of the line of officers. Rha'ngri spoke first. "We
petition for our release. We are bound in t'muvam; we are
not xhu'gha. As such, we are entitled to our liberty."

The chief officer of the guard, a griffin, nodded to his
Randallan, who approached Rha'ngri. "Return to your
cave."

"We petition for our release. We are bound in t'muvam—"

"Return to your cave."

Rha'ngri began again. "We petition—"

"You will return to your cave," the chief officer said,
"or you will receive a beating."

"We petition—"

The Randallan raised two batons, one in each left arm.

"—for our release. We are bound—"

The batons snapped down, one then the other, three
times in all, making a wet, slapping sound on the side of
Rha'ngri's neck. Rha'ngri sank to his knees, but continued to repeat the formula that they had devised the
night before. "—are not xhu'gha—"

Deliberately, raising the batons high and then putting
his shoulder and back into them, the Randallan officer
struck a double blow with all his strength. Rha'ngri fell
face first on the redrock; his arms crept forward as if he
were going to raise himself, but he went limp and collapsed.

Kuf began. "We petition for our—"

In a fury, the Randallan officer spun and beat hard at
Kuf's head, hitting him over and over. Kuf's eyeridges
went white with rage, but he did not raise his beak. He
tried to keep reciting the message under the hail of baton

blows, but the Randallan grabbed his beak and held it closed with one hand as he swung the batons again and again, beating a sick tattoo on Kuf's skull. Without another sound, Kuf sank to the ground. The Randallan officer stood over him, panting with exertion, fur all standing straight up.

Emerging from Kuf's pouch, Thingachganderook stretched across the inert bodies. Unable to speak audibly, and easily killed by a beating, the handsnakes could not participate directly. Instead, they went to the line with the other members of their triples, sharing in the fear and, after the beating, easing the pain and trauma.

The griffin officer scanned the long line. "You will all return to your caves now. These will be taken care of."

The second triple advanced to the prostrate bodies of Kuf and Rha'ngri. This time the griffin began. "We petition for our—"

The Randallan officer leaped forward and hit him, once, twice, many times, until he fell forward, lying across Rha'ngri's feet.

"We insist on our rights as prisoners. It is our right to have our petition heard through to the end, by the declaration of the High King himself," the Randallan of the Christian triple said, quietly and firmly.

The griffin officer's eye ridges went stark white, but he said, "You are right, of course." He turned to the Randallan member of his own triple and said, "You will refrain from the use of force until we have heard the entire petition." The handsnake suddenly emerged from his pouch and slithered around to the other officers, touching all of them in turn before returning to the pouch. Two of the triples turned and rushed off; the other triple stayed with their commander.

The commander looked around once, clacking his beak in anger, then turned back to the Randallan in front of him. "And what is your petition?"

"We petition for our release. We are bound in t'muvam; we are not xhu'gha. As such, we are entitled to our liberty."

The commander sat down, brushing his face with his hand for all the world like a big winged cat cleaning his face. The two Randallan officers stepped forward and beat the petitioner senseless, the blows coming fast, in a burst of fierce drumming, followed by the soft thud of their victim hitting the redrock and the little sigh as the air whistled out of his lungs.

The two Randallan officers dragged him to the side of the gate, then returned and dragged Rha'ngri over beside him. The two unconscious griffins took longer, and the griffin officers had to help, but they eventually got them moved over to lay next to the other petitioners.

The next triple stepped up to recite the petition; the griffin and Randallan were given the commander's bored attention, then beaten unconscious and dragged to the side. And the next triple stepped up.

There were sixty triples in the line. At the ninth one, a party of eight triples of soldiers showed up, forming a line behind the commander. Two triples of soldiers came up to flank the griffin; he nodded to the next triple in the line of petitioners.

Again they came forward; again they recited the petition. The two triples of soldiers administered the beating and dragged them away, this time hauling them off to their caves. Two more triples of soldiers stepped up; the commander nodded again.

"They seem to have the system down," Clio said. She looked as if she were going to vomit. "How long does this have to go on?"

"Till we lose nerve, or they give us a hearing on the petition—or till we run out of bodies."

"We'll run out before they do," she pointed out. "Look—their first triples are already coming back through the line."

"There's always the possibility of a mutiny. This isn't

exactly usual soldierly duty—some of them are bound to
object sooner or later."

"How soon?"

He shrugged.

"Did you know how bad the odds were when you
talked them into doing this?"

Hauskyld glared at her irritably. "I didn't 'talk them
into' anything."

"Would they be doing this without you?"

"Do you have any better ideas? I'm just trying to save
them from the Templars."

"Oh. I forgot." She turned and went back to their cave.
He thought of running after her, but it was vital that the
petitioners in line should not see him even appearing to
desert them. He stayed.

Petition blended into petition, and beating into beating. Once, a triple of soldiers balked, and was allowed to
leave; three times, triples panicked and fled rather than
face the clubs. But otherwise, things proceeded regularly
and neatly. There were only four petitioning triples left
when the messenger triple—griffin panting from the fast
flight, Randallan clinging desperately to its neck as they
flapped frantically to the ground in a steep dive, rolling
off into a somersault at the last second—thumped down
to join the commander. The handsnake slithered out,
touching all three members of the commander's triple;
they stood still for a moment. Then the commander
nodded a dismissal to the messengers, who walked back
through the gates and out of sight.

He gave an order, too low for Hauskyld to hear, and
the soldiers flanking him fell back into the line behind
him. The next petitioners advanced.

"We petition for our release. We are bound in t'muvam; we are not xhu'gha. As such, we are entitled to our
liberty."

"Your petition is to be considered by the High King six
days from now. You will please choose a delegation to
present it to him, of no more than three of these so-called

triples. In addition, you will detail two of the xhu'gha griffins to carry the Terran prisoners with you. We require parole of all prisoners. Ten triples of soldiers and ourselves will escort your representatives. We will depart tomorrow morning. These are the orders of the High King; understand and comply."

"I am honored to receive His Serenity's orders and shall comply regardless of cost to me," the Randallan and the griffin responded together.

The line of petitioners broke up, some of them returning to the caves, others heading for Hauskyld. With an expression that Hauskyld took a moment to recognize as disgust, the commander turned back and gave his orders. The little column of soldiers departed quietly, in poor order, as if they were slinking away from a crime. The commander stayed till they had all gone, then turned and went out; the gate came down with a crash.

Hauskyld looked up at the sky and realized that he had been standing here for almost three hours. He let out a long sigh, feeling almost dizzy. To the small group around him, he said, "We'll meet about it tonight." Before they could say more he was walking into his cave.

Clio was sitting there on the edge of the tub, staring at the wall.

"We've got it," he said. "We meet with the High King in six days."

"Oh. So it worked."

"I guess." He sat down. "I'm sorry that you're angry."

"What if we had just asked and waited?" she asked. "Why did we have to do this?"

"Time's short, and we need all of it to talk. And we can't be sure they wouldn't have ignored the petition."

She nodded, slowly. "How many beatings were there?"

"More than a hundred, counting each triple as two." He sighed. "I'm sorry. It seemed the best way to me."

"It might have been," she said. "I'm sorry, too. You'd think that a good Communist would know that the end justifies the means, but I just can't see it that way. What's going to happen to these people?"

He thought for a long while, but he had no answer; in fact, it didn't seem like a question for a xenist at all. He said so. She agreed, but she still didn't talk much that evening.

17

THE SPENS DESERT was on the western side of Fourmarys, the biggest continent on Randall; on most other worlds it would not have been a desert at all, but Randall had no grasses, a fact which seemed to fascinate Clio. Hauskyld could see some interest in the fact—it was odd to look down on scrub and cactus country when there were obvious flowing rivers and pools of standing water below—but his own interest was much more narrowly focused: he was airsick.

Griffin flight was nothing like being in an airplane. The dense, high-viscosity air of Randall, and the lower surface gravity, made flight possible at much lower expenditures of energy per unit mass, but griffins still ate three or four times what a Terran horse did daily, and carrying passengers they could only remain aloft for an hour and a half, even when thermals were favorable. Thus, a griffin ride involved a great number of swooping stops for food, and a lot of flapping in between, and by the third swoop, Hauskyld was reduced to simply hanging onto his griffin until the last moment, then letting himself fall to the ground. He hoped he had made a favorable impression by not throwing up until he reached the ground, but he doubted it.

Minutes later, bruised and shaken, he would have to summon his strength to run alongside Thwov and mount at the moment of takeoff; twice he had jumped too late, ending up in a heap on the ground and forcing Thwov to circle back and try again.

Clio, on the other hand, was disgustingly cheerful and appeared to be enjoying every moment of it. "Any of the emergency rations contain ginger?" she asked at the next landing. "It's a pretty good antinauseant."

Whoever had designed the medical kit had apparently not anticipated airsickness, and none of the emergency rations contained ginger. But by late afternoon Hauskyld was beginning to feel better anyway. He decided that he was getting accustomed to the process.

Thwov, the griffin he was riding, tried to distract him with conversation. At first that almost made it worse, since the griffin could speak only on the exhale that accompanied a downstroke, or while gliding, and the rhythm of his speech kept bringing Hauskyld's attention back to the rhythm of the flight. Eventually, though, he became interested enough to forget his stomach. Thwov was from a fishing clan from the east coast of Doolan near the equator, an area Hauskyld had not gotten to visit before the war broke out. Randall had never developed much in the way of boats—there were flyable straits between the continents, and even in the old pre-tripling days, the occasional Randallans travelling between continents had hired griffins to carry them. Fishing was done with drag nets towed behind griffins, the Randallan sitting facing backward to work the net.

"How long had that been going on?" Hauskyld asked. "It sounds like it wouldn't have been possible before tripling."

Thwov snorted a disagreement. "Far as we know, we always did it. In fact, the tripling made it harder—between us, we never had much use for the dream-bringers. They're good for record-keeping, but one for every pair is just too many unproductive mouths to feed. And we were never much on this one grabber, one rider rule either; whenever there aren't Royal agents around, we just switch off any old way that works. Otherwise you get all these stupid situations where you can't fish to feed yourself because your grabber has a broken arm—

"Hang on—I see some ripe fruit below, and I'm going to dive down for some. If you'll signal the guards . . ."

Hauskyld made a fist with his left hand, raised it over-head and circled it, then slashed an open hand down at the tiny patch of green below. Immediately one of the guard triples detached and joined them in their slow, spiralling glide down to it.

The little oasis wasn't much more than a few big pud-dles with a fruit tree, but it was spring-fed and probably seldom, if ever, went dry. Hauskyld climbed the tree to pull down fruit; the Randallan guard joined him. For a while, they simply dropped the fruit to the griffins below, picking as quickly as they could while Thwov and the guard griffin gobbled eagerly.

"You might want to grab one for yourself," Xith'da said conversationally. "They're good."

"I might have some trouble hanging onto it."

The Randallan whistled his amusement. "So. Of course. You've never ridden before. You have the Child's Sickness. In us, anyway, it passes after the second day or so."

"I'm glad to hear it."

He was no longer surprised at the the guards' friendli-ness; because there had been only one sovereign for more than ten generations, it would not occur to anyone to violate parole given to the High King—the only possible consequence was outlawry and execution on sight. Even the guards were mainly ceremonial, serving as some de-terrent to bandits and as witnesses against any accusation of violation of parole.

The griffins had at last finished off the fruit; Hauskyld and the guard climbed down and waited beside the grif-fins.

"Oof. Takeoff from the ground," Thwov muttered. "No cliffs handy and nothing we can climb."

Derf, the guard griffin, snorted agreement; then all of them were racing along side by side, the griffins' wings tucked while they gained speed in their gallop, then abruptly open and beating hard a scant quarter meter behind the Terran and the Randallan. As Thwov sprang,

Hauskyld leaped into the harness on his back, grabbing the leather handles near his thighs and sticking his feet into the stirrups along Thwov's long neck, bracing himself against the sharp stall. The two griffins swung upward into the sky, separating to give each other maneuvering room. Xith'da waved a signal; Derf would lead.

Hauskyld waved an acknowledgement and settled into the position that was most comfortable for griffin and rider, sitting directly between the two big wings with his feet extended forward into the neck harness and his hands resting loosely on the grab straps. He looked around with some interest. The bushes and scrub were growing more abundant and brighter green; the land was rising a little, as they approached the continental divide that they would cross in two more days.

He was no longer sick or even uncomfortable; he regretted not having eaten the fruit. He sat with perfect, automatic balance on Thwov's broad back, taking in all the redrock desert stretching to the horizon below him. He had seen badlands desert before, but Randall's was different—less carved and more rounded, as if the deserts of other worlds had been partially melted like cake frosting in the rain. Randall's acid precipitation ate at the soft sedimentary rocks more efficiently but with less force, because lower gravity and higher air density sharply limited terminal velocities.

Griffin flight at this altitude gave barely any sensation of movement. Instead, it was as if he were pleasantly rising and falling in a stationary place in the sky. He looked around again, at the red desert speckled with little green marshy spots and wound with long green lines of rivers. The distant mountains rolled low and crumbly on the horizon, their darker, bluer basalt contrasting with the redrock stretching toward them. The next time they descended, he ate heartily.

18

AFTER THE FIRST day, the journey fell into an easy rhythm—up early, a quick cold meal while the griffins gorged, then off into the sky for the long day's flight, broken only by Thwov's occasional swoops down for food. Now that he was over the Child's Sickness, Hauskyld had come to love the trip. Thwov turned out to be an excellent guide, and as they wove back and forth, making their way up the passes through the Raven Range, Hauskyld began to get a better feeling for what Randallan history had been.

Like the story of most civilized species, it didn't bear much close examination. The triples had come into being in a flash of psychological insight, but they had survived and prospered because they were militarily superior to anything else at the time. A squadron of triples was much more agile than even mounted Randallans; in the air, the Randallan bows and slings, and later guns, gave triples the advantages of range and firepower over griffins alone. Most of the handsnakes wisely embraced the new system early; griffins and Randallans who preferred the old ways were wiped out in a series of bloody wars, the last traditional kingdoms falling about two hundred Randallan years after Hmi'dro.

The great crusades of the triples had worked other changes as well. War had been a seasonal, ceremonial, professional matter before; Hmi'dro had simultaneously invented, in effect, the jihad and the nation in arms, and the deadly struggle had brought forth crossbows and nitroglycerin.

Below them, Thwov pointed out the Pass of Rusted Iron—the Randallan name for it, since only the major features had been given Terran names from the first orbital survey maps. "That was one of the last big battles. It's called that because they just left the enemy dead on the field with their weapons; for hundreds of years afterwards, from the heights, you could see the red patches where the last groups made their stands."

"They were Randallans then?"

"Probably more than half of them. In the last wars the xhu'gha of all sorts were allied. You might say Hmi'dro brought everyone together, whether they liked it or not. "Look—berries. Why don't you signal a guard?"

Hauskyld raised his arm and in a few moments they were plunging down toward the berry patch on one of the mesas within the gorge. There was no experience like this anywhere, he decided; no other known species had flying steeds of any sort, let alone intelligent ones. He leaned into the dive, exhilarated by the wind whipping across his face.

That night in camp, Captain G'tru announced, "We'll be at the High Kings' camp before noon tomorrow. At that time we'll be turning over the petitioners to other guards. I want to congratulate the prisoners on their admirable deportment, and to wish them luck in their petition."

"I'm sure he'd be just as cordial carrying out a death sentence," Clio whispered in Hauskyld's ear. That night, when everyone but the sentries had gone to sleep, she rolled over and touched him on the shoulder, bringing her face close to his neck. Silently, he hugged her. They copulated hard and fast, as if they were strangers angry at each other.

19

FOR THE FIRST couple of years on Randall, Terran xenists had thought that Phmi'phtar must be the capital city. It was shortly before the war broke out that one of Hauskyld's juniors—what had his name been? He had died in the first attacks—had worked out that it was simply the name of wherever the High King happened to be—or the High *Kings*, as Hauskyld had come to realize. The Terrans might have caught on much sooner if True Speech had had plurals in the honorific.

Even if it was not a true city, normally Phmi'phtar was an impressive place. The High Kings' entourage included a "baggage train" of over two hundred triples, two squadrons of lancers, and a squadron each of musketeers, pikemen/grenadiers, and crossbowmen, plus a "life peerage" that added up to about eighty more triples— some for meritorious service, some for connections to leaders of important bands. With just over 1,300 mouths to feed, Phmi'phtar must normally be far and away the largest population concentration on the planet; now, of course, it was dwarfed by the great camps ringing the Terran fort.

The High Kings by tradition held council only after dark. Theoretically this was because the High Kings had to forage for their own food like everyone else—the whole planet seemed to work like one small town and in fact, "High Kings" might not have been as good a translation as "Most Important of the Socially Prominent Triples."

The High Kings fostered the egalitarian illusion by nominal foraging, but in practice, everyone in Phmi'phtar made daily "gifts"—gifts of food and goods to the High Kings which they had gotten in turn from friends, relatives, and old comrades in other bands. Since, in normal times, the High Kings weren't much more than a combined Supreme Court and Chief of Police, empowered to make up the law as they went—as long as they didn't annoy the peerage enough to be deposed—the regular gift-giving sufficed as the tax structure.

"The rates are low, and compliance must be problematic, but they've got a whole planet to draw from and there's a status bonus for paying more, so I'd imagine the deficit's under control," Hauskyld commented to Clio as they walked with the party of Christian petitioners.

"They probably see it as having a lot of good friends," she pointed out.

"Yeah. Did I mention that Captain G'tru accidentally tipped me off to why they could never get more than about a hundred triples into battle right away—just five squadrons?" He took her hand. He knew he was rambling on, but his nerves were fraying and he couldn't quite stop. "For a squadron to be allowed the honor of being on duty, it has to send appropriate gifts from every member—and the cargo convoy can only haul about five squadrons' worth of gifts per day. And the honor includes their fair chance to prove that they can handle the fighting all by themselves. So even though their commanders know objectively that five squadrons isn't enough, they have to let things get desperate before they can justify insulting the vanguard by reinforcing it. Even then they get a lot of complaints—the triples who paid to be in combat resent the freeloaders."

She nodded. "A lot's coming clear, now that we have a key to it. Kuf tells me that they weren't actually crucifying prisoners, either, as they saw it. They were leaving them out to be reclaimed. Then, if we wanted the people who had disgraced themselves by surrendering, we could come out and get them, and if we didn't, nobody had to be bothered with them again."

Hauskyld felt a twisted disgust in his mouth. "So what Sherman did—attacking under cover of retrieving prisoners—that was the equivalent of putting an artillery control center inside a hospital . . . I told him not to. And then his boyfriend got killed that way . . . why don't the historians ever do studies of stupidity?"

"Too much material to cover adequately," Clio guessed.

They came to the first bend in the path. The Pavilion of the High Kings—an enormous tent, decorated with the ceremonial spears and banners of countless war bands, going back for centuries—could never be approached directly; though they stood less than three hundred meters from the pavilion, the zigzag parade route up to it was just over a kilometer long.

At the first bend, the handsnakes had to emerge from the pouches to join everyone in the gesture of submission. Hauskyld and Clio had already worked out that

they would kneel and bow all the way to the ground,
arms behind the back, as the Randallans did; it seemed
easier than stretching out prostrate, all limbs extended,
like the griffins, and it would have been difficult to du-
plicate the position, like a rearing cobra but leaning
backwards and looking straight up, that the handsnakes
used. In any case, all the positions indicated the same
thing—a willingness to be killed at any whim of the
High Kings'.

Silence seemed to be expected of them during the next
straight stretch—at least the chatter, which had been
general up till then, died abruptly after the obeisance.
Menkent, the great red sun of Randall, was all the way
down now, and the mountain air, here in the low foothills leading down to the Stavingchain Ocean from the
Raven Range, was chilly. Hauskyld wanted to hold Clio's
hand, but he had no way to know whether it was permissible.

The obeisance was made twice at the next turn, and
the column formed silently into single file for the final
approach to the royal pavilion. By now the sun was gone
entirely, but the sky behind the Ravens still glowed deep
red. The torches, placed about every twenty meters on
this last approach, were more hindrance than help,
blinding if Hauskyld looked up at them, preventing his
eyes from staying adjusted to the last dim evening light.
Isolde and Mark were rising in the east, but they were too
low to give much light through the tall conifers yet. The
red afterimages of the torches swam before his eyes, and
he occasionally stumbled on the stray stones in the soft,
loamy path. Ahead of him, Clio also seemed to be having
trouble.

After making three obeisances, they entered the pavilion. The tent walls were hung with bright tapestries, and
the crowd within wore brilliantly colored dyed leather,
the Randallans as sashes, the griffins in a chest-crossing
harness, the handsnakes as a hood. They formed a semicircle around what Hauskyld realized must be the artifact

whose name he had translated as the "Throne."

It was one—sort of. The arrangement sat on a wooden scaffolding that was obviously made to be taken up and down quickly. Krish'pha, the Randallan, sat on a chair-like seat with a low back; the chair had an arm on its left side, but not on its right, where the griffin, Vwat, sat doglike on a slightly lower platform, his head level with the Randallan's. The back of the chair continued part way around the griffin, and on it lay Dintanderoderam, his body continuing up the griffin's side and onto his shoulder. The three heads, close together, looked down from a height of almost two meters above the crowd.

The front of the scaffolding was hung with a great wooden bas relief, more than two meters in radius, of the face of Hmi'dro.

Hauskyld, Clio, and the Christian petitioners were prodded gently into the space directly in front of the mask, so that they had to look up to see the High Kings. Four pikemen flanked them. For what seemed a long time—actually perhaps twenty seconds—no one spoke. Then the party made three obeisances, rose again, and waited.

At last the Randallan and the griffin Kings spoke in unison, slowly, as if all three were conferring quickly on each word before speaking it. Probably they were.

"We have heard your petition.

"We have reached a decision.

"Hear it and abide by it, so that peace may be upon all concerned.

"We find that the ancient rules for the forming of the triples do not require formation at birth. We find, there-fore, that when the xhu'gha submit themselves to this Jesus-belief, and after that live as a triple, that they are a valid triple indeed, and as such are free.

"We urgently ask the Jesus-followers among our friends to establish, for the knowledge of everyone, the way by which they do this thing, for we do not wish invalid or spurious combinations formed.

"The Jesus-following triples are free." The three figures slumped back. To make a speech that long while locked in telepathic link was surely exhausting, Hauskyld realized; the natural tendency to have a phrasing of one's own would lead to an at-least-subconscious battle over every word.

The guards sprang forward at once, Captain G'tru in the forefront. Within a few minutes the former prisoners had been led into the surrounding crowd and leather sashes had been put on them; they were welcomed warmly by those around them. At the word of the High Kings, the Christian triples had gone from abominations to regular, accepted members of the people, and there were clearly no hard feelings at all between former prisoners and former guards. Hauskyld and Clio were left alone, still surrounded by armed guards, standing in front of the High Kings.

"Furthermore," the High Kings said, "the teachers of the Jesus Way will be permitted to teach in the xhu'gha confinements. We hope they can form more triples there."

"If one may request the importance of receiving your attention," G'tru said formally.

"We listen."

"How am I, or those who serve under me, to know who is a valid teacher of the Jesus Way?"

There was a long pause. Since no one moved, or appeared to notice that the High Kings were thinking, Hauskyld didn't either.

At last, very slowly, the voices forming not much more than a sibilant hiss, the High Kings spoke again. "You may choose among the triples who petitioned tonight, one triple that will judge all others. When you have chosen, notify me of their names so that I can proclaim their judgship over that area. If the triple you select should later prove unsatisfactory, you may select another after notifying me."

"It shall be as you say." G'tru and his Randallan and

handsnake all made obeisance.

Hauskyld was speechless; Clio shook with smothered laughter. Christianity had just been legalized two minutes ago, and already the High Kings had taken the path of Henry VIII. He was glad it would take a long time for the report on this to reach the Archbishop.

"Is there no other business requiring our attention?" It was clear that the question was ritual; for one thing, the High Kings spoke the words quickly. "Then court shall be dismissed. The Terrans will remain afterwards. No guards will be required; the Terrans' parole is accepted."

Hauskyld knelt and made obeisance. Beside him, he could feel Clio doing the same.

"Dismiss!" one of the Randallan guards bellowed.

The exit actually took quite a long time, because everyone, handsnakes included, had to back out, still facing the throne, and make obeisances at the door, before proceeding single file back up the path. By turning his head just a little, Hauskyld could see that they were permitted to turn their backs and proceed up the trail normally after the first bend. He tried to memorize everyone's position and sash color within his field of vision, and the order in which they filed in and out. Potentially, the data was priceless.

When the last triple had passed the first turn, Krish-'pha and Vwat arose slowly, unsteadily stretching. "We understand that you both speak the True Speech," Vwat said.

"If it pleases you, we do."

Krish'pha whistled low. "There's no reason to be formal in this situation. If you noticed, we no longer speak-as-one. Therefore we are now just people, like other people."

"We understand," Clio put in. "You wished to speak to us?"

"Confer with you, perhaps." Vwat stretched again and lay down. "Excuse my informality, but anymore I find I'm terribly stiff after these audiences. The Royal Physi-

cian said that you're subject to the condition as well—
swelling at the joints with age—''

"Arthritis?" Hauskyld asked. For a moment, he
thought this might be what they had been summoned to
discuss.

"That was the word, I believe. My wings are mercifully
free of it, but my hind legs—ahh. Never mind that, anyway," he said, glancing at Krish'pha, who was wrapping
and unwrapping his lower arms impatiently. "There are
many things to discuss."

"There are indeed," Krish'pha said. "I am told that
you are craftspeople of a kind, working at the trade of
understanding those who are not of your kind, of speaking for your kind to them. This is true?"

"Yes." Hauskyld said, and waited patiently.

At last Krish'pha spoke again. "Do you ever perform
such services for anyone other than the—what is the title,
your High King—the Pope?"

"We can often do that," Hauskyld said. "It is our belief
that such a service to one party is a service to both if it is
done honestly."

"There's truth in that," Vwat said. "Very well, then.
What we need is peace—peace of a very particular vari-
ety. We believe you can help us secure it. We had thought
that there was little hope before the petition of the Jesus-
followers was brought to our attention. Now matters are
somewhat different than they were.

"You are supposed to be a teacher to your people, of
wisdom about my people. I am told that you have memory of how we came to be triples?"

"Yes." Hauskyld and Clio spoke together, then glanced
at each other. The High Kings' ability to gather information was greater than they had realized.

"Do you understand why the xhu'gha are persecuted,
imprisoned, encouraged to do the honorable thing and
kill themselves?" Vwat asked.

Clio drew a deep breath. "Because, though the triples

are superior on the field of battle, a xhu'gha has many advantages over the triple in times of peace."

Hauskyld nodded and added, "Everywhere we have explored, we have found that those with few bonds of loyalty find it easier to rise in society. If most people are bound to each other closely, one who has no bonds can grab the good things more easily than others can—there's nobody to make him feel ashamed of himself, he doesn't have any friends to share with or feel bad about leaving behind, and he has more time to put into it because he has fewer distractions. So if you were to tolerate xhu'gha at all, after a few generations, they would be the rich ones, the ones with real power."

"Exactly." Krish'pha said, in Standard.

They both stared. The Randallan's mouth formed a tight circle of amusement. "We all know your speech. We copied the memory from those who made contact with you." He switched back to True Speech. "This is one of our ways: to give a secret as a sign of trust. We must ask your solemn pledge in return."

"We will try to be of all possible service, consistent with our view of the good," Hauskyld said. It was a part of the Oath of his order, translated into True Speech.

They looked to Clio; Hauskyld realized that what he had said sounded so much like an oath that they thought he had sworn one, and now expected one from her. Clio bit her lip in a little grin that made Hauskyld uneasy, and said, "On my honor I will do my best to do my duty."

It was perfectly appropriate, of course, but he hadn't quite expected it; anyway, her oath satisfied the High Kings. Vwat cleared his throat in an oddly human sound and said, "Since now we see that your Jesus-way can save as well as abolish triples, we hope it may in fact help us to reduce the number of xhu'gha among us. So we now see a need for peace with your Terrans, and it is with that that we ask your help."

"In what way can we serve?" Hauskyld asked.

"Carry our message," Krish'pha said. "Bargain for us if need be. We wish to offer peace to your people, on these terms:

"First, that both sides shall lay down arms completely; there will be no reprisals after the agreed day.

"Second, that this new kind of Jesus-following, created by the now-dead Thkhri'jha, shall be both permitted and, among the xhu'gha, encouraged."

Hauskyld waited, but there was no more. After a moment Clio broke the silence. "Then that is the entire message?"

Vwat ruffled his wings in thought. "Are there other things that we ought to offer, in your opinion? Or perhaps things we should ask that you would be glad to do?"

"You might consider offering terms of alliance," Hauskyld said. "That would help you later if you should wish to make a case for closing this world to . . ." There was no Randallan word. "Colonization."

"Kholini—?" Krish'pha asked.

"The settling of Terrans on this world, in great numbers, permanently . . ." Clio began. "It usually leads to Terran domination. Most peoples would rather avoid it. So Hauskyld is right—you might want to join the Commonwealth rather than be forced into it."

Krish'pha whistled. "This all grows more complicated."

"There will be many years to prepare," Hauskyld said. "It will be fifty of your years before the Gate of settlers arrives. If by then you have joined the Commonwealth, it will be for you to say what they can do. They can go on their way, to another world, or settle here under whatever terms seem reasonable to you. The decision is yours as long as you have formally joined the Commonwealth. But in any case, some things will necessarily change."

"They always have," Krish'pha said. "That much sounds to us like wisdom. Shall we add, then, that we would like to explore the possibility of joining your Commonwealth, and open talks on that matter?"

"That seems good to me."

"Then do that as well." Vwat stood up, stretching his hind legs painfully. "I regret to call a halt to this—we have much to learn from each other. But no doubt there will be time later on."

Hauskyld and Clio bowed deeply and backed out the door; as they backed up the first leg of the path, Hauskyld saw, from the corner of his eye, that Krish'pha, dropping all ceremony, was gently massaging the griffin's hindquarters.

20

THIS IS WHERE we find out if they believe us," Hauskyld said. Clio held the white flag up high; it snapped and popped in the autumn breeze. The fort, less than two hundred meters away, seemed almost deserted—posts that had been routinely manned looked empty. He wondered idly if the Randallans had taken to sniping, forcing the crews on the wall to be more careful about cover. Given the short range of projectiles, it seemed unlikely. Perhaps Sherman had decided to tighten up anyway. "We can't go any further without risking the mines."

It had taken them more than two hours to get here from the rock outcrop where they had waited before dawn. Every fifty meters they had stopped to wait three minutes by Hauskyld's watch and to make the standard Terran gestures requesting parley—easier for Rha'ngri than for Kuf and Thingachganderook. So far, everything was all right—they hadn't been shot at. Now, they were close enough to the fort to easily see the guards running back and forth—which seemed to indicate that someone was at least paying attention.

"Can they hear us from here?" Rha'ngri asked in True Speech.

"Probably not yet. Can you hear them, Kuf?"

"Not quite yet. Wind's the wrong way. But I don't hear

horses or anything else that says they're coming out."

"So now we wait?" Clio said.

"Yeah. At least it's autumn and there's been some rain. I'd hate to have been standing here all day in midsummer." They stood there, looking at the fort, Clio occasionally shifting the flag from one hand to the other. He felt an absurd urge to point things out, to say, "That's my old guardpost—I bet that's Joshua and Gideon standing there" or "I helped patch that wall," anything to make conversation.

Kuf had long ago sat down in dog fashion; Rha'ngri was leaning back against him. Hauskyld took the flag from Clio. "The sun's past noon now," he said. "I guess Sherman's going to take his time."

"I wish I could sit."

"Lean on me if you want," Kuf offered.

"No, better for us to stand. We're diplomats, after all." She smiled at the griffin.

"Should I also be standing?" Rha'ngri asked.

Hauskyld shook his head. "They don't know what's appropriate to you, since you're an alien. So it doesn't matter at this point. Actually, though, Clio, if you'd be more comfortable you could kneel. That way they'd think you were praying."

"Would I have to do the thing with my fingers?"

"The thing—oh, crossing yourself? No. Just kneel and bow your head."

She did. "Much better. Why didn't you do this while you had the chance?"

"I'd feel guilty about faking it."

They lapsed into silence again; the sun sank steadily behind them, their shadows running out toward the fort. "What if they don't respond?" Clio asked.

"We try again tomorrow."

"Looks like that won't be necessary," Kuf said. The gate was rising and the drawbridge was rolling out on its tracks over the minefield.

"Positions, people," Hauskyld said. They lined up,

Clio holding the flag in the center, Rha'ngri and Hauskyld flanking her, with Kuf and Thingachganderook behind and to the sides. As they watched, the door opened
and Kanegawa, the Templar captain, walked out onto the
bridge. He saluted once at the door, and came forward to
the end of the drawbridge.

Saluting again, he walked briskly over to face Hauskyld and the others, standing about two meters in front of
the flag. Hauskyld was startled to see that Kanegawa was
haggard, his eyes sunken and his skin sallow as if he had
not had much sleep in a long time.

"Brother Hauskyld," he said quietly. "Doctor Yeremenko. And—"

"Emissaries of the High Kings." Hauskyld pointed at
each of them. "Rha'ngri, Kuf, and Thingachganderook.
May I present Captain Kanegawa, of the Brothers Templar." As he had suggested, Rha'ngri bowed, Kuf nodded
deeply, and Thingachganderook coiled his head under.

"You are welcome under flag of truce," the captain
said, bowing deeply himself—a good reply, Hauskyld
thought. "I am required to inquire of your purpose here
and to ascertain the status of Brother of Mbwe Sanctus
Hauskyld Gomez and of Tovarich Doctor Clio Yeremenko."

More than anything else, the diplomatic niceties told
Hauskyld he was back among Terrans. The real questions that everyone in the fort wanted answered were
simply, "Why are you here?" and "Are you prisoners?"—
which made those exactly the questions that couldn't be
asked directly.

"We have been engaged, under the terms of my Mbwe-
'ist oath and Doctor Yeremenko's current status as an
alien resident of the Christian Commonwealth, as
broker-agents for an armistice, intended to lead to a permanent peace with a possible application for Randall to
join the Commonwealth at some unspecified future
date."

Kanegawa nodded gravely and slowly repeated the entire message into a small hand-radio. That done, he permitted himself to grin at Hauskyld. "Silly bureaucratic floogershit. All of us here could probably settle this in ten minutes over a beer." Then the radio pinged, and he raised it to his ear. He listened for a full minute to it, and then said, "Your status has been accepted under all the relevant covenants; we have also accredited the ambassadors Rha'ngri, Kuf, and—Thingachganderook?"

Clio smiled. "Your pronunciation is perfect, Captain—perhaps you should handle the negotiations."

"Not a job I'm trained for," he said, smiling back. "But I'm glad we're over the nonsense. You're both getting your old rooms back—sorry about that, ma'am, but Father Sherman insists—and we've fixed up a large, warm comfortable space for the ambassadors; that's near the cavalry quarters. If you'll give whatever signals you need to and then come along with me—"

Rha'ngri turned and raised his fist over his head, circling it three times, and then extended all four of his arms, hands out flat, in front of him. Far out in the morning sky, a dark, circling dot flashed brightly three times. "That will tell them we are not prisoners," he said in his best Standard, his accent barely perceptible.

"Excellent." Kanegawa gestured toward the drawbridge. "If you will follow me—"

"Also," Kuf said, "you need not try to conceal that you're putting us in the stables. We realize that on short notice nothing else is possible. We are not insulted."

Kanegawa started a little; Hauskyld realized that, even knowing in principle that the griffins were intelligent, the experience was probably rather like meeting a talking horse.

When they were halfway across the bridge, Kanegawa asked, "How did you know it would be in the stables?"

"Where else can you put something my size? Most of your bigger rooms must already be in use."

The captain nodded, twice, as if he had just understood something profound. Hauskyld liked that gesture—which surprised him more than anything so far today.

21

EVEN UNDER SIEGE, some tradition was being maintained, anyway—his old cell was just as he had left it, right down to the half-full wastepaper basket. He hoped they would have a decent change of clothing and somewhere to bathe for Clio, but for right now he was mostly interested in those things for himself. He dropped his boots in the middle of the floor, stripped off his grimy trousers, tunic, and underwear, and got into the shower stall, turning the hot water up as high as it would go and scrubbing his itching skin ferociously. He massaged the hard soap into his hair, swirling the suds around and rinsing it out in the stream of hot water, lost in the pleasure of getting clean at last.

The dirty alweather, tunic, trousers, and undershift went into the laundry hamper—it was fuller than he had remembered, so the selection of clothing was not going to be large. Fortunately, the pale blue formal robe was what the situation called for, and it was clean. He dressed quickly, then sat down to comb his wet hair. There was a knock at the door.

It was Kanegawa. "Come in," Hauskyld said. "Is it time already?"

Kanegawa quietly closed the door behind himself. "Not yet. I think there're some things I should tell you privately, and they aren't likely to think I'll be in here."

"They?"

"Sherman's boys. The younger Aquinian officers."

Hauskyld gestured toward the other chair, then took a seat himself. "It sounds like you'd better just tell me from the beginning. What happened after I left?"

Kanegawa shifted in his chair, looking at the wall for a

moment, and crossed and uncrossed his legs. "I think
that Sherman must have had a minor stroke right after
you left. I'm not sure. But it's classical paranoia."

"Why hasn't he been removed?"

"This is a base in a war zone, which means I'm the
next ranking officer. Sherman's got a lot of younger ones
tied to him—he's tossed some senior officers in the brig
and promoted the rest. They're thinking of career, not of
the fort. And he's gotten them to share his fear of the
Templars—he seems to think we're going to take over
Randall, they'll be in deep trouble with their abbot for
losing it to us, and so forth."

"Well," Hauskyld said mildly, "are you?"

Kanegawa grinned at him. "Every order looks after its
own, of course. Yes, I admit it would be a feather in my
cap. But I'd get the feather regardless of what happened
here—and one troop of Templars is not going to domesti-
cate the planet. Look, it's obvious that the Aquinians
have gotten into a war here, but that's not enough by itself
to bring the Templars in. Do you know how many do-
mestications there've actually been?"

Hauskyld shrugged. "You're from a lot later in history
than I am. There hadn't been any approved when I last
left."

"There've been two since. The last pope I knew about
made it real clear—only Infidel worlds with nuclear
weapons and space travel can be considered for domestication. The purpose is supposed to be just to remove
positive dangers from Christian space—that's all." He
looked at Hauskyld for a long moment, obviously sensing doubt. "Do a little arithmetic. The number of habitable worlds we know about is almost twice the number
we have settlers on. We have to keep our frontiers with
the Islamics and the Communists, and we have to keep
expanding outward because sooner or later we're going
to meet the Equivalent Culture we've all been fearing.
We can afford to bypass any one planet."

Hauskyld shrugged. "Suppose I accept that for the

moment. I'm not embroiled here yet. Tell me about it."

"I've pretty much told you. Most of my Templars are being held under arrest, though sometimes they let them out to fight. Same with a lot of senior Aquinian officers. It's almost entirely younger Aquinians in any position of responsibility—which includes Captain of the Watch, and that scares the hell out of me."

Hauskyld nodded. "I noticed there were some unmanned posts."

The Templar captain slapped the red concrete wall with his hand. "Yeah. And the maintenance on those homemade weapons has been pretty shoddy, too. The place is falling apart—and there's still a war on." He looked up. "I figure you're an Mbweist—you're not really committed to anything except preserving this planet. Right?"

"Unh-hunh."

"Then I think you should know that I want to recommend a full withdrawal. Any idiot can see we can't possibly settle humans here until we understand what we're doing—which might be a long time. This place isn't strategically vital—I know there are arguments that it's important for other reasons, but those are none of the Templars' business—so we might as well go to where the pickings are better. I thought you might like to know that if Sherman gets turned over, it doesn't mean domestication."

Hauskyld nodded. "I'm glad to hear that. When you hear what the Randallans are offering I think we'll be in a position to cut a deal—they're actually interested in becoming a member species. Or three member species, to be technical."

Kanegawa smiled. "So I heard. From what I've seen of them, I'd sure rather have them on our side." He glanced at his watch. "It's getting close to time for the meeting. Give me a couple of minutes head start so it doesn't look like we've been together."

22

SHERMAN LOOKED WORSE than Hauskyld had imagined. He seemed not to be sure of where he was; his aides bustled him from one thing to another like a cranky puppy being trained to the leash. He had made it through the greeting ceremonies somehow, though Hauskyld was sure that his condition was obvious even to Rha'ngri, Kuf, and Thingachganderook.

Now he was slumped in his chair, listening to Hauskyld's report whenever he wasn't nodding off. Kanegawa was paying intense attention, asking questions, taking notes, making sure he understood; the young Aquinians were attending only to Sherman.

Clio got up to give her report, fully concurring with Hauskyld's recommendation that they take the High Kings' offer. Hauskyld noticed the Templar captain was nodding vigorously every time Clio paused—he wasn't sure whether that was for Clio's recommendations, or for Clio, but in any case she seemed to be persuading him.

Now that he had a moment to think, Hauskyld noticed that only two of the officers around Sherman were men of any seniority—and those were battlefield promotions within the past year. The rest were just out of their teens. Kanegawa was obviously telling the truth—Sherman must have jailed anyone who had argued with him. Now he was being managed by his least independent subordinates.

As Clio finished, Sherman suddenly sat up, seemingly alert. "Repeat the material on, ah, reproduction again," he commanded.

That had not been part of Clio's report. Hauskyld gave the material again, explaining patiently. Sherman stayed alert, questioning Hauskyld about the exact mechanics, so intensely that he felt embarrassed to be talking of such things in front of the Randallan delegation. As he finished that part and began to go on to the cultural impacts of Randallan reproduction, Sherman waved him silent.

"Now, gentlemen, we know what I had long suspected. This entire planet is Satanic. What we must do is get this world back for Christianity. Captain, your Templars are unleashed; do what you have always wanted to do."

Kanegawa swallowed hard, glanced at Hauskyld, and said, "Father, I don't see any need for domestication here. The local population has submitted to the instruction of the church. And in any case the Templar troop is mounted infantry—we don't have nukes, weather modification equipment, or a pathogen-tailoring facility."

There was an edge in the old priest's voice. "That sounds very suspiciously like insubordination to me."

"I have a duty to tell you the truth," Kanegawa said. "Furthermore, I have a special duty to look after the Pope's military interests here—and he would be well served with the gain of a friendly, intelligent world in this part of our space. It is true that to us some of their reproductive processes are repugnant—but they're beyond conscious control, so doctrine can be developed to cover them. From what Brother Hauskyld tells us, it is already developing. Please, sir, listen to your own reason . . ."

Sherman, his face flushed and red, stood up and bellowed, beating the desk with his fists. "There is nothing at all wrong with my reason. The problem is treachery, and I know it. I know the Templars have turned many of my own officers against me. I know that the Archbishop has conspired behind my back to turn this world over to Satan by sending me Templars who are quite incapable of domesticating this planet through their own sheer insubordination. And I know I was sent to a Satanic world by the same people. It all connects if you see who is behind it." He stared at them, chewing his lower lip, and seemed about to cry, but instead he shouted *"Me retro Sathanas!"* He glared around the room. "First of all, lock

up this fraudulent Templar. Second, I order that all of
these obscene *critters* be tied up on posts on the wall. Yes,
you heard me! Expose them to their friends, show our
contempt for them. Let them see how much they like it,
when it's done to *them!*"

"They are here under our pledge of safety," Clio said.

Sherman breathed hard, his shoulders heaving. For a
moment, his face seemed to clear, as if he had come back
to himself; but then he smiled, a grin with more rictus
than humor in it. "Your pledge. Yours and this Mbweist's. You can join your critter friends on the posts."

"Sir," Kanegawa said, "this is crazy. I must protest
that—"

Amazingly fast, Sherman's hand slapped against the
thigh of an aide who was trying to whisper in his ear.
The hand came back holding a pistol. "Crazy? Is that a
thing to call your commander?"

Kanegawa stared straight down the barrel, his face
blank. "Sir, someone has to tell you. You are no longer fit
for command."

Sherman swung the pistol back and forth, covering the
room. Kanegawa obviously had not been allowed a
weapon, but two other aides were armed. Neither reached
for his weapon. Sherman smiled. "Is there anyone else
who agrees with this Templar?"

No one spoke.

"Then you had best follow your orders, gentlemen."

Slowly, obviously afraid, the aides came around the
table. One of them had handcuffs. They fastened them
on Kanegawa, then led him out. He did not speak at all;
he exchanged one glance with Hauskyld, but it didn't
seem to mean anything.

23

THE GLOW OF the false dawn was showing through the penance compound window. Hauskyld had requested that Kanegawa act as his chaplain—he couldn't think of a way to justify requesting Clio—and now they were together in his cell, both trying to think of something to say. Hauskyld was having trouble believing that this was happening at all, which was probably just as well.

"Now, once more," he said. "If you leave on the Evacuation Gate, give them this list of record caches. I don't think the Randallans will find or bother most of them, and they contain a lot of really important information—if we'd had it before all this started, it would never have started."

Kanegawa nodded. "And if I get the chance, I surrender the fort and talk to the High Kings." He sighed. "There sure wasn't anything about this in the old handbook."

"I suppose not. There are lots of things that are outside the rule books but have to be done anyway." Hauskyld held up the two microphones he had found and pulled just before Kanegawa got there. The Templar gave him a slight smile, but then there was nothing left to say, so they sat in silence.

The troopers who came for him looked vaguely ashamed. Just as they arrived, Kanegawa clasped Hauskyld's arm and whispered "I'll pray for you."

Then he was out the door, walking between the two guards up the stairs onto the parapet. It was only when they began to tie him to the post that he finally really believed this was happening.

The five posts held them up on the wall, arms over their heads for Rha'ngri, Clio, and Hauskyld, front feet lashed to a crosspiece for Kuf. Thingachganderook's fins were pulled to their widest extension and clamped to the post. Hauskyld had only a hazy idea of the handsnake's

anatomy, but he thought that was probably horribly painful.

Menkent was just risen, so the main discomfort was the cramps in his arm muscles—and of course the sore mouth from being slapped there when he had tried to talk to the others. The world seemed to narrow down to just the pain in his forearms and shoulders; he could look around and see with perfect clarity, but nothing he saw made much difference to him.

One guard, off duty, came up and sat down facing Clio; twice, irresolutely, he got up as if to touch her, but the second time an officer saw him and made him leave. On his way past Hauskyld, the guard casually jabbed an elbow into his solar plexus, leaving Hauskyld gasping for breath, and went on his way. After a little while Hauskyld's breath came back and his stomach was only a little sore, and he went back to looking around him as he had been doing. He realized he was beginning to be thirsty—a little vomit had come up when the guard hit him and was burning his throat.

The sun crept toward noon. Out over the mesas, Hauskyld could see a number of triples circling on thermals—as he watched, there were more of them, as if they were taking a particular interest. Hauskyld struggled to clear his mind, to think about this.

Perhaps an oncoming attack? It didn't seem likely. If it were an attack, more troops would be rushing to man the walls—but the guard was less than usual, and the few who were on duty were lounging around, indifferent to the world around them. Even though the triples were now swinging almost into range, no one was even readying a ballista.

At first he thought it was pure hallucination brought on by pain and thirst, then that he was seeing double or more. But he squirmed, waking his arm muscles into fresh agony and driving a small sliver from the post into the skin on his back, and his mind and vision cleared for a moment. A great swarm of triples—two hundred, three

hundred, perhaps more—had popped up from behind
the cliffs by the landing field, wings beating frantically
from the level-ground takeoff. At the instant that the first
ones popped up, the triples circling the fort had plunged
into steep dives, headed directly for the ballistae. The
alarm bells and sirens sounded.

But when the crews reached the ballistae, there were no
polaron blocks ready to go, and some of the bolt lockers
were empty as well. Two of the pivots had actually rusted
into place, probably from the recent rains. Even though
the first wave was barely a reinforced squadron, and the
griffins, tired from circling for half an hour or more,
could do little more than dive straight in, only four bolts
rose to meet them.

Two bolts found targets. A rider plunged from one griffin as another griffin veered wildly and thudded to the
ground short of the wall. The rest of the triples swept in,
landing on the wall itself, among the scrambling troops.
Twenty Randallans, each carrying a brace of pistols and
a battle axe, swarmed from their griffins and headed for
the ballistae. The griffins, wings beating fiercely, beaks
slashing, rushed down the wall, knocking men into the
courtyard below; handsnakes twined everywhere, biting
an ankle here, a hand there.

The Terran troops fought back as best they could with
whatever was at hand. One leaped to a scattergun on the
parapet, pointed it down the wall, and blasted into the
oncoming griffins, killing two and wounding a Randallan on a ballista. The next moment a handsnake flipped
up onto the parapet and bit him. The soldier gripped it
hard in one hand as the convulsions hit him, then fell
down outside the fort, carrying the snake to death with
him. As he fell backwards, Hauskyld recognized Gideon.

At the ballista nearest Hauskyld, an Aquinian officer
leaped up with a machine pistol, tearing the Randallan
there almost in half at close range and killing a handsnake creeping toward him. He spun the ballista around
and let another bolt go, up into the oncoming hundreds

of triples; unaimed, it hit nothing. A moment later, a Randallan musket ball smashed the man's arm, and the gun fell from his hand. Two Randallans leaped on him and threw him, screaming with rage and pain, from the wall.

Ballistae on the other walls were beginning to fire as well, though slowly and irregularly, without great effect. The second wave swept in, onto the captured portion of the wall, reinforcing the triples already there as griffin after griffin thumped onto the pavement.

A party of Terran troops tried to storm up the main staircase onto the wall, but two griffins standing shoulder to shoulder held them back. Gunshots rang out and the griffins fell, but their bodies partly blocked the way, and more Terrans fell to the pistols of the Randallans almost as effective as the human ones at close range.

The first wave of reinforcement had been enough; the counterattack fell back, and the attack carried to the corners, where Terran and Randallan fought desperately to control the machine gun emplacements.

Fully conscious now, Hauskyld strained to look around; even the little additional motion of his neck sent long needles of pain racing up his arms. Off at the horizon, he could see great swarms of triples rising—perhaps as many as a hundred squadrons, all sweeping in over the horizon toward the fort. The big anti-aircraft guns thundered at them, but without any appreciable infrared to guide on there was little they could do; the shells, set for distance only, seldom burst near a triple.

Down below, in the courtyard, humans were running to the staircases to get onto the three remaining walls. The ballistae were crewed now, and occasional shots were bringing down triples. Scatterguns, too, were crewed, but seldom got a free field of fire in the melee.

He could see most of the fort by twisting painfully around, and so far there was no trace of the Templars or of the senior Aquinian officers. Apparently Sherman, lost in his paranoid haze, would not let them out of the brig.

Someone was trying to get a counterattack going from the two corners, but the triples had already landed in too great a force. On one corner, the Randallans overran the machine gun, throwing the last two defenders to the pavement below. At the other, two clever Randallans figured out how to work the scatterguns.

Bracing their feet on the outer walls and leaning far out of the fort, they swung the guns down at the stairway. As the two scatterguns banged almost in unison, the stair dissolved into gory, screaming panic. Two men had taken the brunt of one blast, both their heads were torn to shreds, and their blood sprayed the other troops, the smell panicking them. The other shot had hit the wall high and sprayed back down onto the staircase, wounding a dozen men and killing two. As the smell of blood and the feel of panic hit the men at the top and bottom of the stairs, they turned and fled—adding to the confusion in the courtyard, or crashing into the backs of the almost-organized counterattack.

That group of men, suddenly jostled and confused from an unexpected side, lost precious seconds getting back together. During those seconds, a griffin bounded forward and leaped in among them, slashing wildly and injuring many of them.

Yet they tried to fight on. Hauskyld felt a little swell of perverse pride—but it was all for nothing, no matter who won, and the tears ran down his face. Within a few sickening moments, both corners on this side of the fort were in Randallan hands, and some two thousand triples were less than a minute from landing.

Hauskyld heard a bang on his left side. When he looked around, he saw a young Aquinian, not more than fifteen, standing staring at him. The boy had just shot the helpless, tied-up Rha'ngri squarely in the face; his eyes were wide and staring as he leveled his pistol at Hauskyld.

Abruptly, a griffin behind the boy pivoted and slapped him with a wing, knocking him off the parapet and down onto the ground below. Hausklyd leaned as far as he could to see what had happened to the boy.

His left leg was badly twisted under him, and his right ankle appeared to be broken as well. Hauskyld shouted at the boy not to move, to stay where he was, but he either didn't hear or wouldn't listen—he raised himself on his arms and tried to drag himself away from the fort.

Hauskyld wondered for years afterwards why the boy tried to drag himself in that direction. There was nothing out there but the mines, the desert, and the Randallans. Any hope or friends he might have had would be in the fort; yet the boy dragged himself away from it, using only his hands, dragging the useless agony of his shattered legs behind him for almost twenty meters until a mine blew him in half.

"Hauskyld!" Thwov had come up behind him and cut his bonds; he almost fell from the wall himself before sitting with an undignified thump. "Wipe your face."

He reached down to pull up his tunic front, saw that he had already vomited all over it, and wiped some of the remaining vomit out of his beard with a sleeve. Clio was sitting beside him, shaking her arms; in a moment, Kuf and Thingachganderook were free as well.

Down in the courtyard, Father Sherman was leading a ragged sally, armed with nothing more than a crucifix brandished over his head. A few of his young aides huddled around him, obviously terrified. His white hair shone pink in the sunlight and he was bellowing the old Aquinian Battle Hymn at the top of his lungs. A crossbow bolt suddenly sprouted from the old man's forehead.

He was just close enough for Hauskyld to see that his whole face looked up, focusing around the bolt, as if trying to see it. Then he fell forward. Two of the boys knelt by him; one collapsed with a pistol ball in his back.

There was a strange pause; somehow a sense of what had happened ran through the fort, so that even Randallans and Terrans locked in close combat paused a moment for breath. The moment stretched on; then the loudspeakers buzzed.

"This is Templar Captain Kanegawa. As ranking officer of the Christian garrison, I order all Terrans to surrender to the authority of the High Kings as soon as they can disengage from immediate combat." Then, carefully reading the phonetic script Hauskyld had worked out for him and passed to him that morning, he repeated the message in True Speech.

Suddenly the fight was over. The humans gave up in ones and twos at first, and then en masse, backing away and dropping their weapons. Everywhere there was a clatter of pistols and rifles hitting the ground, and Terran hands were raised. The Randallan officers began to herd them down into a corner of the outer wall, making them sit close together on the ground.

Within minutes, before all the prisoners had even been collected, the High Kings landed in the courtyard. "I must report," Kuf said, and flapped off the wall and landed beside Vwat.

"The prisoners," Clio said. Hauskyld stared at her. "The prisoners. In the brig. We had better make sure that nothing happens down there when they see all those Randallans walking in." She looked at Hauskyld intently. "Somebody might decide to be a hero."

She gave up and ran down the stairs toward the brig. Hauskyld watched her go.

Something smooth and scaly crawled across his arm and onto his lap. *Bless me Father for I have sinned.*

"Thingachganderook?"

Yes. Not much time. I— There was a shrill scream like audio feedback in Hauskyld's mind; he shut his eyes tightly and clamped his hands over his ears, but the sound would not go away.

The sound stopped. *I am sorry. Lost control. Will not happen again. Father, I must confess that I cannot go to heaven. I shall die in a few moments; I shall poison myself. I have now been made xhu'gha twice and it is more than I can bear.*

"I understand," Hauskyld said, dully. "I grant dispensation."

Thank you. I had not known that was possible.

"Do you repent of all previous sin, acknowledging your guilt?"

Yes.

"Do you believe in God the Father and Jesus Christ His Only Begotten Son?"

Yes.

"Are you of a species for which death is the only alternative to madness and defilement of the soul?"

Yes.

"Then you are forgiven. Go in peace."

The memories I carry must be preserved before I die. Will you carry them for me, and let a member of the Silent People read them from you as soon as is possible?

It was too much, but there was no one else. "Yes."

And he was *awash as wave upon wave of sentient experience on Randall washed over him, eons rolling over him, lifting and pulling him back to the first awakening of the Silent People, before the Great Cold and Dark that brought forth the wingpeople, before the Twenty Years' Storms that brought forth the handpeople afterwards, from womb to womb and birth to birth in endless waves, down branch upon intertwining branch, fanning out through a thousand ancestors who then contracted to fewer than ten, each a whole life, piling up back so far that there was no memory before—*

Thank you. There was the moment of waiting to not be, and then he was there by himself and Thingachganderook lay dead across his lap. Gently, he moved the handsnake onto the pavement, and went down to find the others.

Clio grabbed him by the elbow as he got off the steps. "The prisoners are all okay. Vwat and Krish'pha say we'll all sit down to a conference after a feast they want to throw. They say they understand perfectly that the whole problem was Sherman's senility—apparently elderly Randallans get something similar. Are you all right?"

He had not really been listening; mentally he reviewed what she had said. "Yes. I—" He swallowed, realizing he was shaking. "Thingachganderook is dead. Killed himself. I was there—heard his confession—"

There was a sudden, earsplitting, terrible keening; for the first time, Hauskyld saw Kuf. The griffin pressed close against Clio and asked, "Did you get his memories?"

"Yes. And his confession." He stifled an urge to ask why it mattered. Putting an arm on Clio, he staggered on toward the High Kings.

24

THOSE LINED UP to board the departing Gate, to Hauskyld's surprise, were the great majority. Apparently no volume of assurances of peace on the part of the High Kings could erase the memory of the last bloody battle for the fort, or perhaps of the early massacres. There were in fact less than twenty Terrans, counting himself and Clio, staying behind on Randall. He had radioed a full report, including the petition for inclusion in the Christian Commonwealth, but it would get there only days before the Gate itself did, and he strongly suspected that the word of several hundred battered survivors would be taken over that of one xenist, even if his handful of followers did include a Templar captain.

"I want to fly griffinback and explore a wild planet without dragging along all the civilized baggage," Kanegawa had explained. "It beats kicking men awake and making them shine their boots every morning." Now he stood next to Hauskyld and Clio, waving goodbye to his command.

The technicians finished the checkout and activated the Gate. Seen sideways, the reason for the name was apparent; it appeared to be less than a meter thick, a mere steel frame four meters tall by fifteen wide. Yet now, as the men and horses entered it on one side, they did not emerge from the other—to all appearances, they somehow simply packed in on top of each other, impossibly thin. Wagons of papers and museum pieces, whole file cabinets, rank on rank of men and horses, all vanished into a space only thirty centimeters deep.

Naturally the Randallan delegation was greatly excited at seeing all this, and for the millionth time they plied the humans with questions about how it worked. But though they had gotten almost to the brink of Newtonian physics by themselves, there was a still longer gap to be bridged before they could grasp that "the conducing units in the gate set up a hypersymmetry within it so that spacetime is severely distorted, with the time axis folded very close to the spatial one so that c approximates zero within the field."

Of course, the Randallans had seen Gates unload several times—things emerging from such a space, as the hypersymmetry was defolded. The Terrans had been lucky, during the war, that no Randallan had known to trip the manual override on the Gate control panel, bringing the whole huge parade out while the Gate was still hanging from its parachute two kilometers up.

Well, they would someday understand the Gate, as full citizens in the Commonwealth; there were enough willing humans here to ensure that. In twelve or fifteen Randallan years, when the next Gates arrived, the humans on them would find a peaceful, advanced, Christian world. By then the Randallans would already have made the long march through Maxwell and Einstein and Valasquez, perhaps even on to Suraphatet or to Runeberg himself.

They turned to go. The pulsed fusion blast of the Gate lifting off was something better observed from a distance, and it would take them an hour to fly to a safe distance. Clio stood beside Kuf and Hauskyld beside Thwov. Kanegawa with Phreg, a xhu'gha griffin that Hauskyld did not know, and looked a little uneasy.

"Nothing to it," Hauskyld assured him. "More up and

down than an airplane, but a lot more dependable."

Kanegawa grinned at him. "Yeah, but I don't have to worry about the airplane knowing more than I do."

The command was given. They ran across the redrock, the griffins beside them, and with a quick, precise bound, they were aboard and the griffins were airborne. They flapped upwards in a great thunder of wings.

Hauskyld thought of looking back at the Gate, but after all he would see the light of its takeoff, and, a few days later in the night sky, the bright white streak, three times the width of Isolde at full, dimming and shifting to red as the Gate departed this solar system on a blast of gamma, vanishing back toward the heart of the Commonwealth at just over 100 g's. Against those two spectacles, what was an ugly piece of steel in the desert? He kept his back turned, concentrating on once again flying— really flying.

The desert swept away below them. Hauskyld knew he was happy. There was so much to be done.

Part II
Clio: Randall 2902 A.D.

1

PARTLY AS A matter of custom, and primarily because the time was needed for other things, there were two moderately long breaks per year at Randall St. John University, and one of them was just beginning. The last class had just filed out an hour ago, and Clio was busily rearranging her classroom/office/lab more toward the "lab" end of the spectrum. Former students had sent her dozens of new cores and samples during the last few months, and at last she was going to have time for them.

She gave the last crude bench a good scrubbing, because she didn't expect her work would spread out quite this far, but if she didn't do it now, it would still be grubby for the new term. She whistled an old tune as she cleaned. The suds slopped around on the wooden top with a satisfactory plopping noise, and the soapy water was comfortably warm. It was several minutes before she realized that she was whistling the old Internationale. Well, she thought, if any Terrans were around and recognized it, they could ask her to stop.

There was technically one surface to go—the special bench at the back that was adapted to handsnakes—but that was hardly necessary. The handsnakes were such clean creatures by nature that they seldom allowed even a speck of dust to remain on their bench. The griffins, on the other hand, were often clumsy, and these last two rows of benches were always a mess. The ten rows up front, where the Randallans sat on stools, were messy too, but there tended to be fewer spills in the course of a term.

Well, she decided, this would have to do. She hardly ever used griffin benches anyway—they were too low and wide for comfort and of course there were no stools. She dumped the soapy water down the drain (it ran direct from there into the river, she thought guiltily, pollution control being a very low priority at this point in Randall's development) and ran some more hot water from the tap, enjoying for a moment the realization that this hot water came to her without her having to chop the wood for it, and that it would be the last such until she had a fresh crop of students when winter arrived in about sixty days. It was pleasant both to look forward to the manual work and to not need to do it just now.

A polite cough startled her; she set down the heavy bucket of warm water and looked up to find Kuf standing at the door. "May one enter?" he asked in True Speech.

"Sure. Sit anywhere I'm not washing. What's up?" They had long ago reached an agreement: each understood the others' language, but spoke his or her own most of the time. This avoided not only Kuf's inherent lisp, but Clio's difficulty in making a clear distinction between "throat-r" and "palate-r."

"I have come to an old friend for advice. There is a thing I do not understand, and would like to."

"Well, whatever I can tell you I will, but my advice doesn't come guaranteed."

"Always understood between old friends," Kuf said. "May I ask first how you've been?"

"Oh, busy as always." She hauled the rinse water to the

drain and poured it down; a little more soap for the river, which was already foaming at the falls below here. "A lot of teaching in this last term—I'm still the closest thing to a chemist we've got, and I do planetology and gaietics as well. And my research is still coming along—in fact, that's what I start with first thing tomorrow. What have you been doing?"

Kuf pawed the ground. "Not a great deal. I often play your Terran game chess with Vwat—who is old, and has absolutely no desire to do anything else anymore. Nominally I advise the High Kings, but since they now do so little they require very little advice. They are looking forward to handing over power to this new Parliament.

"In fact, it's about that that I want to ask you." He scratched his head with his back leg. "I've been approached by something called the Christian Liberal Party about being a candidate for election. I wanted your thoughts about that."

Clio thought hard. She hadn't really talked with Hauskyld in more than a year, but he was rumored to be the main Terran advisor behind the Christian Liberals, just as Andros Kanegawa was supposed to be behind the much smaller Traditional Royalist Party. (She realized she hadn't seen Andy in a while, either—almost four days.) The Christian Freedom Party had several minor Terran technicians and bureaucrats connected with it.

Irrationally, she thought she preferred the Traditional Royalists, but it was really just a feeling. Kuf was old and smart and would make a fine member of Parliament, and his own outlook was probably pretty close to that of the Christian Liberals. She told him so.

"My doubt was not about that so much," Kuf said. "My allegiance is pledged to the High Kings. I think too that I would serve them well in their Parliament, but I am not sure I would serve them best as a Christian Liberal. I notice that there are some strange things about the whole affair; things I don't understand that younger ones won't talk about in my presence . . . a feeling that I am somehow less in charge than I might think I am."

She nodded. "We would say you're being fronted. Your appearance up front, somebody else behind it."

Kuf's head bobbed up and down, a gesture that had become universal on Randall. "Exactly. I would greatly appreciate anything you could learn."

She thought of seeing Hauskyld again and vaguely wanted to just shuffle Kuf out the door. Feeling guilty, she said, "I'll see what I can find out. You'll be at Phmi'phtar?"

"Yes. Clio, I appreciate this greatly; I know you're not eager for this, but I had no one else to turn to."

Suddenly choked up, she hugged him; his eyeridges turned dark with embarrassment. "We'll find out what's up," she said firmly. "I suspect it's just one more of Hauskyld's little power games. He means well, you know."

"Yeth, but he doethn't alwayth do ath well ath he meanth."

She laughed then; partly because Kuf's Standard, when he used it, was good enough to be startling, and partly because what he said was true. "Well, I'll see him tomorrow, and we'll get to the bottom of this. Would you care to dine together tonight?"

"Surely. I want to hear how the project is going."

She closed up the room, locking the door—that was different too, they hadn't had to have locks on the doors until just these last few years—and they went up the broad walkway into town together, Clio resting her hand on Kuf's shoulder.

2

SHE TALKED WITH Kuf in the Dining Commons until it closed. When she got home, Andy had let himself in and was waiting for her. "Evening, Sister Science. Get onto something good in the lab?"

"Evening, Killer. No—Kuf dropped by." She told him about what had happened.

He was thoughtful for a while. "Speaking just for me, anyway, I'd hate to have the CL's do any better than they're going to—but if Kuf's one of them, they'll worry me less. What did you have in mind to do about it?"

She shrugged. "What I told Kuf. I'm going to look Hauskyld up in the morning, and see if he'll tell me what's up. Whatever he's doing, it's certainly no way to treat an old friend."

"Would you like me to come along?"

"I don't think it would be a good idea." She was a little surprised that Andy had offered; Hauskyld had never quite forgiven the Templar captain after Clio had made her preference clear—how long ago? It had been the summer after the Gate left, so about twelve years Randallan.

"I'm only offering because you seem so nervous," he explained. "I thought maybe you didn't want to see him by yourself."

She thought for a moment as she kindled the little woodchip stove to make up some citruspeel tea. "No, it's nothing personal. It's just that—well, I hadn't thought about him in a while, but somehow I'm coming to resent him very much. I know he's only trying to bolster Randall's case for admission to the Commonwealth, but the destruction that accompanies that . . . I just miss Randall the way it was when I got here."

"You're beginning to sound like one of us," Andy said.

"Poo." She stuck her tongue out at him. "I'm planning to organize the Randallan Socialist Party just as soon as I get a spare minute."

"You should," he said.

"Just what this planet needs. Another faction."

"Well, in a sense." Since the day the Gate left, one of the things she had liked best about Andy Kanegawa was the obvious delight he took in the world around him, but now he looked as old and careworn as if he had spent those years as a Templar officer after all. "At least another voice. That's what was occurring to me the other day. The CL's speak for, oh, 'progress,' I guess, the mod'hruns, getting into the Commonwealth as equals. And my bunch takes the other side, we speak for not losing the culture that took thousands of years to grow. And even the Christian Freedomites have their role in all this—the new emancipated xhugha, the first real individuals this society has had in centuries, they deserve a voice too, even if I think what they're demanding would be a disaster.

"But there's nobody around who just wants to talk about what's good for Randall. Oh, I suppose we all do to whatever extent the traditional ways, or progress, or more rights for the xhugha, are best for Randall. But no one wants to evaluate on that basis, and that's a voice I wish we had."

She sat down and draped an arm around him. "Hell of a politician you are. Trying to start a rival party. No, Andy, I'm not the one for that. I don't have any idea at all of what goes into politics. When you come right down to it, all I know is my job, all right?"

He nodded, squeezing her shoulder. "You suit me fine."

She sighed. "Somehow I always feel like a passenger in history. Anyway, the water's hot." She got up and threw in the citruspeel shavings; the Randallan fruit had at last supplied the Terran craving for something hot with flavor, for, though the fruit itself was too bitter to eat, the shavings from the hard casing made a pleasant, orangey tea. The warm, delicate smell filled the room; she resolved not to talk any more tonight about politics.

When she turned back, he had doused the bigger oil lamps and lit two smaller candles; she handed his tea to him and he accepted it gravely. Neither of them said anything while they sat and drank the tea, nor later when they lay together on the sleeping mats, not touching each other because it was the height of summer here in the Southern Mountains, and hot even at night.

3

HAUSKYLD WAS TECHNICALLY the advisor to the Dean, an old aristocrat being sinecured off by the High Kings, but the Dean was never there. When Clio asked for Hauskyld the next morning, first she was told he was busy, second that he wasn't there after all, and third that if she wanted to write a message it would be taken in to him. As she scribbled the note, it occurred to her that in at least one respect, Randall St. John was the equal of any university.

After about half an hour—which seemed to be the minimum waiting period—she was told that Hauskyld would be glad to see her. She walked up the covered boardwalk to the log building that served as the University's administrative office, knocked once, and went in.

The Dean, as expected, was out. Hauskyld was sitting on the Dean's empty desk; across from him, on Hauskyld's desk, sat Krish'pha, one of the High Kings. Around the outsides of the room sat or stood about ten Randallans that Clio did not know; two of them wore the new cloth sashes often affected by the mod'hruns.

"Doctor Yeremenko. Good to see you. How can we help you?"

"Clio, please, Brother. I just had some questions to ask you on behalf of a friend. If you're busy, then perhaps some other time would be—"

He shook his head. "If the questions aren't too personal I'll be glad to answer them." He put an odd inflection on "too personal" which was probably undetected by the Randallans in the room but was painfully obvious to Clio. She found herself wishing, as she always did when dealing with Hauskyld, that this planet had at least one more woman.

"It shouldn't be any great problem," she said. "It's Kuf. He's wondering why the Christian Liberals want to run him as a candidate for Parliament."

"He's famous. He's a Christian xhugha griffin, and there aren't many of them. We think he agrees with us enough . . ."

"We?"

"Well, it's an open secret who their chief Terran advisor is, isn't it? Are you sure Captain Kanegawa never uses that particular pronoun?"

She flushed. "I'm sure he does. I know why Kuf would be a good candidate for you. But he has the impression that things are being kept from him, and he's beginning to wonder if you have some ulterior purpose—"

Hauskyld shook his head and spread his hands. "Not deliberately, anyway. Some of our younger party staff tend to run things without paying attention to the candidate's wishes—I'll talk to them about it. Probably whatever they're keeping from him is trivial anyway."

He looked calmly straight into her eyes; she looked back. There was a moment then when his face seemed to soften a little, and he almost spoke again, but then it was gone. She was acutely aware of the number of xhugha Randallans in the room. "How good are your odds of stopping the Christian Freedomites?" she asked.

"Oh, I think we'll come in ahead of them. What prompts the question?" He was looking away and down at the floor again.

"Just wondering. They're pretty much an explicitly xhugha party—xhugha plus anyone who's really ticked off at the Throne. Seems like they could really throw a bare wire across the board if they wanted to. What if they win?"

He shrugged. "That's politics. We'll have to find a way

to work with them. They're not my favorites, of course, but I'm the Commonwealth's representative, so if the CF's are what Randall picks, the CF's are what I have to talk to. But I don't think it will come to that . . . the demographic changes are just barely under way, and as you say, their program is aimed mostly at the xhugha. I think we'll be able to win it and rule alone."

"I'm surprised you're counting the Traditional Royalists out of it. Andros seems very optimistic."

He stiffened and turned away. He gave a short, humorless snort. "I suppose he does. Most of the people he talks to are TR's after all. But he's forgetting that the less modern and progressive a Randallan is, the less likely he is to vote. They may have an actual majority, but they won't turn out many votes." He sat quietly for a moment longer, and then asked, "Was that all you wanted to ask about?"

"Pretty much. Thanks for your time. Your Serenity, a pleasure to see you again—my regards to Their Serenities." She got up and left quickly, taking a few steps down the boardwalk to be out of their sight before she vaulted over the rail and trotted toward her lab. Something was certainly up; she wanted to talk things over with Kuf and Andy as soon as possible.

4

THERE WAS SOMEONE in her house, someone who didn't belong there. She wasn't quite sure how she knew—or why she had been in such a hurry to get home when she learned that no one had seen Kuf since the evening before. But something—a moved piece of furniture? The sliding blinds at the wrong angle? — told her that something was wrong, and she passed by the house without going up to it, turning between two buildings and heading back into the campus.

Of course, if there actually was someone in the house, she hadn't fooled them—there was nothing else on the planet that looked even vaguely like her. This way, though, they would have to rush out of the house at her.

She had gone about 300 meters when she began to feel silly. Her general sense that there were things going on behind her back hardly justified this sort of paranoia; even if there were someone there, the most likely reason was that he or she wanted to talk, and, after all, Randall had not yet acquired any nice sense of spatial rights. In any case, there wasn't really anywhere to hide on campus either—whatever was looking for her was going to find her wherever she went, unless right this moment she fled into the wilderness. . . .

She was considering all this as she headed toward her lab, for lack of anywhere else to go, and almost walked into the Randallan standing on the path. She had even begun to excuse herself when she saw the short knife in his middle hand.

She turned and ran, leaving the path and zigzagging across the campus. Though Randallans had far more than human muscle strength on the upper body, their top-heavy structure and long prehensile toes made them poor runners. After a hundred meters or so, she outdistanced him and he stopped chasing her. She darted between buildings again, rounded another one wide, and headed toward town.

Two steps ahead of her a crossbow bolt stuck in the dirt, sending up a brown spray. She dodged sideways between two storage sheds, not looking back, trying to make herself a difficult target.

In town, there would be enough friends and witnesses to stop them, and she could get messages to Andy and to Kuf. Always assuming, of course, that Kuf was still alive. If this could happen to her in broad daylight, it could certainly happen to Kuf in the dead of night.

Or to Andy—

She knew she should be saving her wind, but she put on more speed anyway. She wondered for a moment why they had used anything as old-fashioned as a crossbow when there were good modern rifles under development right on campus. Maybe to pin it on the Traditionals?

There was one more hill to go before the outskirts of town. Her lungs felt as if they were on fire—even after all these years, her body could not quite adapt to the higher carbon dioxide content, and she felt as if she were suffocating even though she knew she was getting enough oxygen. Waves of nausea washed over her, and she thought she might faint; she hadn't done anything this strenuous in a long while.

As she topped the hill, she turned off the road, stooping and rolling to stay off the skyline. Nothing came at her, and as she got to her feet and ran on down the hill she felt safer . . . but she kept running until she got to the main buildings, anyway.

5

I GOT HERE as soon as I could," Andy said apologetically, as he burst into the Royal Office for Bipih. "Are you all right? What happened to the house?"

"Nothing happened to the house," Clio said, "except that when I got home it contained someone who I think was trying to kill me. At least, after I didn't go in, several more tried. Xhugha, I think, because they'd have gotten me for sure if they'd had handsnakes or griffins in with them." Quickly, she told the Templar captain what had happened.

He leaned back on the wooden waiting-room bench. "The clerk here—" he began quietly.

"Speaks no Standard. I've known him for a long time. Don't get any more paranoid than me—it won't look good on you." She slid down the bench, into his arms, and he hugged her.

"If you'd told me what was up in your note—"

"You wouldn't have gotten here any faster, but you'd have been upset and worried the whole way here. I'm glad you're here, and I feel a lot better now, but we need to get down to business." She smiled at him as warmly as she could manage; he smiled back, but there was a coldness in his eyes already.

"Another thing," she added. "Kuf's been missing since I saw him last night. I'm afraid something might have happened to him."

"Connected with the attempt to kill you, of course." He stretched his legs out and scratched his head. "The question is who wants to. Since they couldn't have known you were going to see Hauskyld this morning, they must have decided to do it before they knew about that . . . so it has to be something very specific that Kuf was mixed up in."

"But I don't think he himself knew what it was. Kuf wouldn't hold back information if—"

"I take it the conversation is about who is trying to kill us," Kuf said, hobbling in. There was a soiled bandage tied around his left front knee.

"You're alive!" Clio said, jumping up and hugging him. The clerk looked up, startled, scratched himself, and flexed his middle hands in the gesture that corresponded to a shrug. If it wasn't the usual sort of business, at least it wasn't his, he seemed to say.

"What happened to you?"

"The long moon is close to full, and the middle moon and the short moon were both out, so I decided to enjoy a flight out over the Barrens on my way to Phmi'phtar. I was circling around the Lonesome Peaks when I heard shots down below me. At first I thought it was a fight with bandits, but then two shots hummed by me. I dove to get away, aiming to get around the peaks, but there must have been someone on the peaks already, because all of a sudden there were shots coming from there too. I tucked and dropped into a low valley, then flew out at brush level. Hadn't done anything like that since I was a pup—and I'm not sure I ever want to again. When I finally came back up to altitude, I noticed that I was bleeding; the doctor at the ag station said it was just a graze, maybe from a bullet or maybe from a twig I might have hit skimming the trees."

"Well, we're glad to see you," Andy said. "Do *you* have any idea who this might be?"

"Xhugha, of course. Handsnakes can't use a rifle and if they'd had griffins with them I'd have been pursued in the air. And that area is only a half day's walk from St. Thkhri'jha's."

"The xhugha monastery? You think that's where they came from?" Clio tried to make sense of all this. "But why would xhugha attack *us*?"

Kuf snorted derisively. "You think that because we opened the door for them that they won't bother us by going into the house? Liberating the xhugha has just freed up the grabbers to do what they were originally doing—most xhugha are grabbers, you know, so the conversions into Christian triples will never be able to eliminate the problem. Now that they're out of prisons and don't have to hang their heads, they're starting to feel like they should be in charge—and for some reason we appear to be in their way." He suddenly looked up, over their shoulders. "Where has that clerk run to?"

They had switched to True Speech when Kuf came in; the clerk must have understood everything since then. "He's xhugha himself, of course," Clio said, in Standard. "I think we need to be somewhere else. With three of us, and Captain Andy here armed as always, I think we could safely go back to my house, especially if we went slowly."

There were no better suggestions, so they headed back up the road toward the university, walking and talking quietly, watching for anything out of the ordinary. "You know," Kuf said, "I am xhugha myself, though by choice. But the word is coming to mean only the grabbers."

"I hadn't heard you use that word before today," Andy said.

"I am beginning to feel that my ancestors were right

about them. Of course, that almost got my ancestors exterminated—we owe our existence to the unwillingness of the grabbers to wipe us out. Now, though, there doesn't seem to be the same restraint. . . ."

Andy Kanegawa looked down at the ground, hands in his trouser pockets for a moment. "I think this is something we have done to you."

Kuf shook his head emphatically—a very Terran gesture. "Things had been going that way for millenia. Truly, the grabbers have never needed us except as mounts." They walked on in silence for most of the rest of the way.

As they turned onto Clio's street, she had an idea. "Let's just stop long enough to grab some food, and then get on with this investigation. I'd like to get it over with anyway—it's screwing up my work. Since the xhugha seem to be at the bottom of it, why don't we just head out to St. Thkhri'jha's and see what we can find out there?"

"Sure," Andy said. "Let me see if I can find Phreg. He lives one street over, and I'd rather fly than walk. You folks had better wait here." He darted between the buildings.

"Well," Kuf said, "there are a couple of rich fossil beds out by St. Thkhri'jha's, you know. At least you'll get some work done."

She nodded absently, resting a hand on Kuf's neck, thinking about nothing much except how much she would enjoy flying again.

6

AS BIPIH FELL away below them, Clio's spirits rose. Things looked better from the air, she decided; Bipih itself, an imperial capital before Hmi'dro and then a sleepy supply stop for levy troops on their way north into bandit country, had grown into a beautiful city. The old scars from building the town had healed over in new moss, a brighter, paler green. The new university buildings were coolly elegant, constructed in the ancient style so that their brown and green stone facings led the eye out to the surrounding forested hills.

After a circuit to set direction, they were on their way. Bipih was above the gorge of the Kreeth, in the foothills of the Sarpint Range that divided Floyd, the smallest of Randall's eight continents. Out beyond the gorge, the Lonesome Peaks—three great towers of volcanic stone— stuck up like fingers clawing at the sky. St. Thkhri'jha's was on the other side of them, down where the Kreeth thundered over a falls and joined the broad, sluggish Stondlixh. At present, since it was early summer here in the Southern Hemisphere, Phmi'phtar was about thirty kilometers north, in the next river gorge over; the seat of the High Kings would move about two hundred more kilometers south before heading north again, as the weather grew colder, in the ancient cycle.

The first year after the Gate had left, Hauskyld had tried to strengthen the central government by acting as financial advisor to the High Kings. His first, distressing discovery was that there was no war debt to be financed; the Randallan economy had never really discovered credit and the war that had ultimately beaten the Survey Expedition had been financed entirely out of levied goods—not even monetary taxes, since no one would think of incurring the shame of accepting money from the High Kings. Failing at refinancing the nonexistent debt, he had attempted to work out the annual route that would maximize the High Kings' receipts of gifts.

It had unfortunately turned out to be exactly the traditional route. In retrospect, the reason was clear: given perfect memory, if there were only one maximum on the revenue curve, a few decades of trial and error should suffice to find it, especially since the obvious necessities—the north-south movement with the seasons and the need to route flights so that they crossed straits at narrow points—constrained the problem so thoroughly. Hauskyld had given up in disgust, turning to other business, like the university and civil service.

Now, as she enjoyed the long glide on the mountain thermals, Clio wondered if that had been good. The "modernization" of Randall was coming along rapidly of course—down below her she could see the big circular track of Randall's first experiments with the railroad— she could not shake the feeling that somehow Hauskyld had been the wrong person for this.

But he was, after all, a xenist, and he had turned out to have a flair for administration. True, it was more usual for modernization programs to be carried out by those trained to do it, but on the other hand, Otis, in the Communist worlds, had been developed by a completely untrained Naval Infantry sergeant, the last survivor of a massacred survey team, and Power of God, an Islamic, had been developed by an orchestra conductor and two cook's assistants. There was nothing to indicate that the program was not succeeding, either—the railroads would begin construction within two years Randallan, and the High Kings' official pronouncements were now being televised to many towns and wandering bands.

But something about it all . . . itched. As if something that she had not liked about Hauskyld had somehow infected his program . . . which was ridiculous. And besides, who would have taken his place? Most of the ones who had stayed were flunkies of one sort or another, to begin with—lower level people with a chance to be much bigger frogs in a greatly shrunken pond, people facing disciplinary action, and so forth. The real candidates for the job had boiled down to Hauskyld Gomez, Andros Kanegawa, . . . or herself?

Well, Andy would have been awful at it. He had fallen madly in love with the traditional culture, in a way becoming as thorough a Randallan noble as he had ever been a Templar. He wouldn't have done anything that might disturb tradition—and like it or not, Randall was going to be either a colony or an allied world, and either way change must come. If it was to avoid becoming a colony, change would have to be fast.

And as for her . . . Clio almost giggled. She had gotten to like, even to love, a lot of griffins, some Randallans, and even a few handsnakes. But for her, the most interesting thing on Randall remained the fossil record. Some elements of the Church, of course, were less than eager to dig up more evidence of a purely mechanistic creation, so the paleontological surveys had been cursory, but with the computer time Hauskyld had been able to spare her and a copy of the tape from the first probe's land-imaging, she had made up a map of likely sites and scattered her students to them.

The results were just what she had wanted; the great periods of rapid evolution had occurred in the right order, at the right times, with the right genetic intrusions. She still had no idea what mechanism drove it, but it was plain anyway that her original hypothesis had been correct—the Missing Ninety came almost entirely from worlds with intelligent life. If she could just come up with a really solid plausible theory, her career was assured. . . .

Always assuming someone hadn't beaten her to it. Someone out there might have gotten the same idea and been closer to one of the rare planets where the research could be done. They might even be already published; nor, the lightspeed limit being what it was, would she necessarily learn of it within her lifetime. In fact, if the message was not now within eighty light-years or so, she could not possibly learn no matter where she went. Just the same, she could not help thinking that she might be spending all these years and effort for nothing more than a co-discoverer's footnote.

"Are you thinking about something that bothers you?" Kuf asked, turning his head back toward her.

"Er, yes."

"Well, think of something else. Your knees are pinching my neck."

"Sorry." Clio relaxed and went back to looking at the river valley below and the peaks ahead. Ahead and below, Andy and Phreg were holding a steady course; Andy hand-signalled that they would be going on for some time, and, after checking with Kuf, Clio signalled her agreement.

7

S T. THKHRI'JHA'S DIDN'T exactly look like a fort, but there was that quality in its low, squatty, thick-walled buildings. "Ever been here before?" Clio called to Kuf, as they circled.

"No. That looks like the front gate. Do we land there?"

"May as well." She hand-signalled to Andy; he acknowledged. "Okay, let's go."

Normally, landing griffinback exhilarated Clio like a fast straight run on skis or a long ride on a zipline. Because the griffin's legs were built more for vertical than for horizontal shocks, the griffin had to kill all airspeed before touching down, but the griffin was heavy—more so with a passenger—the griffin did not dare to drop very far. Ideally, the landing was a fast, level glide, no more than a half a meter above the ground at its end. As the speed fell to almost nothing, the rider would roll off onto the ground, and the griffin would rise into a gentle stall, flapping in a hard slap just before the instant of impact. The perfect smoothness, the sense of thought becoming action, the feeling of the big powerful muscles of the back knotting and uncoiling underneath, the swift glide that

turned into a clean somersault, never became routine to
Clio.

But this time was different. As they swept toward the
gate, Clio realized that the two gate towers were taller
than they had looked from the air; there was a Randallan
with a crossbow on each one. The crossbow on the left
tracked Kuf; the other one tracked Phreg. As low and
slow as they were now flying, to change course in any
way would expose them further to the crossbows.

Kuf must have thought that as well, for though he
stiffened a little under her, he held course. Clio could not
take her eyes off the crossbows.

At last, a few meters from the gate, she rolled off and
stood. In front of her, Kuf let himself thud to the ground,
hardly flapping at all, avoiding any sudden movement.

A moment later, Andy and Phreg thudded to the
ground beside her, taking a hard landing that made
Phreg whoof a little. She was still looking into the expressionless face of the Randallan on the tower, looking
up the bolt between his faceted eyes.

At last she looked away. A dozen Randallans, all
armed, were running up the path toward them. One in
the lead appeared to be some sort of officer; he shouted a
command and they all slowed to a walk, finally coming
to a halt about ten paces inside the gate. The officer
approached them.

"What are your names and purposes in being here?"
He used the rude children-and-pets form of address.

"Kuf, advisor to the High Kings, and three associates.
We claim entrance on the Kings' Warrant." Kuf was pure
white at the eyeridges; there was no mistaking his rage.
Clio, Andy, and Phreg stood silent, waiting to see what
would happen.

"Oh, yes. The Kings' Warrant. Do you have a written
copy?"

"You may verify my name on the list of Warrant-
holders. It has been there for seventeen years." Kuf pawed
the ground once, hard. "I remind you that you are called

on by the warrant not merely to provide all aid, but to provide it speedily."

The officer rested both sets of hands on his hips and said nothing. Clearly he intended to do nothing at all.

Kuf took a long, deep breath, obviously containing himself by force of will. Clio looked at Andy; the Templar looked left and right sharply—*Maybe*. He indicated the two watchtowers with his eyes, and glanced down toward his concealed shoulder holster. On Randall, where all eyes were multiple and fixed, eye language was unthought of—and thus invisible. They had been making use of that fact for years.

Clio squinted—*No.*

Andy blinked hard—*Okay.*

A Randallan came running up the road to the gate. The Randallan officer turned perhaps five degrees; the messenger raced up to him. There was an exchange too soft to hear; then the Randallan turned around and gave an order. The Randallans who had come with him abruptly turned and went back into the compound, followed by the messenger. The officer turned back to them.

"I must beg your pardon," he said. "There has been violence here by the more traditional, unChristian elements, and we have grown, I greatly fear, overcautious. I hope you will find us hospitable enough now to make up for our earlier rudeness." He bowed deeply. "In particular we ask the pardon of the Warrantholder."

Kuf's eyeridges were now a gray, milky color; still dangerously angry, but no longer helplessly furious. "We extend pardon," he said. His toes curled in the dirt, and he looked as if he would rather spring on the Randallan.

The Randallan must have seen this as well. He approached gingerly and spoke a little too softly. "If you will follow me, I will show you whatever you like."

"We are interested in this place generally," Kuf said. "We have come to see what has come of your efforts with the Christian xhugha. Let me add that my associate" (he

indicated Phreg) "and myself are xhugha ourselves, so
you are in little danger of offending us."

"I understand," the officer said. "My name is Y'rith-
'hra. I am told to be at your disposal. If you wish to speak
with any of my superiors, we can arrange that quickly."

"That won't be necessary," Andy said, in Terran Standard. "What we really have in mind is a simple tour."

"That is hwhat hwe shall ghive hyou," Y'rith'hra responded, and then returned to True Speech. "This way,
please."

Andy gave him a nod that was almost a small bow.
They fell in behind Kuf and in front of Phreg, trailing
after their guide.

After all the difficulty of getting in, Clio had expected
that at the very least there would be many evasions of
their questions, and that there would be areas into which
they could not go, but after an hour there had been none
of that. It was as if the early hostility simply hadn't happened. They looked at buildings, students, laboratories,
and even a fairly large (by Randallan standards) library.
There were many workshops, but certainly no one was
being mistreated in them.

Briefly, Clio thought they had hit pay dirt when Andy
noticed that one workshop was making long-barreled
pistols; it turned out, however, that they were under
Royal contract to supply the army, and Andy had to en-
dure half an hour of being shown the whole process in
excruciating detail.

At last the internal tour was over. Y'rith'hra gathered
them at the door on the way to the gate and said, "I hope
that what you have found meets with your approval. As
you have seen, what we do here is to give xhugha a
chance to return something in loyalty to the High Kings.
If you have no questions—"

"I saw cultivated fields around this place," Andy said.
"Who tills those?"

"Our new arrivals, for the most part. The labor is

hard, but does not demand thought—we find it helps the early healing of new xhugha. If you would like to stay for dinner with us here—"

"I'm a bit of a gardener myself," Andy said. "Do you suppose we could see the fields for a few minutes—just see what you're growing and so forth?"

There was a long hesitation; finally, Y'rith'hra said, "As you wish."

The fields, however, were even duller than the workshops. Clio had thought that Andy was just fishing and had felt a brief surge of optimism when their guide had hesitated, but whatever the matter had been, it certainly wasn't apparent from the crops themselves, or from the obviously healthy Randallans working among them.

She looked away toward the Stondlixh, most of a kilometer away across the fields. The big river, wide and brownish-red, rolled by down below them; beyond it, the land rolled gently almost to the foot of the Lonesome Peaks. Where it was cultivated there were deep greens and reds in thick rows and beds, the forest between light, lacy green. The sky was a pale orange-pink, not really overcast, but just hazy enough to promise rain later. Low on the western horizon, Tristan was just rising, a dim half-disk.

"What time is it, Clio?" Kuf asked quietly.

"Three eighths past forty-seven," she said, checking her watch. The Randallan clock was worldwide, based on when noon occurred at various landmarks. Thus it was divided into fifty-four units of varying lengths; it had been a considerable nuisance to program her watch to handle it. She wondered why Kuf had asked—griffins had a strong internal time sense, good to within seconds across several Standard hours.

Clio saw that Y'rith'hra was staring at them. "We have just discovered that our time is shorter than we thought," the griffin said. "We do thank you for your time on this visit, but I'm afraid we shall have to decline your invitation to dinner and in fact we must go soon."

"I hadn't realized how late it was," Andy said. "Sorry to have dragged you out into the fields for so short a time."

There was something very strange about the way Y'rith'hra bowed. Clio had the feeling that some elaborate joke that she did not understand was being played out in front of her. The Randallan offered to escort them to the gate; Kuf accepted and they turned back up the dusty little track.

They were within two hundred yards of the gate when Andy very quietly said, "Y'rith'hra, tell your friends I will kill you if they don't stay back."

The Randallan stiffened. "I do not understand—"

"I have a pistol at your back. You have two friends on the towers, aiming toward us with crossbows and you have several more friends in the gully to the right. I've seen you signal them twice. We're not quite in musket range just yet. We are not going to go closer till they leave the gully. If they try to rush us, I will make sure you die." His voice was perfectly level and reasonable; he used the politest mode of True Speech. "I do hope I am not being obscure. I also hope you are not expendable, because if you are, you may consider yourself expended."

"I understand," the Randallan said. "I hope you will understand that I did not want you to be here in the first place."

"We gathered that," Kuf said. "This place will have things to answer for. Signal your friends, as you were told."

Y'rith'hra raised his upper arms over his head and crossed his middle ones on his belly. At once, five Randallans emerged from the gully. Impatiently, Y'rith'hra gestured for them to back up.

"Clio, mount Kuf," Andy said, getting onto Phreg. "We'll have to do a standing takeoff. Hold still, Phreg."

Y'rith'hra turned and looked at them. "You may leave—"

"Through the gate. Sure," Andy said. "Phreg, Kuf,

can we take off from a standing start?"

"I've never done that," Clio whispered. It was a military maneuver, not something commonly practiced.

"No fun. Slow and hard work," Phreg said, "but not difficult." For him, that was an oration, but it didn't reassure Clio. Still, Andy seemed certain, so she stepped astride of Kuf's neck and stood with her knees bent, as she saw Andy doing with Phreg. The griffins crouched below them, their bellies actually touching the ground.

Andy drew a long-barreled pistol from inside his tunic through the special slit. He fired twice; the guards on the towers collapsed. Turning behind him, he shot twice down the road. Clio looked and saw Randallans pouring out from behind the buildings. Two of them howled terribly and fell. Y'rith'hra broke and ran, getting almost three steps before Andy shot him through the back of the head. "Take off!"

"On three jump straight up. Jump high." Kuf's voice was as pleasant and level as it had been when they dined together. "One, two, three."

She jumped upward as hard as she could, swinging her legs out in front of her, spread wide as she had seen Randallan soldiers do at practice. With a single hard flap, Kuf shot up between her legs. She grabbed the straps, almost losing her balance for a heart-stopping moment as Kuf arced over into level flight less than two meters up, flapping with all his strength to get some altitude. Puffing and snorting, Phreg trailed after them.

"Turn left! Fly away from the gully!" Andy shouted.

Futile shots banged out at them from the gully. Behind them, the mob of Randallans was pouring up the road. She heard Andy shoot again, and one of the Randallans leading the crowd fell, thrashing.

At last they were high enough. Kuf and Phreg dove together, skimming the fences between the fields, first trading altitude for speed, then flapping to add speed and climb slowly. About a kilometer out, as they neared the river, still no more than a hundred meters off the ground, they found a small thermal rising from a basalt bluff and circled slowly upward, gaining altitude.

The crowd was now running through the gate and across the fields toward them, but far out of musket range, and the two griffins had gained enough altitude for safety. By hand signals, Clio and Andy agreed to head north into the wilderness.

Half an hour later, they thumped to the ground beside a stream where sugarberries grew. Kuf and Phreg gulped them fiercely; Andy, after looking carefully for stunlizards, went down to the stream and dunked his head. As he got up, Clio saw that his face was white, although the stream was warm. She went down and splashed a little onto her face, letting it dribble down onto her tunic, and went back up to join Andy.

He was sitting by the two griffins, on a rock overlooking the stream. Clio could not think of a thing to say at first.

"You're a good shot," she said.

He smiled slightly, as if it hurt him. "Rocket slugs guided on body heat. They carry a nerve poison. Expensive, but worth it—one shot, one corpse, right out to the maximum range, even if they're under cover, as long as you point it into a generally right direction. And even better on Randall—because you really need continuous thrust to overcome the high drag. As far as I know, I own the last one hundred eighty-eight—umm, one hundred eighty-two—on Randall."

"How did you know—"

"The ones on the tower were over-eager. They leveled those crossbows on us a long way away. When I noticed that—especially after some funny gestures Y'rith'hra made right after Kuf asked you what time it was—I knew we were in trouble. And if they wanted to hold us, they had to have troops down in that gully. When only five got out, I knew Y'rith'hra wasn't playing straight, because to be sure of getting all of us they had to have fifty or so—allowing for musket reload time and the distance and so forth. Even if they had underestimated, it couldn't be by that much—and I didn't think they had, because the troops that stopped us at the gate looked pretty disciplined and professional, and not in a parade ground way either." He drew a long breath. "I haven't been in a fight like that one in five years—not since we wiped out the last major bandit groups. Excuse my rambling on professionally."

"Sure." She sat down and put an arm around him. His shoulders were tight and there was a little tremor in his right arm, something she hadn't felt in a long time. The most peculiar thing about the Templar captain, she had long ago decided, was that he felt such shame at a simple fact: killing made him sick.

Phreg looked up from the bush for a moment to say, "Good standing takeoff for first time. Little awkward on the mount."

"Thank you," she said.

He nodded and went back to gorging. Everyone was upset today—Phreg was talking far more than usual.

For a while the only sound was the gulping and bolting of the griffins. Then Clio said, "I wonder why they got so worked up about you knowing the time, Kuf."

Kuf swallowed hard and looked up. "Because they are in the Traditional Preserve. By a distance of at least—oh, five of your Terran kilometers. Their permit is for much rockier ground eight or nine kilometers west of where they are."

Andy stared at him. "How do you know—"

"The short moon orbits almost exactly over the equator," Kuf said. "The Winged People have used it to navigate since the dawn of time. If you see it rising or setting, and know the exact time, it's trivial to calculate your longitude. And St. Thkhri'jha's is much too far east." He went back to wolfing down berries.

"The Traditionals need to know this!" Andy breathed, his voice straining with rage.

"Of course," Kuf said. "All this is obvious. In fact,

they'd have known years ago if they hadn't changed the major migration route to avoid having to look at the University and the railroad. If you'll just permit Phreg and I to finish our meal, we'll get on with it."

Clio sat quietly for a moment and watched them eat; then she threw her arms around Andy and cried. He held her with one arm, but there was no comfort in it. It was bad enough that Captain Kanegawa had re-emerged from Andy; the aristocrat had also appeared in Kuf.

8

SHE HAD NOT imagined there were still so many Traditional triples on Randall, but then she had lived mostly in the towns. The triples in their thousands sat on the great stone shelves of Gatherplace, huddling together in the way she remembered seeing in her first years on Randall, facing the four of them in the rubble in the center. It was deathly quiet.

It had taken them a full midmoon to set this up; many of the Traditionals would not deal with Kuf or Phreg because they were xhugha. Andros Kanegawa was trusted by some of them, but those were precisely the most modern; "the real Traditionals are out in the hills ignoring everything," he had said to Clio.

Still, they had gotten all of them together. And at least there had been no word of anything dramatic from the cities.

Andy went on for some time, going through all the possible politenesses to try to mollify the crowd about the necessity of listening to a xhugha. It was hard to tell how effective he was being—a Traditional crowd would make no noise until the speaker was done—and perhaps that was why he ran on a little longer than Clio would have.

Gatherplace was carved into the edge of the mesa; although the shelves were large enough for griffins to comfortably sit, it was not known when the amphitheater had been built, or by whom, or even for what reason—there was even the thought of some unknown intelligent species.

At last Andy got down off the rubble pile and Kuf got up. The crowd still made no sound; that was, if not a good sign, at least not a bad one.

The griffin made his appeal shrewdly, playing on their feelings about the High Kings. The High Kings had decided they wanted a parliament; what they needed most of all was to have loyal supporters there, people who were not entirely given over to the new ways, people who understood the value of the old way of life. Though Kuf had been advisor to the High Kings for many years, he could not speak for the Randallan way as the members of real triples could. These encroachments, this creeping erosion of the Traditional way, could be stopped, but only by the concerted action of the triples; as little as they approved of elections—which admittedly were not at all traditional—that was now the arena in which they could fight most effectively, and in the way most pleasing to the High Kings, for their rights.

By the time he finished, Clio was beginning to feel a little better. It seemed to her that short of an actual visit from the High Kings, this was as likely to move the Traditionals as anything. She glanced sideways at Andy; his face was set in a tight little smile that could mean anything.

That did not bode well. The Templar captain knew the traditional culture better than any Terran; even Hauskyld said that.

There was a long pause at the end of Kuf's speech; then one of the old nobles in the front row came forward, his Randallan and handsnake with him. "I speak for Pralbepretraderat. Let us withdraw to counsel among ourselves and return here at dawn tomorrow."

As quietly as they had sat watching the speakers, the crowd turned and was gone. "Well?" Clio asked no one in particular.

"It is traditional to do this for a major decision that is

not the High Kings','' Kuf said. "They will spend the
night meeting and talking, sharing their thoughts. What
they will decide is what they will decide." He sounded
oddly tired; looking at him, Clio realized that her friend
was getting old.

There was nothing else to do; they returned to their
camp, ate, and went to sleep without saying much.

9

THEY HAD EXPECTED a vast gathering the next
day at the appointed time; what was waiting was
one youngish triple. "I was appointed, in courtesy, to explain to you that we have reached our conclusion and we have decided to deal with this grave matter in
our own way. We thank you for bringing it to our attention, and we wish you a safe return."

With that, the Randallan spokesman and the griffin
took a little running start past them. The Randallan
leaped aboard and, with a few hard flaps, they were up
and away. They were too astonished even to shout until
the triple was barely a spot in the sky.

"Well, this isn't quite what we had in mind," Clio said
after a moment.

"What do you suppose they're doing, Kuf?" Phreg
pawed the ground.

"Something that they think it would be wrong to tell
the High Kings about. That was why they did not tell
me." Kuf sat down heavily. "I need to think. I am sure
they were outraged by the incursions on the Preserve of
Tradition, more so than by anything else because of the
threat it poses . . . if the xhugha of the cities cannot be
kept within their boundaries—" The griffin's eyeridges
went white. "War. That's what it must mean. I can't say
how soon, but if they aren't going to vote, and they aren't
going to kill themselves, and they aren't going to give
up—"

"That's what's left." Andy finished it flatly. "And of

course they will want to spend a while preparing it, making sure that they have the polite fiction of retaining their loyalty to the High Kings."

Kuf nodded emphatically. "So there's time, but not much time—we need to slow them down, keep them from doing anything rash and getting things beyond retrieval. This invasion by the xhugha is intolerable at any rate, and in my view a lot of other things have been hard to stomach. They need to learn what their place here on Randall is, useful or not. We should never have let them—"

"Us," Phreg said.

Kuf ignored it. "—out of confinement unless they had Christian-tripled. Well, that's a strait already flown; what we must do now is calm our rebels and reform Serenity's government."

His head swung around once, as if he was somehow counting the three of them, and when he spoke again, it was in the old, formal command mode of the aristocracy. "Andros, you and Phreg see if you can find the Traditionals and persuade them toward caution. Clio, I'll fly you back to Bipih. Then you go to Hauskyld and make sure that he understands the terrible things that may happen—see if we can get Terran help. As for me, I must try to explain to Serenity—who, I fear, will try very hard not to understand me."

There was nothing further to say; in less than a minute, Phreg and Kuf were both back in the air, carrying Andy and Clio farther apart with every second. She thought for a moment she might cry, but that was childish, and she might as well save her tears for the things to come.

10

CLIO HAD BEEN around the outside of Hauskyld's house twice now, creeping along in the shadows, and she was quite sure he was alone inside. With no idea who was in how much power in the city any more, she had played it safe, not going back to her own house. Her neighbors would not think there was anything unusual about her long absence—after all, she was gone almost every break for as long as she could possibly manage. And whoever had tried to kill Kuf and herself might well still be sitting quietly in the house, in the little back room with the curtains drawn, changing the watch at night, waiting for her with a poisoned crossbow bolt or even a big, heavy, splattering musket ball. . . . her shoulders felt itchy, and she crouched lower in the shadow of the tree.

The little log house had only three rooms, and it had plenty of windows. Hauskyld had surrounded the house with brownflower and sharpneedle bushes, so it was too thick and thorny to go in through a window.

He was seated by an oil lamp, writing in one of a set of bound volumes. He claimed the time taken to write by hand helped his thinking. It appeared that he had already filled eight of them and was well into the ninth, but then just writing down all the memories Thingachganderook had given him would fill many more books than that. It was almost midnight, oil was not cheap, and she knew he rose early, but still he continued at his work.

At last, Clio allowed herself a sigh, backed out carefully through the bushes, and went around to the front door as she had thought of doing in the first place. She decided she was not good at intrigue at all; in fact the biggest success of the summer remained a half-dozen microcores she had drilled out in the back country that had allowed her to establish several more time baselines much more precisely than had previously been possible.

She shuddered. She was still here, out in plain sight,

standing at Hauskyld's door lost in thought. No question—she was really a lousy spy. With a little grin, embarrassed at herself, she looked around once, and then, seeing no one, knocked quietly on the door.

She heard the scrape of his chair on the floor, the thump as he returned the book to the shelf, and each step as he came to the door. She would have to remember to talk quietly, she reminded herself.

After all the tension of the last few days, she trusted no one. She was prepared for him to shout a warning and bring the guard to arrest her, to fling open the door revealing a hidden assassin. . . . in fact, he smiled with what seemed to be genuine pleasure. "Clio! Just back from fieldwork? Come on in."

She followed him in. "I—yes, I just spent a while in the field."

"You're probably hungry for real food, and I'm afraid I don't have any—well, some flatbread and some brownflower jam, perhaps? And I'll warm some water—I've got fresh citruspeel. . . ."

"Thank you," she said. She had meant to refuse, but actually after almost two midmoons of field rations, broken only with the occasional feast at a Traditional camp, she found her mouth watering at the prospect. Then too, it was such a pleasure to sit down in a real chair, in a house with a fire in the fireplace. . . .

She looked around the room curiously. Randall had no real tradition of the graphic arts except sculpture, but one of Hauskyld's bright young men had noticed that the long fibrous needles of a tree that grew on the south coast of the Continent of Davy could be made, with a crude spinning wheel and loom, into something not unlike canvas. There were so many kinds of vegetable dye available that there had been no problem in coming up with paints, and now most of the mod'hrun homes had a few paintings on the walls.

Something caught her eye; she got up and looked. The earliest efforts had imitated the Terran geometric, abstract patterns, but then someone had shown the Randallans some drawings, and a rash of paintings looking like those of Terran children had followed.

But this was something new entirely. The painting was a quite accurate representational drawing of the High Kings on the Throne, repeated several times from different angles as Randallan artists often did—some effect of the faceted eye, she supposed, since the different views tended to be arranged in a hex. But there was no mistaking it—this looked like the High Kings.

"Like it?" Hauskyld asked. "One of the students at the Royal Law Academy has begun to do those. Half a dozen others are imitating him now; I think realism has come to Randall. Not too surprising—it correlates with individualism, which tends to increase with modernization." He set the tray down. "At least the flatbread is fresh today," he added, "and I think, personally, that I did a marvelous job on the brownflower jam."

"I'm sure it's wonderful," she said, sitting down. She broke off a piece from the hard, flat wafer, dipped it in the hot water to soften it, dribbled a little bit of the wet runny jam on it, and popped it in her mouth. "It's delicious," she said, bubbling around it.

"Good—I'm glad you like it. I think it's the best I've ever had it come out," he said.

"I think you're right." She smiled at him.

He sat back, smiling, playing nervously with his fingers. "Er . . . Clio. I think I know what you've come for. What you might want to say to me."

She felt a stab of fear.

"No," he went on, "let me finish. I know that for—well, for several years, I've behaved like a fool about you and Captain Kanegawa. And I just wanted to say that after your last visit—well, I felt like an idiot. There was no excuse for being so rude. And I have no reason to feel the way I've let myself feel. I've been praying for guidance, and, though I can't claim to have really remade myself, I think you'll find me better behaved and easier to get along with in the future."

She was too astonished to know what to say. For a moment, she looked around the room, letting her eyes come to rest on the painting of the High Kings. When she looked at Hauskyld again, he was looking nervously everywhere except at her. Finally, she said, "I'm terribly glad to hear it, Hauskyld. I'm sure we'll be friends again, and there's no need to talk further about it. But—I had something else I needed to ask you about."

Quickly, she told him of everything that had happened since he had last seen her—the attempts to murder her and Kuf, their investigation of St. Thkhri'jha's, the fight to get away, their attempt to rouse the Traditionals to their own defense, the deadly probability that civil war was rising out in the Preserve. He interrupted with occasional questions, but mostly he just listened intently.

At last he leaned back in his chair and thought for a while. "I suppose," he said, "something of the kind was inevitable sooner or later. Now, the question is what we can do to minimize the damage . . . and that will need some careful planning. Captain Kanegawa is exactly right, by the way—the first priority is to keep the Traditionals from attacking any Royal forts or offices. If they do, the lines will harden so fast that there won't be any other way but war. I'm glad he's doing that, but I'm not sure what we can do here and now."

"One of the things I came here for was because you have the High Kings' ear," Clio said. "I was hoping Royal troops could be used to remove the illegal settlements."

He whistled. "Big gamble. Good if it works, disastrous if it doesn't."

She leaned forward in her chair. "I don't see what the matter is."

"If the Traditionals get the idea that their threat of war is what turned the trick—and remember, they're very much a nomadic, warrior culture and likely to see it that way—it increases their feeling that the cities can be bullied. And there's a long list of concessions they're apt to demand—number one being the return of the xhugha, and maybe the Christian triples as well, to the concentration camps. When they don't get it, again, being warriors, they're likely to actually launch a war—and the xhughawi and mod'hrunwi would fight. No question about that. The High Kings would end up bypassed in the process; it would be the end of central government for a few years, until the xhugha won and exterminated the Traditionals."

She was startled. "Until the xhugha won?"

"They've got most of the technicians. They're willing to adapt more quickly. And they could make the move to true taxation sooner, which would mean they could pay for more of a war effort. But even if you don't think I'm right, if the Traditionals win there's going to be a massacre the other way."

She wanted to deny it, but it was true.

He sat crosswise on the chair, staring into the fire, shadows from the oil lamp playing on his white hair. "This planet is next to last, I think," he said. "In a few years I'll be going on to another, but that's probably where I'll die. I'm not complaining—probably ninety-nine plus percent of humanity lives on just one planet for its entire life—but I wish this was going to be a more graceful exit. The problem is that the Randallans are physically and psychologically too much like us—everything they learn from us favors the Randallans over the griffins and handsnakes.

"And I'm afraid they're on the same course as humanity. They're getting individualized, tearing off the web of social connection . . . and with it goes their sense of security and a lot of their traditional morality. It's a step they have to take before they can enter the Commonwealth as equals of course—and the same step they'd have had to take to enter the League or the Islamic Association. And if they were opened to colonization, things a thousand times worse would happen to them. But still it will cost them more than they can imagine.

"What we need right now is *time*. The parliament idea is mostly intended to buy time, get them used to the idea of avoiding violence among themselves, until cultural adaptation smooths over some of the cleavages. It's not much, but it's what we can do."

"Then we're not going to do anything?" She was surprised at the resentment in her voice; childishly, now that they were friends again, she had expected him to have a solution ready, as he always had before.

He held up his hands, as if surrendering or asking for mercy. "No. That's not what I mean. We must do two things—hope Captain Kanegawa succeeds, and look for opportunities to cut the xhugha down to size—*without provoking a Traditional attack!* All I'm saying is that I don't have any idea of how to do the second one."

She was quiet for a long time, turning it all over in her mind. She had not noticed at first, but the picture of the High Kings was uncanny. All that multitude of faces— even the carved one of Hmi'dro under the Throne—appeared to be watching, waiting for something that they didn't really dare to hope would happen. She sighed and looked down into the fire. "So the Randallans will get to determine their own future—at the expense of becoming bad copies of Terrans."

"Well, all the species of the Commonwealth will absorb a little bit of Randallan over time as well."

"And griffin and handsnake?"

He stirred the glowing coals with the poker. "It goes without saying, doesn't it?"

They talked about her work, without much heart or interest, for a few minutes. Yes, she had made quite a bit of headway; the origins of several great pulses of genetic material that had fallen on Randall were now established, all on worlds with long histories of indigenous intelligent life. But no, the cause of those pulses was no clearer than it had ever been.

Talking about her work brightened her considerably;

she realized that Hauskyld had probably been right, years ago, when he had said that the major danger for many of the Terrans on Randall was not xenophobia—the xenophobes had gone home—but an extreme xenophilia, a wish to see Randall forever undisturbed, even by its inhabitants. A xenist specializing in culture study was to some extent protected against this by his awareness that, though every case was unique, none was special. For the rest of them, it was more than likely that they would fall in love with their first new planet, however unrequited and unjustified it might be, and that first love would ache as it always does. Well, she would be catching a Gate out of here soon after the next Gate arrived, which was only seven years Terran—eleven Randallan—or so. With luck her work on this problem would be done and, spreading outward at the speed of radio relays, would have prepared her a place on some other, more civilized world. She would miss Randall, of course, but then she still missed Mars.

When they finally said goodnight and he showed her out the door, she was beginning to believe all that herself, and even to feel a little better. On Hauskyld's advice, she did not go home, but to the Royal Post House in Bipih, where a Terran would be given a room and a meal on the assumption that it must be High Kings' business. There were frightening sounds behind her twice, once when both Mark and Tristan were behind a cloud, but she got there without any trouble, and slept till almost noon the next day.

When she woke the next morning, a note from Kuf lay on the floor by the door; he was two rooms down, waiting for her at her convenience. Hastily, she dressed, threw her kit together, and went down the hall.

He opened the door only partially at first, blocking it with his body. "Yes—oh, good, Clio. Come right in—quickly."

He backed out of her way and let her in, then sprang forward to close the door fast behind her. As he moved past her, he revealed the High Kings, Vwat sitting on the floor, Krish'pha on the sleeping shelf, Dintanderoderam in loose coils between them. She heard herself gasp in surprise.

"Yes," Vwat said. "From what Kuf has told us, our influence will be needed to avert terrible tragedy. He has brought us this far; we were hoping to press on tonight. There are those at court who will know why we have gone and we must expect pursuit. Meanwhile, I am told by Kuf that you are not a bad chess player in your own right—and that, at least, is something we can do silently." He flicked out the cloth painted in the chessboard pattern on the floor. Clio sat down facing him. She was glad that none of them dared to speak much.

11

T HEY HAD NOT been able to sleep enough the day before, and, after flying all night, Kuf and Clio were tired; but the High Kings were worse, most especially Krish'pha, who seemed to be coming down with a cold. The sun was just rising as they landed among the sugarberries in a small bog where a low basalt outcrop partially dammed a creek. Here in the shadows of the trees it was cold, and Clio shivered as Vwat and Kuf gorged on the berries. She bent to pick some for herself, and offered some to Krish'pha. He refused curtly and went off to sit by himself on a rock.

The sky overhead was pale reddish-gray, and the bog had a sweet, tangy scent; summer was coming quickly. As she watched, Tristan rose in the west, seeming to jump from the horizon.

Kuf looked up. "Serenities, I regret the necessity, but we need to be airborne again soon."

Hastily, Vwat stuffed a few last mouthfuls of berries in. Dintanderoderam, who had been letting his head hang out to eat a little and breathe, went back into the pouch. Krish'pha came grumbling back from his rock.

"I promise Your Serenities," Kuf said, "as soon as we're safe and among friends—"

"We understand," Vwat said. "A High King is lucky if he ever can do what he wants—more often he does what he must. Shall we be going?"

As soon as they had gained altitude—hard work since there had been no hills near to take off from—Clio saw that it was going to be a beautiful day. The gentle, rolling glide and swoop of Kuf's flight was soothing, and the morning sun was pleasantly warm, not yet hot. Below her, the brush, broken with patches of forest, was a deep, vivid green. She could see creeks and rivers cutting through it; here, beyond the eastern slope of the mountains, there was plenty of water—in fact, the loose conjunction of all three moons would bring rain tonight, and that might mean trouble with Vwat's arthritis.

She put the thought aside for later. For right now, the sky was just moving over from its dawn pinkness to a pale, hazy red. Tristan was shooting up the sky; at this time of year, the short moon would pass north of Menkent sometime well before noon.

They had the advantage of the falling land below them, and with the warmth of the sun they were able to stay airborne for longer with less effort. The Continent of Floyd was shaped like an elongated kidney, with the bight facing east; as they flew south into the broader part, the cool sea breeze off the bight helped a great deal. Tomorrow, when they were farther in and trying to head east, the wind would be against them—

She was thinking of tomorrow again. Clio sighed—it was hard not to.

"Are you bearing up?" She was startled; Kuf seldom spoke in flight.

"I'm not going to fall off yet, anyway."

"All right. In another six hours we should be deep in the Preserve of Tradition—complete wilderness, lots of broken country. That should give us more places to hide and Their Serenities an easier trip."

At every stop, Kuf checked the time on Clio's watch, then scanned the sky. "The short moon rose at the perfect time," he said. "Right when we needed it for the more difficult navigation. We shouldn't be doing much back-tracking, anyway."

After they took off again, Clio found herself unexpect-edly sleepy, struggling to stay awake in the hypnotic rhythm of rise and fall. "Mind if I talk?" she asked.

"Please do. I need to stay awake myself."

"This may not help. I'll be speaking into a recording device. I want to get some of my findings recorded."

"Still at work on that? Go ahead. May I interrupt if you say something interesting?"

"Not much risk of that." She unclipped her belt re-corder and began to talk, describing the Gatherplace and explaining why in her judgment it was unlikely to be the construction of griffin, handsnake, or Randallan. Then she talked about what that might mean for her work.

"This adds a special urgency to the problem of the paleotopography of Randall. I do have the satellite pho-tos and the computer extrapolations from them. Unfortu-nately for me, a lot of what drives Randall's plate tecton-ics is tidal energy, which means a lot more intra-landform deformation than usual—so the features are all relatively new. We know handsnake memories go back about eight thousand generations, which is no more than half a million standard years; it wouldn't have to be terri-bly long before that. Anyway, there are several identifia-ble ancient river mouths that go back that far, and they're all potential places to search for some remains of a city. Obviously the two here on Floyd are the best immediate prospects."

"Do you mean there was someone else here long ago? That the Gatherplace was some other species's place?" Kuf interrupted.

"Well, yes, that's the idea."

"Talk with Dintanderoderam when we stop for the

night. I think he might have some memories of use to you."

But by mid-afternoon, the High Kings were just too exhausted to go on. They landed on the thick moss in a clearing, near some big patches of edible fungus. It was all they could do to eat some of that before going to sleep.

12

THE NEXT MORNING, while the griffins gorged, Clio sat with Dintanderoderam across her lap, helping him to stay warm and incidentally taking the chance to pick through his memories. There was little question that something was back there—in the oldest memories of the handsnakes, they frequently referred to themselves as the Younger Ones or the Later Ones; there were memories of several ruins and of a much less eroded Gatherplace. There were no memories of handsnakes making anything more than crude nests— someone else had built on this world before.

Is that not your idea? Dintanderoderam asked. *That this is a world with a richer history, because of what has drifted down from the stars?*

"Well, yes," Clio said. "But it's always surprising to see the predictions exceeded. I had thought Randall might have many surprises—but four intelligent species, so far, and without even having looked in the oceans yet, or thoroughly explored the South Polar Island or the more distant archipelagoes . . . it's almost beyond belief."

Not hard to believe if you are right. If intelligent worlds spread life more widely, then surely the genes for intelligence fall heavily on the world that gets the most diversity.

"Sure. I suppose. But it's still amazing. No other world's been known to have more than two intelligent species." Shifting her weight carefully to avoid disturbing Dintanderoderam, she pulled down a handful of sugarberries, giving some to him and eating the rest herself, savoring the sweet apple/pear taste. "And there are some real problems, too. A couple of the 'intelligent' worlds appear to have made most of their contributions a long time before the intelligent species we know of evolved on them."

Perhaps they too had earlier intelligent beings.

"Maybe. But then that argues that extinct intelligent species contribute more than ones that survive. Pretty bizarre, if true." She shivered in the cold; Dintanderoderam lacked her temperature regulation system, and to be awake in this temperature, he had to draw heat from her body. The touch of him was icy cold even through her trousers. She wondered idly if Vwat ever complained of coldness in his pouch.

Constantly. The handsnake shifted. *If I could make this more comfortable for you—*

"It's fine. I didn't realize you could hear my thought—"

It was unusually clear. As many of your Terran jokes are. He rose shakily, arching back till his first set of fin-hands could tear off bunches of sugarberries. Carefully, he coiled back down onto her lap. *A peace offering, from a nosy king?*

"Accepted," she said, laughing, and took one of the bunches. Dindtanderoderam curled to eat the other. "I wish we could have a fire, but we just aren't a big enough party to fight anyone off if we had to, and if no one has guessed your whereabouts, we certainly want to keep it that way."

Agreed. But it is surely cold.

Kuf and Vwat trotted back from where they had been feeding. "May we strip this bush?" Kuf asked. Without waiting, the two pitched in and began gobbling down the berries.

Vwat looked much worse this morning. His hindquarters were stiff and unmoving, and there was a blue tinge on his chest where the blood ran close to the surface. As she watched, he pumped his back legs hard, one after the other, trying to stretch his pelvis a little more, as if trying to break a rusted machine part free.

"Where's Krish'pha this morning?" she asked suddenly.

Sitting by the creek, feeling sorry for himself. Lately he does not communicate with us much.

"He had things he had to do," Vwat said.

Clio concentrated harder on her eating, though she wasn't especially hungry. Finally, Kuf said, "I'm afraid we must take off, Serenities."

Quietly, Dintanderoderam left her lap and slid into Vwat's pouch; she noted that Vwat gave a little involuntary shiver. In a moment, after being called, Krish'pha came sulkily over and stood next to Vwat.

"I think if we walk up this hill, Serenities, there will be an easier takeoff down the windward slope." Kuf turned to lead the way.

"I am tired," Krish'pha said. "I hate to walk."

"Then fly yourself," Vwat said, and started after Kuf so abruptly that Krish'pha was left standing for a moment. Clio followed discreetly, bringing up the rear.

Kuf proved correct; from the top of the hill, there was a gentle slope down to a bend in the river. Clio rested a hand on the griffin's shoulder for a moment. Then Kuf took a deep breath and ran down the slope, on the edge of tumbling over, until he had reached more than airspeed, actually using his wings to hold himself to the ground. Clio leaped into the saddle, and they bounded into the air with a hard flap and shot forward into the valley, picking up a light thermal from a patch of bare rock that the sun had reached.

Kuf climbed quickly upward, banking back the way he had come. Below them, Clio saw Vwat jumping awkwardly down the slope, Krish'pha trotting along at his side as he bounced up to speed. There was a heart-stopping moment as they skimmed the far bank of the river, then Vwat found the thermal and circled slowly upward in it.

"He almost didn't make it," she said.

"The sun will help him today. I hope. Last night's rain was bad for him, and the conjunction gets to its closest tonight—we'll have heavy rains after midnight." Kuf circled back to get closer to the High Kings; Clio gave a handsign to follow and Krish'pha acknowledged. "Vwat's not all. I'm almost more worried about Krish'pha. He may be getting ready to die. He's been sulking and refusing to share in the bond."

"Dintanderoderam told me the same thing," Clio said. "This would be a bad time to lose the High Kings."

"If we lose the High Kings, it's the end of it all. They have not named their successors. Vwat and Dintanderoderam both say they've wanted to, but Krish'pha has refused. That in itself would be a good sign, a sign that he wasn't yet ready to die, but I think it's just this stubbornness of his."

"What happens if they die without naming successors?" she asked.

"By tradition, there is a grand gathering of the leaders of the bands, speeches are made, bargains arranged, sometimes duels fought—until there is unanimity. I cannot imagine they can reach unanimity now."

"You're right," Clio said, almost in a whisper. She was not sure that Kuf heard her, but in any case he didn't say any more. They flew on through the morning sunshine, Clio trying both to keep a nervous eye on the High Kings and to spot good feeding places with easy takeoffs near them.

13

THAT EVENING, WHEN they landed, Krish'pha seemed to be in much better spirits. He was interested in what went on around him, even talking a little bit with Clio about her scientific work and with Kuf about some minor political business and he did not go off to sit by himself.

Unfortunately, Vwat was much worse. He had felt better during the day, but as evening came and he tired, his hind legs had stiffened alarmingly. Moreover, the great wing muscles of his chest and back were swollen and sore, and unable to exert fine control, he had bumped down hard on landing, further straining and stretching his aching joints. As the damp cool of the evening descended, it was certain to get much worse.

"We'll have to chance some kind of fire," Kuf said.

Vwat started to disagree, but Krish'pha cut him off. "We'll do what's necessary. You need to fly tomorrow and you can't if this gets any worse. Chances are there's no one to see it anyway—it's entirely possible that no one knows where we've gone."

Clio did not feel quite so confident, but if it got Vwat to accept the fire, it was better to have him believe it.

They kept the fire well-banked, among the trees, but still, since it had to warm a griffin, it could not be small. Vwat grumbled a little at the indignity of sitting with his back to it, but as the heat soothed his aches he relaxed and after a while he was able to eat with something of his old appetite. Kuf produced a small chessboard from his pack and the two sat close to the fire to play a quick game before going to sleep.

Dintanderoderam stretched out by the fire, enjoying the warmth and obviously asleep. Clio and Krish'pha dragged up a log to sit on. "How did you come to be here?" the Randallan asked suddenly.

She started to explain about Kuf's concern when the Christian Liberals had approached him, but the High King cut her off. "No, I had meant, why are Terrans out here? Hauskyld has pointed out the dim star to me, your home sun, and he says the light from it takes eighty-five of our years to reach us—fifty-six, I believe, of your Standard ones. Why did you Terrans come so far?"

"We came in stages," she said, "one world at a time over the centuries, first our robots, then survey expeditions, then to settle, then to build more ships. It continues even now—our outmost probes are already more than 200 light-years beyond this point."

"I can understand the urge to explore," Krish'pha said. "That too is not the question. I thought perhaps your research would explain why the Terrans in particular have come to dominate other worlds. We are at the current edge of your space—I presume it extends in all directions about the same distance?"

She nodded.

"I thought so. And in all that space, you've met nothing like yourselves, nothing that sets out to bring the galaxy under its hand?"

"We've met nothing as advanced as we are. One civilization had spread to a very nearby star-system, less than a light-year away. And others had probed—we found pictures of our own past in the libraries of Haywood. But you're right, Terrans are the only ones who regularly cross deep space." She laughed.

"I fail to see the joke."

"Just something I remembered. There's an old story of my people, made up—oh, probably a thousand of our years ago. Before we had space travel, anyway. On Terra, there were creatures called lemmings. They were small rodents, I think; they bred in great numbers, much like the littlebeasts here. But instead of succumbing to plague when there got to be too many of them, what the lemmings would do—most of them, I suppose there must have been some deviants or there wouldn't have been any more lemmings—was rush into the sea. All of them at once; they'd travel hundreds of kilometers just to walk into the sea and drown. No one knew why.

"The story went that a Terran who had studied lemmings for many years learned to speak their language, and he met a lemming who had studied Terrans in the same way. They fell to talking, of course, and finally the Terran asked, 'Why do you run into the sea like that?' The lemming said, 'I was going to ask why you don't.' "

Krish'pha laughed. "The point is well taken, I suppose. But still, what do you get out of it? The ones who

stay home surely get nothing back from the ones who
venture out. And I cannot imagine their wealth is so
great that the stay-at-homes can afford to launch the
huge colony ships that Hauskyld has told me of—the
ones with a million beings aboard—and not feel the expense."

She smiled. "Tradition, I suppose. Each planet expects
to do it, because all the others did. It's not much more
than one of our centuries from colonization to being able
to launch further colonies, so there would certainly be
some strength to the tradition."

Krish'pha shrugged. "It still fails to account for how
you started."

"Another Terran parable. How did the cat learn to
swim? Bad example—no one brought cats here. Anyway,
the things hate water, but they can swim if they have to.
So the answer is, it had to." Krish'pha looked very
puzzled; Clio thought for a moment and then decided to
tell the truth. "One reason few intelligent species take up
starfaring is that . . . okay, let me begin at the beginning.
As far as we've seen, there are two great branches of
science—a physics/mathematics branch and a biology/
cybernetics branch. Only the physics side can get you
into space—but that's also the side that best lends itself to
really destructive weapons."

"I should think plagues would be a terrible weapon."

"They are. But they take longer to work, and they leave
the enemy more of a chance to hit back than some of the
physics-based things do." She had skirted the edges of the
permissible already—she wasn't going to compound it by
mentioning nukes or crams to the leader of an as-yet un-
affiliated world. "And the biological sciences also tend to
foster an attitude of not wanting to kill the enemy off
entirely—sort of an ecological point of view. Anyway, the
result is that those species that *can* go to space tend to
destroy themselves before getting there."

"And you Terrans were just lucky?"

"Not by much. I'm coming to that. We had built a few

cities in space before the war that wrecked our planet broke out. A few of those cities, untouched by the war, were just barely able to support themselves with resources available in space, and we survived there. Eventually we were able to modify a few planets in the Home System to fit our needs—Mars, where I come from, was one—but even that was a desperate undertaking and most of our people stayed in space.

"It would be several centuries before Terra would be habitable again, so when our probes found habitable planets circling nearby stars—and the Runeberg Gate made them available to us for minimal energy cost within a subjective eyeblink—we had little to lose and much to gain. And once we had the habit of migration and expansion, we kept it because it turned out to be convenient for other reasons—a good way to dump surplus economic production, an outlet for splinter groups, and something to do instead of having more wars."

Krish'pha sat and thought about that for a time. "I suppose," he said, "everything was bound to happen at one time or another." He stretched and nodded toward Kuf and Vwat. "From the look of that board, they're well into endgame. I suppose we should think of sleep."

14

WHEN CLIO AWOKE, her first thought was that it was already morning, but then she realized it was just a clear night with three moons in the sky. She looked to see Tristan rising in the west, and wondered what had snapped her awake.

Around her, silvered by the light of the innermost moon, the trees were silent—odd for the wind not to blow on Randall. Nothing moved. In a few hours, as Tristan approached Isolde and Mark, the tidal effects would begin building toward thunderstorms from the mountains, but for right now even the wind was stopped.

She looked to Kuf, asleep, she had offered to stand a

watch tonight, but he had pointed out that being with the High Kings they could neither fight nor run effectively— therefore, they might as well sleep.

The strain of the last few days had aged Kuf. The bases of his scales were not as pink as they had been, and she realized that some day he would be wholly slate-gray like Vwat.

Vwat was gone; so were Krish'pha and Dintanderode- ram.

She thought of waking Kuf, but something about the strangeness of the night stopped her. She got up quietly and crept along, not sure where she was going, some- thing—she didn't know what—guiding her along.

The light of all three moons, even filtered through the trees, was more than enough to see by, and the ground was level in this part of the forest. They had come down off the great plateau that formed much of the southern part of Floyd, and were now in the hills below. With Randall's strong tides, rivers ran brackish far inland; in the last half-day of flying they had begun to see the fresh- water pattern reverse, the trees now avoiding, instead of clinging to, the streams. The ground was damp and soft everywhere; in a moment she saw the footprints, a griffin walking beside a Randallan, and followed them.

She had gone less than a hundred paces when she found them. They sat facing each other, talking in low voices, Dintanderoderam lying between them.

Something in the way the handsnake lay told Clio he was dead. She did not know why the other two had not suicided yet; all she could think was that she was about to see that happen, and she did not want to—she loved them. Moreover, she could not bear to think of what would happen when the High Kings died without suc- cessors. She started to go back to Kuf, already trying to find a way to tell him.

Her boot turned over a stone, and the little reptile un- derneath—the size of a shrew, but built like a four-armed monkey—sprang up and swung hissing away into the brush. There was a moment of silence; she turned her head to look back. "Come here, Clio," Krish'pha said, gently.

Her feet turned and pushed her to where the High Kings stood.

"We owe you an apology," Vwat said. "We had not realized that you would be awakened or might follow us. There are things it would have been better for you not to see."

She thought they might kill her. Tristan, now risen higher, shone down on their faces, the faceted eyes like a staring, empty mask. "What happened?" she asked.

"We conferred. We have decided what the High Kings must decide. The way we have chosen, our brother could not go—must not go—so he has died." Vwat's voice, too, was expressionless.

"You're not going to—" she stammered, looking down at the corpse at their feet. A wind was beginning to rise, the trees rustling faintly.

"We have much work to do." Krish'pha rested one of his upper hands on Vwat's neck. "Do not move our brother. It is our way that wherever the High King dies, his body lies, to be remembered until it is good to forget." Abruptly, the Randallan flung his arms around the griffin, and the two rubbed faces together. Then Krish'pha, without another word, walked away into the trees.

"We will return and go back to sleep," Vwat said, when Krish'pha was no longer visible. "You must say nothing of this to Kuf, or to anyone."

"What about Krish'pha?"

"He has his purpose. I have mine." The griffin turned back toward camp and walked away, his hindquarters stiff. "Try to forget that you saw us together, or what you saw us doing. And—speaking as High King—whatever else, even if you must record this somewhere, tell *none* of *my* people. They must not know how things really were."

The wind picked up as she ran after him; the smaller branches whipped. Triple shadows ran madly around on the forest floor. She caught up quickly and said, "What are the duties you spoke of?"

"The less you know, the better." He kept walking.

"What were you talking about with Krish'pha?"

He turned; he reared his neck straight, and he spoke in the oldest, most formal form of True Speech. "Know this, then. It serves our purpose that a Terran know. There were two hard tasks to be done. We settled which of us would do each task. And then we shared a memory through our brother. Our brother died and we parted." He extended a wing, resting it on Clio's shoulder. "And you will never speak that to any of my people."

She bowed low and then, knowing somehow it was right, she dropped and made full obeisance. When she looked up, at the touch of his wing, it had become suddenly darker as clouds blew in from the east to cover Mark and Isolde. When the clouds reached Tristan, it would be completely dark. The wind was now tearing at her hair and clothes. She stood, looking up into the flat, shining surfaces of Vwat's eyes. He was dull gray all over, and in Tristan's light he looked more like a statue a thousand years old than a living being.

"We need to get back to camp. It will storm soon and you should be inside your shelter for that," he said. He did not speak again as they walked.

As she slid into her little one-person shelter, a kind of hybrid sleeping bag and tent, she realized that waking up in it would be evidence that all this had happened. She fell asleep with Tristan still shining on the fabric, but the wind rising. Or perhaps the swift moon did go behind a cloud—her last conscious perception was of darkness falling.

15

FOR A MOMENT, when she woke to the rain spattering on her shelter, she tried to believe something else had happened during the night—that she and Krish'pha had simply unrolled shelters and snuggled in between the griffins, who were less bothered by weather. But she could not make herself believe it; the memory of the night before was clear and vivid. She pulled her clothes out of the drying pocket; the capillary pumps, powered by her body heat, had made them warm and dry, though they still had a musty smell of sweat. Wriggling around in the narrow space, she got dressed, and lay still for a moment in the dry warmth.

With a mental wince, Clio wrapped her old alweather around herself, unfastened the shelter opening, and slid out into the cool rain. She switched the pump over to self-drying, made sure the evaporator was protruding, and stuffed the shelter into its bag. She did all this without thinking, her mind locked onto the task at hand. The bag went into her pack; she pulled out a strip of dry meat and chewed it, sitting on a rock, looking at the two griffins as they lay asleep in the flat dimness of predawn.

Kuf showed the strain of the last few days on every surface. The folds around his mouth—had there been any at all when she first met him?—were deep, bluish smears among the fine gray scales. His ribs showed a little now, between his collarbones, and the flexible girdle of floating ribs behind his wings stood out in stark relief, heaving even now as he slept. His forepaws occasionally ran irritably over his face, as if he were brushing away a bad smell.

Vwat seemed to have gotten younger during the night; there was a color in his skin that hadn't been there in years and he seemed to sleep in perfect peace.

As she watched, he woke and looked at her. "Are we ready to leave as soon as Kuf and I eat?"

"Yes."

He nodded, extended a forepaw, and woke Kuf. "Up. Eat. We have far to go today."

Kuf rose, a little puzzled, and said "Is Your Serenity feeling better this morning?"

Vwat did not reply. He had already turned to the bank above them, where he crouched to crop the wet, succulent *dhyvrha*, shaped like Terran cauliflower, but rusty red and too bitter for Clio's palate. Kuf looked around twice, but seeing nothing to offer any explanation, he followed Vwat up onto the bank and ate.

As they ate, the light grew brighter and the rain stopped. There were a few large patches of clear by the time Vwat raised his head, stretched his back legs, and said, "Without a burden, I can take off from where I am. Kuf, I believe there is a steep drop you can use just over the hill. You will guide me and provide whatever guard you can. If I should be unable to finish the trip, you will carry my message on for me."

"I understand and will obey regardless of the cost to myself." Kuf spoke formally and made an obeisance.

"Your loyalty moves me," Vwat said, and took off, circling upward. Clio and Kuf walked to the small cliff, perhaps a hundred meters high, in silence. Slinging her pack on and snugging it tight, she got into the harness, gripping the straps but leaving her feet on the ground at the lip of the cliff. Together, she and Kuf sprang forward over the cliffside and into the air. Kuf flapped hard to get altitude. They circled several times, looking for a thermal, but there were none this morning.

When they had flapped high enough, they turned eastward. Vwat fell in behind them and they flew in silence.

After their first stop, the remnants of the night's storm had cleared and the sun was out. Thermals began to rise from the land beneath them, and the flying became easier. As they climbed to a comfortable altitude, Kuf said, "Let's push on as long as we can. The short moon will set soon and I'd like to get a bearing before we land."

"Sure. That was a hard first leg this morning."

"Yes, it was." He swung left, diving a little, and picked up a big thermal rising from a large gravel bar in the river below. They circled slowly up, Vwat hanging behind and below them. "I assume that if you know anything, the High King has ordered you not to speak it."

"Yes."

"Do you have any other orders I should know about?"

"No," Clio said. "I don't think so."

"Well, then we know what we have to do." The griffin sounded neither happy nor unhappy; Clio could think of nothing to add. As they circled upward, Tristan set and they calculated their position. They were further east and south than they had expected to be, making much better time now that Vwat did not need to carry anything.

16

I T WAS LATE that afternoon when they found the Traditional encampment, at T'xhur, one of the old gathering points for Royal armies against bandits and rebels on this continent.

They flew in low over a ridge, diving to get the maximum benefit from the likely windrise on the other side. As they soared on the uprushing air, the floodplain spread out before Clio. The bright green suggested it was swampy and wet, with deep organic-rich soil—probably one of the broad valleys scooped out by glaciers pushing down from the plateau, back during the Great Cold and Dark the handsnakes remembered.

The river here split into two broad, sluggish channels; sidechannels and bayous fanned out from them, dissecting the floodplain into low, weedy islands. Gaudy tents in the patterns of more than fifty different bands covered the highest few of the islands, which lay close by the main far channel and the opposite ridge. The islands were joined by wide wooden bridges to a central island, from which sprang five tall takeoff towers. The rest of the island had been paved in black gravel to enhance thermals; the overall effect was that of a launch pad complex, which in a sense was what it was.

"Vwat will want to land somewhere near the center," Kuf said. "He'll probably make us circle the camp once to find the appropriate clan. That should tell us something about what he has in mind."

She looked again at the encamped islands surrounding the takeoff field like brilliant irregular shreds of crazy quilts. Figuring that the largest island held about as many tents as the other islands put together, and that on that island there were something more than fifty rows of eight tents, each of which would hold three triples . . . 2,500 triples, easily the biggest army since the war against the Terran fort. Still, it was small enough compared to the half million Traditional triples scattered around the planet. There had not been time to gather more than the troops available from Floyd; other armies were doubtless on the way, but the first of them could not be expected for a midmoon yet.

Far and faint, a shrill whistle sounded behind them. She looked back to see a patrol of three triples. The lead griffin's rider flashed his heliograph: "ORDER: ACCEPT GUIDANCE . . . ORDER: ACKNOWLEDGE."

She told Kuf and handsignalled Vwat to follow them. Immediately Kuf cupped his wings into a stall. She grabbed the heliograph from Kuf's harness and sent: "RECEIVED. . . . REPLY: GUIDANCE ACCEPTED . . . WILL FOLLOW LEAD . . . <YOURS> . . . QUERY: ACCEPTABLE? . . . QUERY: STATUS . . . <OURS>?"

The patrol leader blinked: "RECEIVED. . . . REPLY: ACCEPTABLE . . . REPLY/PROVISIONAL: PRISONERS . . . ORDER: DESCEND . . . <SLOWLY> . . . WE WILL DIVE . . . <TO OVERTAKE> . . . ORDER: ACKNOWLEDGE."

Clio acknowledged, signalled Vwat, and told Kuf. Kuf stalled again and began to flap hard, dropping almost vertically toward the swampy valley floor. From the muddy water below, Clio could smell the rich scent of decay. She looked to make sure Vwat was still with them, and saw that the diving patrol had already overtaken them, sweeping beyond them and heading toward a corner of the valley, stalling to lose airspeed so that Kuf and Vwat could follow.

The heliograph winked again. "ORDER: GIVE IN-FORMATION . . . QUERY: IDENTITY . . . <WINGMAN> . . . <<YOURS>>?"

Clio sent back the sign for the High King. For a long time, as they flew over the swamp toward the encamp-ment, there was no reply, and she decided they must simply not have believed her; but then the patrol ahead of them veered abruptly, heading back toward the center of the camp.

They flew on, now quite low over the swamp, the heat and stench gripping Clio like a hot, clammy fist as the insects whirled around her. She rolled down her sleeves and pulled her gloves and bug hood on. Through the mass of flies and biting insects, it was hard to see where they were going, but Kuf's better-armored eyes were less bothered, and they stayed on course. She could hear him snorting the tiny things from his nostrils, and held on tight through the lurch of one hard sneeze.

As they neared the camp, perhaps because of the smoke of the forges and cooking fires, the bugs were suddenly gone, and she pulled her hood back to see that they were headed for a low hill at the center of the biggest island. "REQUEST: LAND ON MARKER . . . REQUEST: AC-KNOWLEDGE."

"REPLY: WILL COMPLY." She slipped the helio-graph, hood, and gloves back into their harness pockets and got ready for the landing, repeating the message to Kuf.

The patrol leader swooped over the hill, dropping a streamer on the very top. Kuf circled in, diving below the top of the hill and along its mossy face, perhaps three-quarters of the way up. Clio rolled off, seeing the mud puddle too late and coming up dripping wet and dirty, temporarily blinded. She wiped her face with the sleeve that had stayed dry.

With a great flapping, making a steep descent, Vwat landed on the streamer at the apex of the hill.

Around them, the patrol split into individual triples and descended at three points around the little rise, forming equal angles. It was, Clio realized, the honor guard position for the High King; clearly she had been believed.

From the top of the hill, Vwat gave a great, bellowing cry; Kuf dropped into the deepest obeisance and stayed there, so Clio followed suit. "Hear and follow," Vwat announced, his voice booming. "I will give orders from this hill to the entire assembled army in two hours' time. Do not disturb me before then; assemble around me quietly. See that my assistants are fed and made comfortable."

From behind her came a Randallan voice giving the traditional acknowledgement of a Royal order. From the corner of her eye, she saw Kuf rising; she got up slowly herself. There was a quiet click of a tongue; she turned to find a triple standing behind them. "You'll want to eat and bathe," the Randallan said. "Follow us."

As they walked behind the soldier-triple, between the long rows of bright tents, their feet squashing in the mud, they could see that triples were already beginning to move in toward the central hill. The traffic increased as they went along, till it was only with difficulty that they crept along through the press.

At last they came to a small pavilion and, after climbing onto the paved platform and drying their feet, went inside. There, sitting on mats, were Andy Kanegawa and Phreg.

Andy looked up in surprise; Clio saw at once how much hope they had brought him—and how little he had had before. He hugged her, wet dirty tunic and all, and she tried to think of any way to make the news sound good.

A triple brought food for Clio and Kuf while they told

the other two what had happened. Clio's promise to the High King handicapped her; she planned to tell Andy as soon as possible, but the presence of the griffins prevented that for now.

They had finished eating, and Andy and Phreg were beginning to press questions, when guards returned and asked them to come to the hill where Vwat was to speak.

The pathways through the camp were less crowded now, since most of the triples had already assembled below the hill. As they approached the gathering, they saw that Vwat still sat on the hill, head bowed, as Clio and Kuf had last seen him. Below him, in a great semicircle extending 150 meters from the hill, almost back to the line of tents, the ground was solid with triples, sitting and waiting silently.

The air was thick with the smell of mud and bodies. The griffins stood or crouched, their gray bodies almost blending into the olive-green muck worked into slippery goo by so many feet. On top of them, to avoid getting the mud in their fur, the Randallans sat silently, handsnakes coiling around them. There was silence, except occasional splashes and muttered apologies, as the latecomers found places. All the heads were pointed toward the hill, the hexes of the eyes expressionless as always.

As the very last stragglers arrived, Vwat spoke. "Thank you for listening to me. You need not. I am xhu'gha—I was part of the High Kings, and I bring you the last orders.

"I know that my being here requires some explanation. Let me give you that first, then. For long, the handperson High King, Krish'pha, has secretly embraced the Jesus-way. This has brought great pain to Dintanderoderam and I, but we have borne it in silence. We have seen that Krish'pha was partial to the interests of these 'mod'hrunwi,' and even more to the xhughawi, and for the sake of peace we have put up with it.

"Yes, for the sake of peace!" The irony in his voice stung like a whip.

"But, when at last these incursions, these intolerable abuses by the xhughawi came about—so that you rightly rose up to put an end to them—then we prevailed upon Krish'pha to come with us and to lead you in this war to restore your rights, as the High Kings should do. To this end we set out to come here with a loyal xhugha retainer and a Terran who has been sympathetic to our cause.

"On the way here, Krish'pha chose to become xhu'gha, as his Jesus-way taught him, and deserted us, going to join the xhugha forces. He is with them now. Dintande-roderam destroyed himself honorably; in his distress, he could not give me his memories—thus the lineage of the memory of the High Kings is lost forever.

"Hear then, the last message from your High King.

"Go to this place of St. Thkhri'jha. Destroy it. Kill all the xhughawi in rebellion. Forbid the Jesus-way. Restore the ancient customs.

"Henceforth, xhughawi shall live only as slaves; the exceptions I make are the Winged Ones Kuf and Phreg, who have proven their loyalty beyond all doubt. All others—kill or enslave without exception.

"Carry the war throughout the world. As Hmi'dro proclaimed the First War Against the Xhugha, so I proclaim the Second.

"Choose for your new High Kings whichever triple most distinguish themselves in the first great battle.

"My duty is discharged. I thank you for your tolerance of a xhugha. Good-bye." Then he bowed his head, opened his beak wide, and tore into his own chest. The scaly hide ripped apart and deep red blood burst forth onto the hillside. He sank slowly to the ground and lay face down, the blood throbbing out, then slowing to a trickle as he became limp.

There was a long silence; then a great shout went up, and triples ran to wait at the tents of their band captains. The band captains themselves gathered in the middle of the field, arguing eagerly and trampling the mud.

No one bothered to look at the body of the High King.

A griffin, wearing the mark of a minor captain, broke from the circle and approached them. "We request the advice of Captain Kanegawa," he said.

"Certainly." Andy gripped Clio's arm, tried to smile at her, and was gone, following the griffin.

"Are you all right?" Kuf asked.

She realized that she was sobbing, that tears were pouring down her face. "They didn't—they didn't have to— they told me that—"

"Stop." Kuf leaned against her, gently, with the bony outer edge of one wing. "You were ordered not to speak. I can tell you, anyway. We all know that the High Kings made this agreement, and that each of them went off to start this war; we will all have forgotten it by nightfall."

"It is our way." Phreg spoke softly. "History is always with us here, because of the dreambringers. We would sink under its weight, paralyzed by the number of possible roads at every decision if we did not destroy parts of our history. This is what the High King has begun for us. It is not the first time, nor will it be the last. We know that Krish'pha has said something of the same kind to the xhughawi and that war is sweeping down on us— war until one side prevails or another." It was the longest she had ever heard him speak.

"But—surely a middle way—"

"Not for us. To act, one must be one thing or another, not both. Sometimes, we must settle which it is we will be, and then we spill blood. It is sad, of course. Death is always sad. But it is necessary."

She could think of nothing to say; a hand resting on each griffin's shoulder, she walked with them back to the tent. On their way, they passed many quiet gatherings of triples, waiting for the captains. Neither Clio nor either griffin said anything.

17

THE ROUTE THE army took back towards St. Thkhri'jha's and Bipih was more direct than the one Kuf and Clio had taken to T'xhur, but the necessity of keeping so many griffins fed and keeping the gash'hwar caravan, with its reserves of ammunition, close enough for immediate resupply, slowed the pace to a third of what Clio and Kuf could have done alone. The heliographs winked constantly, rotating squadrons forward and backward along the several columns, down to feeding stops and back up into the air.

It had been a relief to be rotated down to this little pond in a clearing, to eat before continuing. They were never sure whether any attention was being paid to them—the army ignored the two Terrans and the xhugha griffins most of the time. A couple of times a day the Council of Captains called in Andy or Phreg to discuss strategy, but that seemed almost a superfluous courtesy. "They know what they're doing better than I do," he said. "They have generations of experience with the triple as a weapon. I don't. About all I can tell them is that they might be facing more accurate or better massed fire from the ground than they're used to. And watching the way they move the army, I'd be even less use to them on logistics."

Phreg nodded gravely. "They know history as well as I do, though it was kind of them to ask. All I could tell them was there have been nine remembered battles in the passes approaching Bipih from this side, two right where St. Thkhri'jha's stands today. The attackers won four times, one of them at St. Thkhri'jha's."

Kuf kept his face down, browsing the soft plants by the bank. There was of course no call at all for a xhugha Christian courtier; his skill at chess was hardly of use here. Clio leaned quietly against him; all this time on the road had made her lose weight, and she was glad of that for Kuf's sake. She thought of eating a few more handfuls of the bland, damp plant but decided against it.

The heliograph of the squadron overhead winked at them, relaying a message from the command squadron. "We have about six minutes to takeoff," Clio warned. She flashed the acknowledgment back.

"Better get all you can in," Andy said quietly. "They're going to try to push this last flight all the way to the mouth of the pass."

"Over an hour's flight," Kuf said. "But it's about the only place for an evening camp."

"You sound like you don't like the idea," Clio said.

Kuf chewed hard and swallowed. "Bad idea to go into a battle at the end of a long flight. And we're getting to within a day's land march of St. Thkhri'jha's. If they surprised us . . . we might lose more than we had to. And that might slow us down." He put his face back into the greens, taking in another huge beakful.

Clio wanted to ask more, but both Kuf and Phreg were still packing in food as quickly as they could, and they would be taking off soon. "How much difference does a delay make?" she asked Andy.

"Maybe a lot. This is likely to be a mobilization war. There are a lot more Traditionals than mod'hruns and xhugha put together, but the Traditionals are all over the planet—so it will take a lot longer to get them together. The xhugha/mod'hrun forces have to beat the scattered Traditional armies before they can coalesce. Anything that slows down the Traditional armies makes them more vulnerable to being picked off one by one."

"Sounds like it could go either way."

He shrugged. "That's the way it always is. If it didn't look that way, why would anyone fight?"

The griffins were ready. The run and the rise into the sky didn't exhilarate Clio as it usually did, and somehow the absence of that joy was more depressing than anything so far.

Even now, after several days of flying, she had not quite gotten used to the sight of a sky full of triples, squadrons flying in V and box formations, some moving forward to take over the lead, others falling back. The whole complicated dance, coordinated by the star-flashes of the heliographs, now formed a great bow across the sky with the center leading and the tips trailing. The control squadron was within the bow, behind the center; there, the mirrors winked constantly.

Below them, the land was changing again. Randall's temperature gradient with respect to altitude was unusually steep; the top of the great plateau to the west was relatively cold, and through the passes of the Sarpint Range the winds rushed down from it to the sea. In their flight from Bipih, they had flown low to take advantage of that. Now, two kilometers higher at almost the practical ceiling for loaded griffins, they were riding the upper tidal wind. The first line of hills at the front of the Sarpint Range was visible now in the distance; from the dark, rolling line, long thin river gorges fanned out across the plains, dark, almost blue strips in the green of the forest below.

The xenist in Clio thought hard about what processes might have created that pattern. Clearly the rivers here did not join each other; was it simply that the surface had been scoured too evenly by the glaciers? Or, more likely, the rivers ran in channels ground by the glaciers, and given a gentle gradient and Randall's lower gravity, there was simply insufficient erosion for much stream piracy. That too might account for what must have been a relatively rapid deposition of soil after the last ice age—fast enough to build up the soil for that heavy forest below.

She had gotten so engrossed in thought that she was not paying much attention to the flight itself; she was startled when she looked up to see the first hills actually rising below them. The great bow was tightening and thickening, getting ready for the descent to the river valley at the mouth of the first pass.

Far away in front, the scouts' heliographs blinked wildly. At first, Clio was reading it casually, more out of boredom than anything else, but then her heart jumped sideways. "They've spotted fortifications," she said. "The xhughawi have gotten to the pass ahead of us and dug in on the ground."

"I saw," Kuf said.

Signals were flashing throughout the formation now as the commanders responded to the threat. Kuf and Phreg plunged steeply downward and to the right, as the whole left tip of the bow dove across the path of the center toward the Lonely Peaks several kilometers away. The right wheeled sharply, reversing direction and hooking in from the other side as it descended; the center—the great bulk of squadrons, scrambled to reorganize and descend at a right angle to its former course. The command squadron swung down out of the confusion to join the right flank. The army continued downward to around half a kilometer above the ground, where the wind off the hills was a little more favorable to their course.

It was going to be a long flight to reach the Peaks, and foraging would be poor there, but, Clio realized, there was little choice. In a war zone, they would have to land where they could take off quickly; with the element of surprise gone, and prepared fortifications barring their way, they would have to change plans drastically. Further, with the distance added to the already overlong flight by this last-minute detour, they would be exhausted when they arrived. It looked like a bleak, cold camp tonight. And since she couldn't help Kuf fly, there would be nothing she could do for at least half an hour.

Andy's heliograph was flashing to her left. It took her another instant to realize he was talking to the command squadron. "SUGGESTION: RETREAT . . . SUGGESTION: DESTINATION . . . ENEMY OCCUPIED . . . <PROBABLE> . . . <<HIGHLY>> . . . REQUEST: ACKNOWLEDGE."

She was glad once again that Andy was along for this. It had not occurred to her, but the Lonely Peaks were certainly the best place to divert to in the area and the xhughawi might well have thought of that. If the Council of Captains agreed with Andy, the course change would have to come soon—many of the griffins were already beginning to tire, and the rest would be quickly exhausted in a fight. They were simply in no shape to seize a landing area against any defense at all, and they had to land soon.

One of the captains began to return signal. "REPLY: CONCUR . . . QUERY: REQUEST FOR SUGGESTION—"

Something exploded among the command squadron. There was another burst, then another. Griffins veered and fell away; some dove into buttonhook turns to escape the attack, but others fell all the way to the ground, dead or dying. Clio looked down and saw little bursts of flame and smoke below. With a hand signal, she indicated them to Andy.

He acknowledged and pointed to two squadrons already diving on the enemy. There was at least no question now—they must divert back eastward at once for if the xhugha had prepared this trap, they would have others in store.

Something crashed overhead, a rumbling, clattering noise like thunder mixed with hail on the roof. Clio looked up to see the sky full of tiny, bright lights, rapidly dropping toward them. As she looked, two more explosions burst overhead, and more of the bright burning objects dropped from them.

The first of the burning things dropped past, a bundle of burning rags wrapped around something heavy.

A griffin screamed to her right. One of the blazing things had stuck to its back, clinging to its hide. It was beginning to thrash frantically, losing altitude and threatening to tumble as the Randallan turned and tried to cut the object off with a knife.

There were many more explosions overhead; the sky was filled with the hot, burning things. Clio caught Andy's handsigns and looked around.

A cloud of smoke burgeoned from halfway up the nearest of the Lonely Peaks. As she watched, more rockets rose from the cloud on pillars of red flame; the flame disappeared, and the rockets became black dots, but she knew they were on their way.

The air was full of screams and cries, and heliographs flashed everywhere. She looked to the command squadron; there was nothing there. Not many of them had been killed by the fire from the ground, but the rest had been forced to scatter in all directions, and now could not find each other quickly enough. The army was without any central command.

Down below, two squadrons tore into the hidden emplacements in the woods, the xhugha gunners fleeing into the brush, shot or speared through the back as they ran. It would have no influence on the rest of the battle, of course, but at least the Traditionals were hitting back somewhere, and that gave her a moment's comfort.

The air around her stank of acrid burning; she had to shift her weight as Kuf swerved violently to avoid a burning bundle, which dropped no more than two meters off his right wing. She drew a breath, trying to think. There would be no retreat; there was no one to call for it and in any case signals were hopelessly confused. If anything, what was waiting at the Lonely Peaks was certain to be worse than this. The battle was lost already—what remained was the dying.

She signalled frantically to Andy and Phreg. Andy tried to wave off the suggestion, still working his heliograph at the nearer squadrons. They ignored him, intent on pressing on to attack the mountain, refusing even to acknowledge his signals.

After a moment's hesitation, Phreg dove steeply to the left. Andy's arms flailed for a moment—this was clearly not his idea. Kuf followed.

"Can you hold this course, Kuf?"

"I think so." His wings beat hard a couple of times; they had now gotten entirely out of the army's formation, and were virtually out of the battle. "If we don't have to fly too far."

They kept on, trying to stretch the glide as far as possible. Phreg was perhaps a hundred meters below and in front of them. There was nothing to say.

Ten minutes later, the land began to rise steeply under them and Clio doubted that Kuf would be able to climb much. What she could see beneath them was heavy forest, impossible to land in. Further up the slope were patches of scrub where they might have a better chance, but the ground was coming up fast and Phreg and Andy were even lower.

Kuf's muscles heaved under her, and she could hear his hard breathing over the flapping thunder of his wings. They climbed, slowly, but enough . . . the ground below dropped away a little, and they shot forward toward the brushy clearing on the slope ahead. Still below them, Phreg had gained just enough altitude to stay above the trees; his wings flapped constantly, with no room to even attempt a glide.

To give Phreg room, Kuf swung wide, aiming higher up the slope and to the left, flapping hard himself. Clio lost sight of Phreg and Andy below them; she looked, but had to stop and concentrate on the landing. They shot in among the four- and five-meter-tall trees, weaving to find an open space. Suddenly Kuf's wings opened out to spill speed, and as he stalled upward Clio dove, landing in a clean roll among the minty-smelling ferns. A few paces beyond her, Kuf thudded to the ground, folded his wings, and lay down panting.

She got up gingerly, checking herself for sprains and broken bones. She was shaken and bruised, but nothing seemed to be broken.

Trees blocked the view in all directions. Kuf's landing had been brilliant, considering the conditions. She looked back to see if he was all right; he raised his head a little and gasped, "I'm fine. Need to breathe a little. Phreg?"

She turned again. They were nowhere that she could see, but she couldn't see much. She climbed a tree and looked.

There was no sign of either of them anywhere. It was entirely possible that they were all right—after all, even this clearing would hardly be visible from far away—but she had little idea of where to start looking for them.

She was about to climb down when something caught her eye. She remembered the battle, and looked again at the sky.

A few triples hung on, circling above the forest, pursued by—she couldn't see what the things were, but they were bigger than a griffin, and the triples were obviously fleeing them as well as they could. As she watched helplessly, two more triples went in for whatever landings they could find.

A distant boom like thunder turned her head toward the Lonely Peaks. There were muzzle flashes and, moments later, more booms.

Clio climbed higher, to the point where the tree swayed dangerously. She could just see down into the broken country of the valley floor where the the Traditional army had been forced down. As she watched, great plumes of white vapor billowed upward. Strangely, the smoke clouds were big, but there were no explosions from the valley. As she watched, the smoke—if that was what it was—fell back, lying in a thick layer on the valley floor, visible through the trees, streamers occasionally rising and blowing downwind. There were more flashes from the Lonely Peaks and, a few moments later, more smoke billowed from the plain.

The last of the triples was spiralling down into the cloud. One of the—airplanes?—dove at it, and abruptly the triple veered off and fell, shot perhaps? Or simply diving to avoid its foe?

The triple dropped into the dense white fog and was gone.

The airplanes—by now Clio was quite sure that their

wings were not moving at all—wheeled and turned, headed for the peaks. She watched for a while, to see what else might happen, but nothing rose from the heavy smoke clinging to the rocky ridges and gullies of the forested valley below. Occasionally the big guns on the peaks would boom and another cloud of vapor would rise.

Two of the airplanes fell out of the sky, tumbling out of control into the clouds below. Below her, she heard a cracking noise—off to her right.

She looked down; something spat again from the forest, like—

Andy's pistol. She marked the place, down the slope in what looked like a bare spot among the trees. As she did, she noted with satisfaction that yet another airplane was falling out of control.

She scrambled down the tree and ran toward the spot as quickly as she could, barking her shins on stones and fallen logs, and falling twice, almost slamming into the trees as she left her clearing.

Andy leaned up against Phreg's back, the pistol pointed into the sky. There was something strange about the way he sat. A pair of distance goggles was clamped to his face.

"Andy!"

"Clio." His voice was flat. "Bastards are getting out of range. Don't want the slugs to drop toward the ground—they might lock in on someone from our side. Propeller planes! Two Randallans pedalling them like bicycles, one steering with a rifle on the front. Fucking six-armed monkeys . . . got some of them. Kill one, the plane goes down. Think I just made ace."

"Why are you sitting like that?" She realized after she spoke that she had screamed it at the top of her lungs.

"We hit a tree coming in. Phreg broke his back leg, and I think my back's broken," Andy said. "Nothing will move below the waist. Fucking ratfuckers are getting out of range." Tears ran out from under the distance goggles.

She stood there, unsteady on her feet, wanting to hold him but afraid to touch him, wanting to tell him, wanting not to tell him. Finally she just blurted it out. "I think the xhugha used poison gas in the valley. The whole army's probably dead."

She wasn't at all sure he understood. He just sat there with tears running down his face. She couldn't think of anything she could do for him. Tears were running down her face, and she was beginning to sob. She sat down next to the griffin, then curled against him as her sobs came harder and faster. After a long time, she fell asleep, and she was only dimly aware when Hauskyld and a party of armed Terrans arrived in the helicopter.

18

Hᴉs ɴᴀᴍᴇ," ʜᴀᴜꜱᴋʏʟᴅ said, "is Hregh'dhum. He's sort of the xhugha combination of Hitler and Oppenheimer—a certain genius for raising rabble, and for building weapons. Unfortunately he's a lot more coherent than Hitler and has a lot less conscience than Oppenheimer. The ground for this was being laid at least three years ago—that was what was going on at St. Thkhri'jha's. And now, I'm afraid, a certain reading of Krish'pha's last speech supports Hregh'dhum's claim, as an untripled Randallan, to the throne. More importantly, so does his Mod'hrun Army."

Andy stared at the floor, his hands resting on the wooden tires of his improvised wheelchair. "And there's nothing you can do? The Pope's representative—"

"I'm doing what I can," Hauskyld said mildly. "We aren't going to bless him. I haven't much to enforce my authority with, except that a few of Hregh'dhum's advisors have figured out that we must have better gadgets than they've seen so far and so we might be valuable to them, and, of course, I've made sure they know that there are a lot more—and better armed—Terrans on the way. Other than that I doubt I've got any way to reach and

raise even a hundred troops." He sighed, looking down
at the Templar captain. "Clio, can you explain this?"

"You didn't tell me that much," she said. "Rather sit in
the sun, Andy?"

"Yeah."

She turned his chair around and wheeled him a few
meters along the Dean's Office boardwalk to a sunny part
of the porch, the wheels making a thumping and thundering sound. Hauskyld followed silently.

They all waited there in the sun, uncomfortable and
blinking. Finally, Hauskyld sighed. "All right. I probably can't convince you of much else, but please believe
that I had no idea what they were planning or how far
they'd gotten. And the Church *will* have to act, but there
isn't much to be done just yet. For right now, all we can
do is make our disapproval public."

Andy sighed. "I keep thinking of what a beautiful
place this was when we came. Now—my god. Racism.
Genocide. Religious war. Poison gas. Concentration
camps. Is there any other benefit of civlization we haven't
given them yet?"

Hauskyld seemed about to answer, but then he looked
up and waved. In the distance, Clio could see a griffin
approaching them. "Kuf!" she said, as he drew closer.

"The new Bishop of Randall," Hauskyld said. "With
full power to name clergy, excommunicate, specify doctrine, the whole works."

They looked at him in some surprise. "I see," Andy
said. "Ahh—I hate to ask, but how many divisions *does*
the Pope have?"

"That was my question," Clio said.

Hauskyld's eyes didn't leave the approaching griffin.
"How many did he have in 1998 when the Church had to
go into hock to set up Vatican Supra and be in space at
all? Or even when the war came in 2047? But within a
hundred years of that, there was a Christian Commonwealth—more or less by force of moral persuasion. And
there still is one, to back Bishop Kuf up if need be. It

seems more to me that the great forces here on Randall, and everywhere for that matter, have been ideas, not guns. At least in the long run, one being with an idea is worth an army."

"Just now I'd like to have the army, though," Clio said.

"Me too. But Kuf will be getting into earshot, and just now what we need is ideas—and maybe some confidence. A bishop can checkmate a king, you know."

"I hope he'll still have time for chess," Andy said. "It doesn't sound like there are many other pleasures ahead of him."

Then they all bowed their heads, and Clio and Hauskyld knelt beside Andy's wheelchair, as they waited for the new Bishop of Randall. Clio could hear the other two praying and, again, felt vaguely embarrassed that, after all these years in the Commonwealth, she could not bring herself to believe in God, and had to go through the motions without any belief in any of it.

Clio felt the Bishop's shadow fall across her, and knew she was about to receive his blessing. To her deep surprise, she wanted it very much.

PART III
Kuf: Randall 2911 A.D./
Arimathea 2928 A.D.

1

THE SLAVE WINGPERSONS stayed a long way from
Kuf. He was used to that by now, but Nyth was
not, and kept edging back and forth. Perhaps it
was the sickening sight of the iron clips at the parasol
joints on the slaves' wings, perhaps the way they kept
their heads down, as if always expecting a blow. "Calm
down," Kuf said gently. "Even *they* know we're on their
side. If this last scene is disturbing you, perhaps you'd
better leave early—the authorities would be happy to
make something of it, interference with property rights or
something."

Nyth shook his head from side to side. "I am trying,
Excellency. I am still not sure why you called me from
the monastery."

"That will get clearer. And when it does you might not
forgive me," Kuf said. He saw that the rest of the line was
still sitting and waiting; the Terran technicians continued to fiddle. Clio and Andros still had plenty of time
to get here and, of course, they had turned out to be
right—only the underlings were here at the moment, ex-

217

cept for himself and Nyth. Nyth was probably thinking
along the same lines . . . "Appointing you was the kind
of political decision you'll become all too familiar with.
The bishop has to be a wingperson because the Church
is locked in a battle with Hregh'dhum and his Modernization Authority over the rights of wingpersons and
handsnakes, and handsnakes can't speak publicly. And
furthermore, the bishop has to be a good administra-
tor—someone with experience running something large
and complex, like a big monastery. And especially the
bishop needs to be free of any habit of deference to
grabbers—yes, I use that word, and I suggest you begin
thinking with it. It tends to maintain an accurate per-
spective."

Nyth nodded. Kuf thought he might say something,
but he did not—and that reminded him again of why he
had chosen this particular successor. As Hauskyld had
pointed out, the situation he was leaving behind called
for someone stubborn and literal-minded—potentially a
good martyr, if it came to that.

The Spens Desert was as he remembered it; a short way
off around the hills, if he had cared to look, he could
have seen the already-crumbled ruins of the Terran fort,
and just over the horizon lay the vast remains of the main
encampment of the siege. Here on the field stood the
remains of over twenty Gates, all the arrivals of the early
years of the survey expedition, their metal still bright
despite the acid rains of this desert. He had seen a few
such uncorrodable metals at the University, half a planet
away; apparently the day would come when they were
common, but just now the bright star-stuff, twisted and
tormented by the fusion blast of the one Gate that had
lifted from Randall, was a remarkable sight.

The next Gate was being readied now, and Kuf was
still having trouble believing that he would be riding it.
Hauskyld, Clio, and Andros had all told him repeatedly
that one did not "ride" a Gate—because there was no
time inside it, one simply stepped through to somewhere

unimaginably far away, years into the future. But he had seen the previous Gate take off, climbing on a throbbing pillar of white fire into the sky, and seen the brilliant comet in the night sky when Gate had headed for Arimathea. He simply could not imagine being on top of that and not being aware of it, whatever his Terran friends might tell him.

"Friends coming, Excellency," Nyth said.

He looked up to see Clio, Hauskyld, and Andros approaching. Hauskyld brought Andros's wheelchair to a stop next to Kuf and said, "Well, at least it's a nice day for your departure. Nyth, it's good to see you again—if you don't mind, I'll hang around after the departure and get your first official blessing."

Nyth nodded. "I had been planning a blessing for all those left behind. I think we are all going to need it."

"I'm afraid you're right." Hauskyld turned toward them again. In all the years he had known Terrans, Kuf had never gotten used to their habit of pointing their heads at things. He knew, of course, that their field of vision was much narrower than his and blurred somehow in the periphery, and he could understand their having to do it to see, but it still always looked to him as if they were going to bite.

"Last check," Andros said. "Anything we could send Hauskyld racing back for?"

"I've got my record blocks in this case, and my clothes and things all went with the cargo wagon yesterday," Clio said. "If I don't have something, I'll just have to jump backwards through the Gate real fast."

Nyth looked puzzled; Hauskyld assured him that that couldn't be done.

Kuf suspected that getting used to the style of Terran humor would be one of Nyth's more difficult tasks—made more difficult by the fresh settlement, less than three months ago, of a million Terrans on the South Polar Island. Supposedly their ships—strange idea, huge craft that floated on the water like logs—would begin arriving at the river mouths in Floyd within a few years, and meanwhile there would be a swelling flood of air traffic between the island and the continents. The changes that had destroyed the Randall of his birth had been only a shadow of what was to come.

"Is there some reason for this little gathering, or are old friends sharing stories?" a voice said behind them.

Kuf swallowed his anger, again. Of all the Hregh'd-humists, Phrath'chra was easily the most offensive. "Ah, Bishop Kuf," the Randallan voice went on, "good to see you here. Or are you still bishop?"

"A bishop is a bishop," Hauskyld said. "Technically both Kuf and Nyth are bishops at the moment, though authority will rest with Kuf until he enters the Gate. These are important points of protocol for an ambassador—I'm surprised you didn't know them yet. You'd better plan on taking some time to brush up on your manners after you arrive on Arimathea."

"I do apologize," Phrath'chra said, his tone equally polite. "As a purely temporal official, I am not as familiar as I should be with the workings of the Church—I am afraid that in me the practical side of affairs has won out over the undoubted great merits of the more spiritual side. I had merely wondered which of the two spiritual authorities respect was due to, given that there seemed to be some division of authority here—if I may point it out, there are relatively few griffins to whom one has to pay any respect at all."

Kuf wondered how the Terran word "griffin," perfectly simple as a description when the Terrans used it, could be so offensive spoken by Phrath'chra. He supposed it might be the tone, but it seemed more likely that the real difference was that Standard, unlike True Speech, did not have separate noun forms for intelligent beings. . . .

"You missed your opportunity," Andros said. "You might have practiced on a number of wingpersons in your own household."

Phrath'chra took a breath, some angry response about to burst from him, but at that moment the whistle sounded its warning. The Gate was ready, and entry would begin soon.

Everywhere, Terrans who were staying embraced those who were going. Water ran from their strange, tiny, pulpy eyes, a disgusting thing that frequently happened when they were upset. The Gate would be seventeen Standard years—a quarter of a Randallan century—getting to Arimathea, where most of the Terrans would be reassigned to other worlds, never to return to Randall. Even if a few did come back, those who had stayed behind, without the time contractions, would be old or dead. Kuf had mastered the mathematics of that, but still couldn't imagine it. He hoped that the future, when he got there, would prove to have been worth the effort.

Dismissing the gloomy thought, he began to walk forward in line. Hauskyld hugged his neck, and he rubbed his beak against him; the old xenist was scheduled to leave within a couple of years, bound outward away from Arimathea on a twenty-four lightyear voyage to a distant system, so that with a combined signal separation of almost fifty Standard Years, it was likely that neither would live to learn what had become of the other. It seemed strange to part in this way—as finally as death, and yet so normally, in the prime of life.

Hauskyld embraced the others, gave a bare nod to Phrath'chra, and said, "God be with you"; then he turned back toward his groundcar and was gone. They drew closer to the Gate as more people walked into it.

The gray, foggy appearance of the surface was supposed to be condensation caused by the odd temperature effects as the velocity of light dropped, within a millimeter, from three hundred million meters per second to around a meter per trillion seconds. It seemed to Kuf that he should be able to see beyond it, that there were shadowy shapes and colors there; he strained to see more closely and then realized that he was only four or five meters from the Gate. Clio was already pushing Andros's wheelchair to the sheet of gray.

Kuf took his last look at his bishopric for at least fifty of its years. The redrock still glowed in the warm sun as it always had; the sky was pink and the few high clouds were white and feathery. He felt the grit under his claws and looked at the short moon shooting down toward the eastern horizon. And then, because there was really nothing more to do, he advanced to the foggy surface and moved forward.

And walked into the receiving area of the Arimathea Orbital Port, seventeen years later, in less than a blink. For a moment, as neuron firings caught up with him, he felt as if he were standing divided by the field, his head in the receiving area, his back feet still on the rocky landing field in the Spens Desert. Then, as his rear legs came forward from the field, the last ghost of Randall was gone from his nervous system.

He had no time to look around; Clio was guiding him into a short line of the more distinguished arrivals—she was among them, along with Phrath'chra as ambassador, Andros as the ranking military officer, and so forth. An array of dignitaries faced them, and there was a lengthy exchange of titles and names, most of which Kuf was unable to remember for even a moment. Clio had told him that this first presentation was unimportant anyway—the tradition was that station officers must greet the leaders of every group coming aboard—and the really important ones would come after. Still, he did try to keep a good picture of them in his head, listening carefully through the several repetitions of their names, despite the confusions—his Standard was supposed to be very good, but what exactly was the difference between a Deputy for Special Operations, the Deputy Operations Specialist, and the Specialist Deputy for Operations?

After being introduced, Kuf completely lost interest in the ceremony. He was glad that, unlike the Terrans, he could closely examine anything in his field of vision without anyone's knowing.

The reception deck was big enough for whole colonies, but most of it was empty now—Gates arrived only about fifty times a year, even at a major transfer station like Arimathea. The floor extended perhaps three kilometers beyond them, a great expanse of concrete broken occasionally by patches of carpet or what he assumed were the maglev tracks Clio had spoken of. The floor, as did the ceiling a hundred meters above them, curved slowly upward, until in the distance he was looking straight down at the floor. As he watched, a small car carrying a couple of workers ran across the seemingly vertical wall. He was relieved that it didn't bother him; this base had plainly been built for short-sighted Terrans, to whom the distant car would have been a blur at best.

At last the presentations were over and the more serious introductions could begin. A small car had pulled up, and two Terrans and something Kuf supposed must be a freep got out. At least the huge scooped ears, each as big as its head, and the short armless torso and long thin legs matched the descriptions of freeps.

"I am Brother Raul Trati," one of the humans said, "of the Brothers of St. Chang. This is Monsignor General Yhg wlaa Toth-Ftari, of the Templars. And may I present his Excellency, the Archbishop of Arimathea, Erik Uterra."

They all knelt, until the Archbishop gestured for them to rise. "I must apologize," he said. "We average only about one Gate per week here, so of course the two most important of the year are arriving on the same day. If we could do the formal presentations quickly now, I promise you my much fuller attention later."

"Certainly, Your Excellency," Andros said. "I am Father Captain Andros Kanegawa, of the Templars. This is Dr. Clio Yeremenko, Acting Second Xenist of the Randall Survey Expedition. This is . . ." He rattled on through them, doing a creditably quick job under the circumstances, Kuf thought. The Archbishop nodded gravely to each, seeming unhurried and interested despite what he had said.

At last Andros reached Kuf's end of the line. "And may I present His Excellency the Bishop of Randall, Kuf."

Kuf bowed low, pressing his face to the deck. From the other end of the line, near Andros, there was the hissing sound that Terran voices used for urgent, private, or embarrassing matters. By the time Kuf came back up, the disturbance was over, but the Archbishop seemed to be in a hurry to leave. He got into the maglev car and extended an arm in blessing; then the door closed and the car sped away.

A whole rank of cars came up on another track; in each of them there was a Terran or a freep. Brother Raul cleared his throat and spoke. "We've arranged for you to get to your quarters. Captain Kanegawa, the ambulance car will take you to the surgery, of course. If I may have the company of Dr. Clio Yeremenko and of Ambassador Phrath'chra in my car . . ." They came forward, Phrath'chra walking with an odd stiffness as if he were angry, and Brother Raul gestured for them to get in. Two attendants helped Andros into a car marked with a large red cross. "I believe that General Toth-Ftari has suggested that Bishop Kuf ride with him. Our other guides will be announcing the names of their passengers."

Kuf walked forward toward the freep; the general bowed low, and Kuf returned the bow by curling his head down to press against the floor. "We can get in the car and depart at once," he said. "Raul is the one in charge of getting everyone in—I'm purely diplomatic baggage here, part of having non-Terrans represented in adequate numbers at adequate ranks. If you'll follow me in, Bishop, the maneuvers will be less complicated." The freep hopped forward into the compartment and sat on a chair on the opposite side, facing what Kuf assumed were the controls. Kuf followed him and sat on the floor, making sure his tail was well clear of the door.

The door slid quietly shut beside him. The floor pushed against their feet, and the car lifted a few centimeters above the track and drifted forward onto a short curve that led to another straight section. As they reached the straight section, the car accelerated smoothly until they were racing along as fast as Kuf ran to take off.

They slipped onto another track, this one apparently a main one since many others came into it. General Toth-Ftari leaned back and turned to face Kuf.

A Terran stepped onto the track in front of them. Kuf was sure the car would hit him, but it slowed without Toth-Ftari's doing anything. "They drive themselves," the freep explained. "I wanted to talk with you alone a little; this seemed like an opportunity."

Kuf nodded.

"Did you hear what happened while you were being introduced to the Archbishop?"

"No," Kuf said, "I didn't. It sounded like some of the Terrans were arguing with each other, but I couldn't tell which ones."

"Your ambassador tried to protest your being introduced, on grounds that you were only travelling as the personal servant of that Communist scientist." The freep had that strange habit the Terrans did of pointing his head, probably because like them he had only single-lensed eyes and couldn't scan much of the environment at any one time.

"I am not surprised." Kuf hoped that would sound ambiguous enough. By now they were whizzing along long corridors painted in bright colors with many doors set in the walls. The few larger open doors revealed workshops of some kind. They made a steep, banking turn and shot along another corridor, lined on one side with plants and trees in pots of dirt, and on the other side, with windows, letting sunlight shine in. Beyond the glass hung the heavy round shape of Arimathea itself, blue-green and white against the black. Kuf was lost for a moment in looking at that.

"Excuse me if I am rude or somehow violate your customs," Toth-Ftari said. "I would not mention such things ordinarily. But the problem I need to trouble you with is one that would have come up anyway, sooner or later. You know of course that it is really only these mad Terrans who have taken up travel between the stars in such a big way. Few of the rest of us, even the very advanced worlds, bothered with it before the Terrans reached us, and many of us still find it incomprehensible that *they* bother."

"I once overheard a friend of mine ask a Terran that very question," Kuf said.

"Did the answer make any sense to you?"

"A little." They rounded another corner and entered a tight spiral, presumably descending to a lower level of the great structure. It felt like the worst tailspin ever done. The freep had a tight-mouthed expression that, Kuf suspected with horror, indicated great pleasure in the ride.

"A little is more than we ever managed. We only do this because they pay the clan back home. This is a remarkably pleasant way to travel—I never get tired of it. Well, here is what I need to put in front of you. Many of us intelligent species have discovered that, although the Terrans are often very nice personally, as a whole the Commonwealth does not offer all the opportunities it seems to. Is that reasonably obscure?"

"I think I follow you," Kuf said. "There is a certain . . . habit of bias among them. They don't quite think that beings who don't look like them are very bright, or capable of feeling, or something of the sort. It's quite noticeable among some of them on Randall that they prefer to deal with the *thnikkha*—the Ambassador's species—rather than mine . . ."

"Yes. Exactly. In fact, you will find that the more you look like them, the better you get along with them. Well, there are those of us who find that it's worth our while to maintain some contact and communication outside the usual channels of the Commonwealth Temporal Authority or the Church. Sometimes it's useful to know that others are encountering the same discrimination, so that we can all push together to outlaw it or minimize its effects, for example."

The spiralling had stopped and the wave of relief as they glided into a kind of roofed park was so overwhelming that it took him a moment to answer. "How legal are such things?"

The general nodded, approving of the question. "Usually completely. Sometimes they do come a little close to the line of the Protocol Against Cabals, but not often . . ."

"Is there some reason why you approached me and not the ambassador?"

"His shape, of course. And we had seen some of the advance reports that arrived here by radio a few weeks ago. We knew about the political problems between your species and his—and we thought you were both more likely to need us and more likely to be sympathetic."

Of course, although a Gate could travel very close to lightspeed and could accelerate or decelerate to within a ten-thousandth of c in only about a week, the difference in time of arrival was still significant. So they had known what to expect before the Gate got here . . . that too was worth remembering.

Then a thought froze him. "Do you think the Archbishop is likely to be sympathetic to slavery on Randall?"

Toth-Ftari shook his head and made a brapping noise—laugh? general comment? digestive noise?—"No. Especially not after the spectacular rudeness of that fool of an ambassador, but even without that the Church has no tolerance for slavery of intelligent species—it costs them converts in the long run. No, your petition should go well, and I should add that it will be helped along by myself, several monocorni, and a coordinatus . . . you might consider that the first fruits of our prospective friendship. Anyway, here is your door—your quarters will open to the pattern of pores on the tip of your beak, if you press it against the red triangle."

That must have been why Hauskyld had taken that print. Strange to think of that . . . seventeen years ago or only this morning, depending on how you saw it.

The car slowed, swinging onto a curving track that brought them to a door in the wall. It settled with a barely perceptible thud to the floor, and the door slid open. Kuf got out, the general following. "Right here," Toth-Ftari indicated, pointing to the red triangle. "Just put your beak tip against it."

Kuf did, and the door slid open. The general's neck swayed sideways, indicating that they should go in. "This panel of switches is all that you need to know about, I think. Triangle opens the door, of course; if you also press the square under it, it will close after you. The square below *that* makes it close immediately. The rectangle turns the lights on and off; the longer you press on it, the brighter the lights get, to a point of course. The pentagon is temperature; the indicator number beside it is the room equilibrium temperature you've set it to—while you hold the pentagon down the number will cycle up and down, one degree at a time, between 10 and 45 Celsius. Sorry about the panel being so low to the floor, but I'm afraid all we have to put you in are these general all-species rooms, and that's about as high as the panel can safely be."

Kuf quietly resolved, as soon as the general was gone, to play around with the switches himself and see if he could make sense of them. At least it didn't sound like any of them did anything dangerous.

"That low thing over there is an adjustable mat," the general went on. "Press the switch above it to make it firmer or softer. And—if I may be a bit indelicate . . ." He hopped neatly to the other side of the room, landing balanced on one leg, and struck upward with the other foot at a triangle on the wall. A door slid open. Kuf followed curiously. Toth-Ftari pushed a rectangle on the wall, and lights came on. "Er, manure and urine and . . . any other organic material you don't want to keep, go into that low trench on the floor. Clean water comes out here into this basin when you pull this; twist right for hot, left for cold. The big basin can be filled if you press this button and pull this. To drain it, press the button again. If you'd like a spray of water from above, this turns it on and off, this regulates temperature the same way the one on the small basin does, and this one controls the flow rate, anything from fine spray to bucketloads. And this—" he squatted and picked up a length of flexible hose with a big nozzle on the end. "This can be connected to the water outlets by pressing it against them. It will spray water into—harder to reach places, like, er—well, some people for example use it on the anus. To clean it, I mean."

Toth-Ftari was now rocking back and forth, the big ears a distinct orange shade. Kuf assumed this indicated embarrassment, but he was at a loss to do anything about it. "Any questions?" the general asked. "Are you clear on everything, Excellency? Is there anything you need?"

"I'm fine," Kuf lied.

"If you need anything, the call box is right above the mat. Just speak into it and press the button, and it will take you from there."

Kuf committed that much to memory, then repeated that he didn't need anything just at present. He ushered the general out, and was gratified to find he could close the door on the second try. After a few moments, he checked to see what he had done first, and discovered the temperature was set higher. He adjusted it to a comfortable twenty-five, and then, remembering the thinness of the air here, pushed it up to thirty.

He sat down on the mat and considered a nap. He knew more than seventeen years had gone by, and it was hard for him to imagine not being tired, but it felt exactly like he had gotten up this morning on Randall only a few hours before.There was no hope of sleep; he got up and went into the toilet room.

Bishop's dignity or no, this was a wonderful room to play around in. He had a good deal of fun dumping water over himself, though he was nearly scalded before he got the temperature adjustment right. The manure disposal was gratifyingly simple, so he made use of it.

He was about to clean himself in the usual fashion, by curling around and using his beak. when it occurred to him to try the hose attachment. He fitted it to the faucet, grasped it in a forepaw, sat back, pointed it at his anus, and turned it on.

The water roared out of the hose with far more force than he'd expected, stinging painfully. He jumped straight up, letting go of the hose, scraping his wings on the walls, and banging his head on the ceiling. The hose whipped around like a Silent Person in frenzy, spraying water everywhere.

He shut the water off and looked around. The water had knocked some large, brown turds against the wall, where they had stuck, and the puddled water on the floor had brown flecks floating in it. Ordinarily the smell did not bother wingpeople as it did grabbers, but the addition of warm water had brought it powerfully to his attention.

He plucked the turds off the wall with his beak and carried them carefully to the disposal. Using his forefeet and his tail, he managed to push most of the dirty water into the disposal as well, and rinsed more of it in, using the hose cautiously. He hit the button and the mess disappeared.

At least he would have a chance to try using the overhead water spray to get clean. It worked surprisingly well, and he was beginning to enjoy it, when there was a mysterious pinging sound.

He stuck his head out to hear better; the sound came again, seemingly from the door to the park outside. He shut off the water; there was another ping. Kuf got out of the big basin and trotted to the door—a pink light flickered at another ping. Puzzled, he pressed the door open button, congratulating himself on remembering which it was.

Clio was standing there. "You're wet," she said.

"Yes." It seemed like the simplest thing to say.

The door slid shut. He hit the button again, and it opened. Clio was shaking and her face had that odd, screwed up expression that Terrans got when something was amusing, but she stepped through the door without comment. "They gave me our schedule, so I thought I'd come by and go over it with you."

"How did you know where to find me?"

"Remember that list of ID numbers Hauskyld gave you, the one he said not to lose?" she asked.

Kuf patted his pouch.

"If you need to get to someone, you call a maglev car by pressing one of the buttons on the little posts." Kuf recalled seeing posts at intervals along the ride to his room. "A car will come to you. When you get in, it asks for your ID and you push the buttons to indicate that; then it asks for the ID of the person you're trying to find. You can select home, work station, or last known location. If you need to get back here, you put in your own number and select home."

Kuf resolved to go nowhere unaccompanied. "All right," he said.

"Did you hear what happened in the receiving line? I can't believe he did that . . ." Clio said.

"General Toth-Ftari told me about it; I was too far away to hear for myself. It makes sense of a sort. Phrath'chra's argument won't hold in the light of Church doctrine, not the way I preach it or the way any Vatican pronouncement I've gotten to read runs— which I hope are roughly commensurate. So his only hope of getting it made doctrine is to persuade the Archbishop that it's purely a local tradition . . . Caesar's domain, which we have an unfortunate historical habit of blessing. So he had to make it look like a deep, emotional reaction, rooted in tradition. If the Archbishop learns that slavery had existed for less than a decade Randallan when we left, that removes any pretext . . ."

"Well, he certainly antagonized the Archbishop. Which is probably to the good—because apparently we're going to have some kind of private audience right after my big lecture tomorrow. And Phrath'chra won't be seeing him until after we do. So—with a little luck—" she shrugged. "I just wish I'd known how much politics gets into xenics. I'd've stayed home and been a baby machine, I swear."

"There are worse ambitions."

"Spoken like a bishop. Do you notice a strange smell in here?"

"Um, no," Kuf said. He thought he had gotten the bathing room clean; obviously not.

"No, it's something I haven't smelled in a long time, like—" she looked around—"your delivritube's lit."

She trotted to the other side of the room, pushing another triangle—which must be the universal door open sign. A panel slid open to reveal a bundle of flowers.

"Roses," she said. "Red roses. Andy must have—no." She looked at the card. "They're from the Archbishop. The computer routed them here since it knew where I was." Her voice sounded strange.

Water was running from her eyes again. That could mean a lot of things with a Terran; he wasn't sure what to say. "I haven't seen these for a long time," she said finally. "I'm sorry. I know it's silly."

It wasn't at all, but he didn't say that. He just quietly thought about how long it would be before he tasted anything familiar again, or really stretched his wings and flew off for some solitary wandering. After a while, she dried her face, hugged him, and left. Tired now, he lay down on the mat and went to sleep.

2

AFTER A WHILE, during Clio's presentation, Kuf stopped listening and watched the audience. He had heard all this material several times anyway, in Clio's lectures at Randall St. John. He knew that her insight and patient gathering of evidence had paid off as far as anyone on Arimathea could tell; radiofaxes of her papers were spreading across Terran space now, and though they might meet with news of the same idea from somewhere else, for a large part of Terran space she would be the originator of the idea, just as she had wished. Kuf sometimes idly wondered whether it still seemed worth it—and if it did, what she was going to do now that it was done.

She was leading up to her conclusion; from what he had gathered, more than half the audience was lay, and would be hearing a clear version of it for the first time. He recognized General Toth-Ftari, who was sitting very quietly, either quite attentive or trying hard not to go to sleep. Brother Raul Trati was leaning forward and listening intently—this was not surprising, since the Changists were predominantly a scientific order.

The big surprise was the delegation from the Communist worlds. Hearing of the lecture, they had all but begged to attend. Kuf supposed that, given the long time they would be away from home and the huge expense of sending them here—the cost of a Gate trip was proportionate to the square of its distance, and the available payload to the fourth root, and they had come more than forty lightyears, twice the normal maximum—they could hardly afford to miss anything that might be important. Anyway, they all appeared intensely interested, and one with light-colored head hair—the kind that in Terrans indicated aging—seemed to be eagerly taking notes. With some surprise, Kuf realized it was Ambassador Kirlov herself.

The room became quieter and more attentive still.

Kuf's attention shifted back to Clio; she was presenting the linchpin result, the hypothesis that had taken the most effort to support. "So, in a nutshell, that's it: The Missing Ninety, that ninety percent of genetic material in space for which we cannot account by any normal atmospheric convection plus solar wind, comes entirely from planets with intelligent technological life. And the planetary history of those worlds, when compared with actual drifting genetic material, indicates that the material is released by nuclear war. The intelligent, technological species grows through war and conquest; it makes nukes; it uses them against population centers. Millions or billions of the species are burned in the firestorms and the heat of those great burnings lifts their remains—including their DNA and RNA—into the outer atmosphere, from which solar winds sweep them to the stars. It is the nuked planets that pass on their heritage to the others, to an overwhelming extent.

"This seems to call for some measure of philosophic speculation; I leave that largely to the philosophers. I would note that the peace that the growth of the three Terran Systems has brought to many worlds is likely to lead to a decrease in this process; it may, in some future time, be necessary to preserve the interstellar ecological balance by deliberately seeding space with the appropriate materials—which is certainly less wasteful than the 'natural' process." Her style of Terran Standard seemed stilted to Kuf, like that of the textbooks and the preserved lectures. She had told him that this was some sort of a custom or convention, but had never satisfactorily explained its purpose to him.

"And I find I cannot resist one other note, one of warning. We are the children of this process, after all. Terra itself is one of the most recent sources of genetic material, and by my estimates even now the first seeds scattered by the Terran Nuclear War are falling on distant worlds, to find hosts and become part of the lives of those worlds, just as for billions of years other seeds fell on Terra. Who is to say that the tendency to apocalypse does not travel with them? I submit to your examination this proposition: during our first millenia of recorded history, our mission was to burst the bonds of Earth before we destroyed ourselves—to race our creative ability against our destructive. We won—barely. For the next millenia, our project—not just for Terrans, but for all intelligent life—is perhaps to end the process that brought us into being, so that it will not end us.

"Or—if that is not our job—what is?" She waited a moment, seeming to turn her head to look at everyone in the room. Kuf thought for a moment that that might be a hostile gesture in a Terran, but clearly he was wrong—the room burst into applause. "Thank you," Clio said softly.

A line was forming to congratulate her. This was one of the most attractive things about Terrans, Kuf thought—their enjoyment of sheer mental accomplishment. It was perhaps why Vwat had been so able to get along with them, captured by the intricacies of their game of chess.

Kuf had joined the line and was advancing toward Clio when someone spoke his name behind him. He turned to see General Toth-Ftari. "The Archbishop asked me to tell you that your special audience is going to be rescheduled because of an urgent . . ."

"Yet another change in plans," Brother Raul said, joining them. "I'm sorry to break in, Iggy, but one minute after he asked you to get the Bishop, he sent me with more information."

"Dui yfand duwari."

"Exactly. What the General just said, Bishop, is a proverb which roughly translated means ' "Temporary plan" is redundant.' We had had to cancel the special audience because of extraordinarily urgent matters with the Communist delegation—but now they've requested that Clio Yeremenko, and you because you're familiar with her work, attend the meeting, and the Archbishop

has agreed." The line was breaking up suddenly—Clio
had apparently been told by someone else, and was now
slipping out the side door in a cloud of apologies.

"We can catch a car through this door," Toth-Ftari
said, "if there's nothing Your Excellency needs to do before the meeting begins."

"Nothing at all," Kuf said, puzzled. He was in the car,
sitting on top of the folded-down seats behind Toth-Ftari
and Raul, watching a simulated beach glide by, before it
occurred to him that the general, unfamiliar with his
physiology, had been trying to find out if he needed to
defecate.

The car swung abruptly into a nondescript gray corridor surfaced with some smooth material, past dozens of
seemingly identical doors. After about another kilometer,
it slowed and turned inward to the wall, then settled to
the floor. The door opened, and they got out.

Raul placed his hand against the red triangle, but the
door did not open; instead, a tiny, bright yellow light
came on. "Max secure," Raul said. "It wants an ID from
all of us."

Toth-Ftari hopped forward, flattening and extending
one of his huge ears. He pressed it against the plate. "Not
very dignified," he said, "but you should see what
cadgers have to do." The yellow light stayed on.

Kuf stepped up and placed his beak tip against it;
another light came on. He hoped the machine could tell
how many of them there were.

The door slid open and they went in. Clio was already
there, sitting at a low table with Archbishop Uterra. She
looked up when they came in.

"We seem to all be here," the Archbishop said. "The
Communist delegation will be here shortly. I thought it
best that we all confer together first.

"You're here because you're as appropriate a group of
people as I could come up with on very short notice.
Raul, of course, is my chief aide. General Toth-Ftari is
commander of the armed forces here in the Arimathea

system and is the ranking Templar in the Archbishopric. Yes, I'm afraid military questions might well come up, Raul—try to develop a poker face because you're going to need it. Dr. Yeremenko is here because the ideas she presented this morning might well have bearing on the matters we'll be discussing. Also, she was born and raised in the League of Communist Worlds, and may be able to provide us with some insight. Bishop Kuf is here, first of all, because he's the only bishop of an outsystem planet—and the only non-Terran one—that I have on hand. Secondly, he's better acquainted with Dr. Yeremenko's work than anyone we could get quickly. I would have liked, of course, to have Father R'hpn here, but he's out on mission to the cyberfacility crews on Icebucket, three hundred lighthours away."

The Archbishop leaned back in his chair. "When you find out what this is all about, I'm sure you'll all see at once that it must not be discussed outside this room. Saying that, of course, makes me feel surer that it won't be.

"Here's the nub of it: war broke out in the Home System about eighty years ago. All three Systems are involved and they are all fighting each other."

There was a dead silence. Kuf wondered if Toth-Ftari was thinking what he was—"Not *our* war, Terran."

"But how—" Clio said. She seemed to be having trouble breathing. "How did it happen?"

The Archbishop spread his hands. "What we know is what we got on the maser tightbeam, and the path from the Vatican at Centaurus to Arimathea, through the relays, is almost eighty light-years. All three sides have been avoiding opencasting because they're trying not to give away any strategy."

Toth-Ftari made the brapping noise. Kuf decided it must be disgusted laughter. "What strategy? Five hundred realtime years of computer simulations—twenty-five billion simulated wars—and all they know is that the attacker always wins." He brapped again.

"*Wins*. The attacker always destroys every space-based habitat and wrecks the ecology of every planet."

"What about—don't they even try to conquer . . ."

The general shook his head and made the brapping noise again. "You can't occupy. No star system can send enough men to permanently occupy another . . . but they can always send enough nukes and crams to wipe them out. But of course—while you do that to them, they do that to you . . ."

The Archbishop stared at him. "Why can't you defend us? Can't you even try to—"

Brap again. "One unmanned Gate can deliver as many as a billion cram weapons, at a gigaton each. And they come at lightspeed—no reason for them to decelerate. Pick one up on radar and his bombs are on top of you before your circuits have interpreted the signal and gotten it to the screen. And they can come in from any part of the sky. No, you can't stop them from killing you—all you can do is kill them back. This is not a job for a general. A butcher or an undertaker would do you more good."

There was a long silence. Finally, Clio asked, "But what is it all about?"

The Archbishop shrugged. "The official version didn't convince me, and I wouldn't expect it to convince anyone. So what I know is what I've read between the lines. Apparently the resettlers on Terra got into arguments over boundaries—mostly about which continents some islands should count as part of. That led to all the bad old things you can find in the history of planetary colonization before the Great Division—squatting, stakepulls, burnouts, blight-spreading, all of it. Finally the weapons got loose, and now war is spreading out along the borders between all three systems. Or rather it has been for something like eighty years. And some nuclear weapons have apparently been used within biospheres—which I need hardly mention tears all the peace treaties to scraps."

Everyone was very quiet, thinking hard. Kuf tried to imagine what the Terrans must feel. . . . he could imagine how he would feel, he supposed, if the grabbers had tried to claim Randall for themselves alone. But the Home System was so far away, generations back. . . . it must be more like a flag or a pledge—something to which you were abstractly loyal, but rarely had to pay any concrete attention to.

Except that now it mattered terribly.

At last the Archbishop sighed. "Well, ugly as it all is, there's one little ray of hope. The nearest parts of the LCP to us have a much shorter pathlength through their tightbeam relays. Apparently the delegation from the LCP was dispatched here as soon as they got word. They have something to suggest. I want you to listen closely to them, and then give me your candid assessment. Please feel free to question them."

"They showed up just when you found out about the war?" Toth-Ftari asked.

"Within a few weeks. I can't think of any way they could do that deliberately, though—or what they could get out of doing it." The Archbishop seemed distant, abstracted.

"What's their proposal?" Raul asked, leaning forward.

"I only know it's some kind of a peace plan—or so they call it. They'll tell you about it themselves." There was a silence just long enough to get awkward, and then the Communist delegation came in. Kuf thought for a moment and realized that they had probably been in the other room, waiting for the archbishop to activate the door with a hidden button. They might well have been listening to the archbishop's briefing, too—there had not been any information in it that should be kept from them, and to give them a chance to listen might be taken as a sign of trust.

"Welcome, friends," Uterra said, a slightly formal tone in his voice. "Let me present my advisors: Brother Raul Trati, General Yhg wlaa Toth-Ftari, Bishop Kuf of Randall, and Doctor Clio Yeremenko. And the delegation: Ambassador Patience Kirlov."

He gestured at a tall, dark-skinned, gray-haired Terran female, wearing tunic and trousers, who bowed gravely. "Deputy to the Ambassador Ajax Madison." This was a small, light-haired Terran male. "Military specialist Colonel Darla Du Cange" was a short, stout Terran, probably female, with very flat features; "technical affairs specialist Doctor Emily Minh" was another female, almost as tall as Ambassador Kirlov. If Kuf had understood the titles correctly, Kirlov (or should she be called Patience? he'd have to see what the Terrans did) was in charge, Madison was a general flunky, Du Cange was a military flunky, and Minh was a highly educated flunky. He admired once again the Terran word "flunky"— without it he would never have understood what most Terrans did with most of their time.

Everyone bowed gravely again, and then they all sat down and the meeting began. Archbishop Uterra explained that everyone knew the situation; Ambassador Kirlov expressed her gratitude for that. There was an expectant silence, and then the Ambassador spoke again. "What I carry with me is an offer so delicate that it could well destroy my home Union of Kolontai—let me explain that a Union is a group of inhabited planets within twenty or so light-years of each other, the biggest possible genuine administrative unit, similiar I understand to your Archbishoprics. There are fourteen settled planets, and about thirty permanent vacuum-environment colonies, within our Union, so we're slightly smaller than the Archbishopric of Arimathea.

"More to the point, we're a lot closer to each other than we are to the Home System—and that's what I'd like to bring up.

"Our offer, in brief, is this—we'll let the people back at the center fight if they want to. We have no quarrel. We promise no attack on you in exchange for your promise of no attack on us."

"Obviously we need some assurance that this isn't a trick," Toth-Ftari commented.

Madison, the ambassador's deputy, said, "Remember we had no way of knowing whether word of the war had reached you yet. Instead of sending envoys, we might have simply launched an attack. Either would have arrived with no warning; but now that you've seen the envoys, we've thrown away surprise. So there is no attack coming."

"Unless you're here to keep us talking while the attack closes in," the general said stubbornly. "I would prefer, of course, to believe that you are telling the truth, but I'm not sure that's consistent with my duties."

"We certainly understand that." The Terran bared his teeth—which was a friendly gesture, despite what it looked like. "Colonel Du Cange has already told me she's concerned about the possibility of an attack from one of your worlds nearer us than Arimathea—that you may keep us talking here while a surprise attack is launched."

"Not likely from a standing start."

"My point exactly. We might be tricking you—but is it a likely or practical trick?"

Toth-Ftari nodded once, solemnly. Kuf thought about it for a moment; the logic ultimately led nowhere. If the Communist offer was in good faith, they had already made the decision irrevocably; if not, the attack could arrive at any time, even a decade from now. And if the archbishop planned treachery, a Gate full of cram bombs could easily beat any warning the Communist delegation might send home. . . .

Raul was talking. "Have you attempted to extend this idea to other Unions and Archbishoprics? Or perhaps even to some of the Caliphates?"

Dr. Minh answered. "Certainly. Of course there had been no replies at the time we left. But we're hoping to stop the spread of the war and confine it to central space. We've set up an opencast code to indicate compliance—if you decide to join, you'll be provided with the code, which you'll broadcast. Then anyone else who has agreed—or will agree in the future—will know of your decision. We're hoping that even the star groups that don't defect from the war will respect neutrality, though of course that may be a vain hope."

She unrolled a chart; Raul and Toth-Ftari leaned forward over it, and after a moment so did Clio and the archbishop. Most of the symbols were unfamiliar to Kuf, so he didn't bother to look closely at it. "You can see the results here. If we can get about half the groups we can contact to go along with this, the war peters out in a couple of centuries, with most of the damage confined to the center. The situation gets better if everyone respects neutrality, but we can hardly expect that, I'm afraid. Feel free to take this chart and check our calculations—after thirty-eight years in a Gate things may be out of date, or maybe we were working from the wrong assumptions about the Christian Commonwealth."

Uterra took the chart, rolled it, and handed it to Raul. "I'll expect a complete report as soon as you can get it to me. I would like to thank your delegation, Ambassador— you've given us a very straightforward proposal, and heaven knows that's rare enough in such business. Dr. Yeremenko, do you have any comments offhand? What are the implications of your theories for this?"

Clio shrugged. "None I can see. This war is going to spread a lot of DNA around, of course, but that's just a further acceleration of an existing phenomenon. On any time frame we could care about nothing will happen fast enough to make any difference."

Ajax Madison leaned back in his chair, his hands folded across his mouth. "May I ask a question?" No one said anything. He asked Clio, "Don't your results, um, imply that planet-wrecking is built into our genes somehow? That we're all the products of dozens of nuclear wars . . ."

There was a long pause. Finally Clio said, "You could read it that way."

Madison pressed further. "So intelligence is . . . bound up with destruction?"

"Possibly." The Terrans seemed to be avoiding pointing their faces at each other. Kuf felt awkward himself; the quiet hung in the room like a bad smell.

A thought came to Kuf. "Does it make any difference?"

Everyone started; he realized they had forgotten he was there. The archbishop bared his teeth slightly. "I think I know what you mean, Kuf, but perhaps you should explain."

Kuf drew a breath and found an idea. "The young of my species kill and eat their siblings. I did, when I was young. But murder is rare among us, and cannibalism unknown, when we are adults. Clio tells me that most intelligent species do not mate entirely in accord with instinct . . . indeed there is great variation within a species. So, even if we all share this drive for planet-wrecking, *we can refrain.*"

"Or does the deputy mean to tell me that he instantly rapes every woman he feels attracted to?" Raul chimed in.

The ambassador laughed softly. "The point is well taken. In any case, we have no reason to despair yet."

"I quite agree," Uterra said. "If there's nothing further, I think we need to retire to consider all this. I'd like written assessments from all of you," he said, gesturing at his side of the table. "Ambassador, if we could convene again in forty-eight hours, we'll have some preliminary questions for you then."

"That's quite agreeable," Kirlov said.

With a series of bows, handshakes, and other courtesies, the room began to clear.

"Kuf." The archbishop stood at his shoulder. "If you could remain here for a little while, I'd like to talk with you privately."

"Certainly," Kuf said, recognizing the order.

The archbishop's hand twisted in a peculiar gesture; there were bare nods from Toth-Ftari and Raul. Raul caught Clio's arm and guided her out as the Communist delegation left through the other door. Toth-Ftari's head swiveled around once; apparently satisfied, he nodded again and left. The door slid closed behind him.

Uterra turned his chair around to sit facing Kuf. Kuf sat. Their eyes were almost exactly level with each other; Kuf had noticed before that this seemed to be important to Terrans. "I hope you haven't been feeling lost in the shuffle, Kuf," he said. "Ordinarily your case would be the most important business for my attention, but now this . . . offer has overshadowed everything."

"It's quite understandable," Kuf said.

Neither of them said anything for several moments. Then, Uterra said, "I thought we might confer privately first. Are you aware of what was in Brother Hauskyld's dispatches?"

"He told me he would tell the truth," Kuf said. "But I haven't read it."

"I'm sure he told the truth," the archbishop said. "The question is what I can do here to help." He hesitated for a long time. "There's no question in my mind, of course, that the Church's missions have inadvertently touched off this . . . problem."

"Slavery," Kuf said.

"Yes." The archbishop turned his face away, pointing it to the blank wall. "This situation is quite uncomfortable. Do you know enough Church history to know why?"

"I've read the data files," Kuf said. He thought for a moment, about what Toth-Ftari had told him, about things he had seen. "I know there have been other problems, as you call them. But I don't think that's why you're uncomfortable."

The archbishop turned and faced him squarely. "Oh?"

"I think you're not very comfortable around non-Terrans. Especially unfamiliar ones. I suspect that's a feeling that you have to contend with all the time."

The archbishop's face pointed down toward his folded

hands; he appeared to be muttering something to himself. Finally, he said, "You're right, of course. I try not to let it show; evidently it does, and I apologize for that. I am not comfortable with things that don't look Terran; my natural preference would probably be for the Randallan ambassador rather than for you, though even he's strange . . . you can add to that the fact that the cannibalism that you mentioned a few minutes ago is peculiarly repugnant to many of us, especially in light of the details Hauskyld provides. To say that it is a natural part of your reproduction, and effectively necessary, excuses it but does not make it less repulsive.

"But that is not the issue. As long as we are being frank, let me explain Randall's importance to us. You know that we call your sun Menkent."

"Yes."

"The name comes from the Arabic; the Arabs were a Terran people who developed much of our art of navigation and named many of the bright stars. In the skies of Terra, Menkent is one of the brightest stars. But in Menkent's sky—"

Kuf nodded. "Terra's sun is barely visible to Terran eyes on our clearest nights. I know—Hauskyld has told me of this. Menkent is almost at what he calls the limit of vision."

"Yes. The point is that Menkent is visible about as far as any star with a lifebearing planet can possibly be." The archbishop clasped his hands in front of him. "I promised you frankness, didn't I? Well, here it is then. During the terrible years after the nuking of Terra, when only a tiny fraction of us survived in space, before we first ventured to the stars near us, we thought a lot about what we might find. And when the Runeberg Gate opened up the sky to us, those concerns became urgent. We had barely glued together a peace—the Great Division—between the three Systems by drawing arbitrary lines in space, and we did not even agree to that without a century of bloodshed and suffering. And the fear came to us—some day, we would meet others like us. The Equivalent Culture, we call it. Even on some worlds we have occupied, there are intelligent species with whom we cannot manage any relation other than unending war, so that we're forced to simply fence those planets off forever, sending down a mission once in fifty Standard years to see if they can accept us yet. And those are cultures—like the one on Randall—that more or less *have* to accept us, at least by the logic of conquest. The Equivalent Culture . . ."

"Might end up in eternal war with you," Kuf said. "So you worry a lot about meeting them."

"Exactly." The archbishop nodded, as Hauskyld sometimes did at an unusually apt pupil.

"And—" The realization struck Kuf. "If they're exploring a new region, because Menkent is both bright and likely to harbor life—Randall is one of the most likely places for them to come."

The archbishop nodded more vigorously. "Then you've seen it. Of course we cannot tolerate an ugly or brutal culture on Randall. The first contact will be difficult enough; we want our best face to show. So from my self-interest, as an archbishop who would like to be remembered favorably, and from the Church's self-interest, we are going to act strongly. At a minimum we'll condemn every aspect of slavery on Randall, and place the temporal authorities who enforce it under anathema. We'll certainly lay on special decrees against the pinioning of griffins and the use of handsnakes as forced labor for record-keeping. We'll actively recruit both species into appropriate Orders." He sighed. "And if you had turned up twenty days earlier, I'd have said we'd be sending some battalions of Templars to back all that up. But with this war. . . ."

"I understand that," Kuf said. He hesitated a moment. "There is a question I'd appreciate your answer to. A question for you as my spiritual superior . . ."

"Surely, if I know enough to answer it."

"Why Randall?"

The archbishop cocked his head and appeared to be listening for some distant sound. It took Kuf a moment to realize that the Terran was thinking hard. "You might also ask why Terra, or any other world. Every species sees itself as the culmination of all its history . . . and the part of that since spaceflight is short. Even we Terrans have only been in space for less than a thousand years—and those of us who actually travel in space, because of relativity, have experienced a very large part of that time. Hauskyld, after all, has lived through something like five hundred years of history. So we say, all of us, every species, why us? What did we do that we should have to play this part in history? And whatever happens to us seems unique."

Kuf thought perhaps the archbishop had not understood. "I was thinking of two physical accidents. We have received more than our share of the genetic rain. And we orbit a star that's practically a beacon to every spacefarer in this part of the galaxy. It's not surprising that Clio found remnants of three previous destroyed civilizations, one so old that the only remnants were on one of our moons. I was wondering how we were so . . . fortunate in our location."

The archbishop bared his teeth. "I wish I could tell you that."

Kuf nodded. "So do I."

The archbishop laughed, but the sound was sad. "Well, I suppose someone has to be there. As for what to do about it, the Church has a traditional answer—whatever we can, and leave the rest to God." He stood up and stretched. "I'm enjoying this conversation. I trust we'll have many more. Unfortunately, my next duty is beginning to press on me—and it won't be nearly so pleasant. I'd like to talk privately with the ambassador from Randall . . . er . . ."

"Phrath'chra."

"Yes, Phrath'chra. He needs to be brought around to a

more reasonable point of view, especially since he's due soon to send a message back to Randall and we don't want him hedging on the slavery issue. I had hoped to begin by talking to him alone—"

The archbishop stopped for a moment. "We can begin his education earlier than that. He needs to see some practical equality. Would you do me the favor of stopping at his door and telling him to come and see me? Not too politely?"

"Certainly, Excellency." Kuf bowed and left the room. This might all be much simpler than he had feared. The archbishop might be a bigot in his heart, but his head was on the right side, and it was the head that ruled. He pressed the button and waited for the car.

He got into it and cued it to go to Phrath'chra's last known location, which the screen at the front of the car indicated was his room. The car rose and sped back up the gray corridor to the simulated beach, and Kuf congratulated himself on his developing ability to use the things. They were even sort of a fun way to travel, once you got used to them—though he still wished the gravity were low enough and air viscosity high enough to make using his wings worthwhile.

The car climbed a well and then slid down a corridor that looked out on space. Arimathea was a beautiful world, but not as beautiful as Randall—at least not in Kuf's eyes. Where a bare majority of Randall was ocean, ninety-four per cent of Arimathea was, and almost all the land was in a narrow band around the equator. He had been told that the climate was lovely, but since the surface gravity was almost half again what he was used to, and the air actually thinner, he saw little reason ever to go there. Arimathea Orbital would have to do.

When the car turned into the archbishop's private garden, Kuf realized that Phrath'chra probably lived close to him. In fact, the first two turns were familiar. Then the car took an unfamiliar turn and approached a low, blue building. It slid onto one of the turnoff tracks and settled gently to the ground; the door opened.

Kuf got out of the car, watching for a moment as its door closed and it rose and glided away silently. He turned and looked for the door; he could see the plate glowing through a big pink-flowered bush, so he assumed the door would be there too. He went around the bush.

Ambassador Phrath'chra lay in front of his door, his neck bent at a strange angle. His tongue protruded from his mouth, thick, black, and dry. Kuf crouched to look at him more closely.

There was a loud shout behind him. He turned to see a Terran in a General Labor Service coverall pointing and shouting at him. "The ambassador is dead," Kuf said. "We need to get Security."

The Terran backed away, slapped at one of the car call posts, and turned to run. The post began to flash a light and make an unpleasant whooping noise that couldn't be anything but an alarm. Well, evidently the Terran thought he had done it and no doubt Security would want to talk to him.

He looked down at the dead ambassador again, noting the thin linear mark in the fur around the neck. Grabbers had relatively delicate spines, and anything strangling Phrath'chra might well have broken his neck in the process. A large male Terran could do it bare-handed, especially if he jerked suddenly.

There were a few scrabbled marks in the dirt around Phrath'chra's feet. He had been taken from behind, probably by someone crouching between the bush and the wall. They would have triggered the door signal, then crouched and waited; when Phrath'chra emerged, they would have leaped onto his back and drawn a cord or wire tight around his neck. He must have died almost at once.

A big car glided to a stop, and several security people jumped out of it—some male and female Terrans, a freep, and a large, brown, long-furred being with a single horn protruding from its forehead. It walked on four legs like a Terran horse, clutched a baton in its prehensile tail, and appeared to be in charge. It came slowly forward.

"You are identified as Bishop Kuf of Randall?" it asked.

"Yes."

"We'll have to hold you, Excellency, for questioning and as a suspect. I'm Captain Q'shnh—remembering my name will make some of the paperwork easier."

"Captain Q'shnh."

"Right. If you'll just go with these constables, I need to examine the site here."

There was nothing else to do. Kuf got in the car; impatiently, a Terran indicated that he should get into the back part of it. As soon as he did, a clear barrier slid up between Kuf and the other occupants of the car, locking in place with a loud clang. The car rose and sped off into a network of gray, featureless tunnels like the one the archbishop's conference room had been located on.

Kuf realized abstractedly that such corridors must be what the Terrans put in wherever they saw no reason for beauty. That thought was strange, too—that there should have to be a reason to make a place attractive. After an interminable sequence of turns and descents, the gravity getting a little greater with each descent, they glided about a kilometer down a straight passageway and through a door. The car backed against a wall; a door behind Kuf opened, and a door matching it opened in the wall.

He got out, since that was clearly what was intended. The room looked very much like his, except that the walls around the bathing room were transparent and there were cameras mounted in every corner.

The door closed behind him and he was alone. There were no controls on the inside for opening the door. The room was very quiet.

He lay down on the padded surface to take a nap; there seemed to be nothing else to do.

3

KUF HAD NO idea how to call an attendant, but when he woke there was a plate of bread and cheese near him. It wasn't especially tasty, but he was hungry—in fact the portion was a little scant. He wondered how often they planned to feed him.

After he finished the food, he went into the bathing room, closed the smaller basin drain, opened the cold water tap, and drank deeply until he was full. He plunged his face into the water and shook it to remove the crumbs, defecated, cleaned himself—the hose, now that he could control it, was a positive pleasure—and sat down to pray and meditate. No doubt something would turn up.

After a long meditation, and composing a hypothetical letter back to Randall, he was just beginning to think of a nap when the door slid open and Clio and Toth-Ftari came into the room.

"Hello." He was unsure what else to say.

"Good afternoon," Clio said, with just enough force to tell him that it was afternoon locally. He had known that already, of course—his internal time sense was accurate to a couple of minutes per Randallan midmoon, about twelve and a half days. It had not occurred to him before that the prison might be set up deliberately to disorient him, but now he realized that that was surely the case. Probably for other species it was very productive of confessions, at least for those with anything to confess.

"Have you been treated decently?" the freep asked. "Do you need anything?"

"I haven't needed anything yet," Kuf said. "If I did, what should I do?"

"Speak aloud," the general said. "At least in theory you're monitored all the time. In fact I'm sure they're listening even now."

"In that case," Kuf said, "it might be of interest that your xenists estimate that even in this inactive condition

I need about 35,000 of your calories daily. I would guess about eight of those meals they're feeding me—though if that's inconvenient, they can always make the deficit up with any simple carbohydrate or even cellulose."

"I hope you recorded that," Toth-Ftari said, speaking to the ceiling.

"With that out of the way," Clio said, "what the hell happened?"

"I found the ambassador dead. As I bent down to look at him, a technician saw me. I told him to call Security, which he obviously did. Unfortunately Security decided I was the leading suspect. That's about as much story as there is. They haven't questioned me yet."

Toth-Ftari bounced agitatedly on one leg. "That's just like them. They'd rather be able to explain it as a power struggle imported from Randall than actually find out the truth. We have a three-person senticide detail, and our first senticide in two years, and their main concern is to avoid having to do anything." The bouncing accelerated. "Raul and I will have to lean on them."

"*We* think you're innocent, for what that's worth," Clio said. "The problem, of course, is if not you, then who?"

"A Terran or something built a lot like one," Kuf said. "I've had time to do some thinking." He told them about what he'd seen of Phrath'chra's body. "Neither a freep nor anything built like me could have used a thin cord that way to strangle him. And frankly I'm too big to hide behind a—what is that bush, anyway? They're all over the Archbishop's Garden."

"A rosebush," Toth-Ftari said. "I looked at the site too. It would have to be a species that wears clothes, like a Terran, or has quite a hide—because the thorns on that bush are long, and sharp as needles besides. That kind of rose was bred by the Terrans for game fences . . ."

Not just because they were pretty. That fit, somehow.

Clio scratched her head. "So whatever it was had to have prehensile forelimbs, and either wear clothes or be tough-hided enough to hide in that rosebush. So what does that leave us? Terrans or what else?"

"On a long-term basis we have freeps, monocorni, and coordinati here. None of them has the forelimbs, and only the monocorni have the hide. And since no Gates have come in from the center, or from other intelligent worlds in the past year before yours, I doubt we have anything else. So it was a Terran." That obviously brought the freep great satisfaction. "The question is what Terran would have a reason to kill a Randallan ambassador. A lot of them don't like non-Terrans, but they're hardly going to kill them because of it. And besides, to hide behind the door like that—this wasn't some sudden emotional reaction. The ambassador hadn't talked to much of anyone—in fact hardly anyone had seen him."

"Except those witnesses," Clio said.

Toth-Ftari made a strange bubbling noise as he exhaled. "I had forgotten about them."

Kuf waited patiently, but both of them seemed to be lost in thought. "Are there things I should know about?"

"Sorry," Clio said. "Just that the time of death is pretty well fixed, partly from autopsy and mostly because two gardeners and a biobalance tech saw Phrath'chra wandering around in the Archbishop's Garden not long before you found his body. And the central transit computer has no record of anyone other than you taking a maglev car into the area—though all that proves is that the killer planned intelligently. That's about—"

A high whistle sounded through the little room. Kuf winced at its shrillness. A curiously flat and mechanical voice said, "General Toth-Ftari?"

"Yes."

"There's been an outbreak of rioting on the Adult Recreation deck. We'd like permission to call up some of the Templar garrison to help contain it."

"Granted. I'll join them en route if you can expedite me a car. Use Ave and Corpus Christi Companies of the

Two-twelfth, if that will be enough."

"Thank you. That should be sufficient. A car is being expedited, ETA one minute your location. Complete." There was a scratchy hiss, and another voice came on. "Dr. Yeremenko, we remind you that under the Dangerous Offenders Protocol you cannot remain alone with the prisoner. Would you like a car to return you to your quarters?"

"I guess so," Clio said.

"Request definitive formulation."

"Yes, dammit."

"ETA six minutes your location. Complete."

She hugged Kuf around the neck, pressing her face to the side of his beak. "See you later, you dangerous offender. Take care of yourself."

"Thank you for coming," Kuf said. Toth-Ftari bowed, Clio raised an arm at him, and the door slid open. They stepped through it, and it closed quickly with a loud clang that rang off the bare walls.

4

THERE WERE THREE more meals, both large and very much more to Kuf's taste. By his internal clock it was 20:32 when the door opened again and, to his surprise, the archbishop entered. He carried a slim tube about a meter long, which he leaned against a wall. Uterra's head swung from side to side; it occurred to Kuf that he might well not have seen this part of Arimathea Orbital before. "General Toth-Ftari sends his regards," Uterra said. "And I'm sure you'll be happy to know we've overruled the software and reclassified you to something milder than Dangerous Offender. Are you getting enough to eat?"

"Yes, thank you." Kuf sat carefully on his haunches, aiming to be just below the archbishop's eye level. "What did the rioting turn out to be about?"

The archbishop made the flapping noise with his lips

that Kuf had learned expressed mild disgust. "A group of drunken technicians got themselves worked up over the presence of atheists here, and started smashing things. Smashing things, particularly things that aren't yours, is well-known to be great fun, so a lot of people joined in, and they tore up and wrecked a good portion of the movable stuff on the Adult Recreation deck."

"Atheists?" Kuf said. "You mean the LCP delegation?"

"That's the one. Some of us find it very interesting that such fighting should break out just exactly when it might do great damage to the peace initiative, and wonder whether it might have anything to do with the murder of the Randallan ambassador."

Kuf thought for a long moment. "I suppose it's possible. But it's hard to imagine how they found out what was going on, or what they were trying to accomplish—or even who they are."

Uterra nodded. "Well, there are possibilities. It's not discussed much but there are lively Communist and Islamic undergrounds here in the Commonwealth. And of course various crime syndicates. All of them might have reasons of their own, though what those might be I wouldn't know offhand."

"And of course there's your own intelligence service," Kuf said.

"I hadn't thought of them, but for the sake of completeness I guess I should. Why would you suspect them?"

"Well, if there are underground movements connected to the other systems here in Christian space, it stands to reason that as retaliation, if nothing else, there are Christian undergrounds in Islamic and Communist space. So I assume we have people who spend their lives running such things . . . and those people, in effect, are always at war anyway."

"And they might not want to see a permanent peace. You're right." Uterra ran a hand over his head, mussing his hair. "Yes, there are people who fit just that description. And furthermore they're not subject to local control. By dint of good police work, we know who most of them are—and if we decide to accept this proposal, we will probably have to round them up as a precaution."

"Should you be saying this in a prison cell?"

"No problem. Raul is monitoring, and erasing as he goes. One more of the privileges of rank. Anyway, I'm sure he's made a note of this by now. Any more cans of worms you can think of to open?"

Kuf wasn't sure what Uterra meant by that, but the thought of worms, canned or otherwise, reminded him that in his subjective timeframe it was sweetworm season in the northern forests back on Randall. He felt a little twinge of loneliness, and shook his head once, hard, to drive the feeling out. "So," he said, "what are my prospects of getting out of here?"

"Not good in the short run—but Toth-Ftari is working on something. We've gotten them to modify conditions so you'll be as comfortable as possible, though, and I brought something I thought you'd like." The archbishop retrieved the long tube from the wall by the doorway and slid several rolled-up sheets out of it. "Wall holos," he said, "with built-in power. The red dot in the bottom margin is the on-off switch. I had them made from the pictures that Hauskyld sent. They'll attach to the wall if we just press the corners—to take them down, you just press again, and when they're free they'll roll back up." He unrolled the first one and pressed it onto the wall.

Unlike what Hauskyld had called "realistic" paintings, and made such an obscure big fuss over, the holos, once in place and with the power on, seemed like windows, with real depth. Sunlight actually visibly shone through one of them. By moving his head, Kuf could see more of the scene through them. Only the unmoving figure of a soaring wingperson in the background of one, and the perfectly stationary herd of wild gash'hwar in a forest clearing in another, showed that these were not true portals.

"Now," the archbishop said, as he hung the last one,

"if you're willing to talk, I'd like to know what these are pictures of."

"Well," Kuf began, "this one is certainly familiar, because in the days of the War against the Terran Fort, I was one of the prisoners there. Now it's the Shrine of St. Thkhri'jha. That high rock pillar is where he preached his sermon—"

"And the desert itself—what's that like?"

Kuf found he had no words. He wanted to say something, but he could think of no answer to the question.

The archbishop bared his teeth, the heavy lines around his eyes deepening. "In our line of work, Kuf, we see far too many shrines. But I haven't seen anything from a planet new to me in several years. Now what's the desert like? Terribly hot? If I turned over a rock, what would run out at me?"

"I'm told many Terrans find it terribly hot, especially with the higher carbon dioxide content," Kuf said. "And if you turned over a rock, the Terran Standard words for what you'd find would be 'randigator' or 'mindripper' . . ."

The memories flooded back, and he found it easier and easier to talk. Uterra prompted often, and in the end it took almost five hours to look at the five pictures. By the end of the time, Kuf had been persuaded to call the archbishop "Erik," and the two had begun to talk like old friends.

At last Uterra sighed. "We have to get you out of jail, Kuf. There are hundreds of these pictures and all kinds of other things. I want you to give a general course, sort of an introduction to Randall, next year at St. Paul's Orbital College—and I plan to attend."

"If you can tolerate my lecturing," Kuf said. "May I ask—this may be inappropriate, Erik."

"Anything you like," the archbishop said. "I've certainly pried enough into your affairs."

"How did you come to be so interested in other worlds, when—"

"When I react so badly to alien species?" He shrugged,

and Kuf was afraid that he had offended him. "I trained to be a xenist. But during the deep psyprobes they do before you can work toward an advanced degree, I turned out to be a bigot . . . those things happen, I understand. I suppose you could say I like to exercise the part of me that loved studying xenics. Or maybe I'm just an incurable tourist."

Kuf laughed. The strange noise startled Uterra, and required an explanation, but afterwards they both laughed. When the archbishop left, with a promise to see that some books would be delivered soon, Kuf felt almost happy. He took a moment to look over the holos once again, then stretched out to go to sleep.

5

I T WAS ACTUALLY several days. Kuf had read three of the books and begun some tentative notes toward the course he would teach, when the security officers came to get him. This time they were respectful, almost deferential, and they did not raise the clear screen between him and themselves. However, they either knew nothing or were under orders not to tell him anything of what he was wanted for.

The small room where they eventually dropped him off held a conference table, at which were seated General Toth-Ftari, Brother Raul, the archbishop, and Clio. "We seem to be forming a regular social club," Raul commented. "I only wish we could meet about something pleasant now and then."

"Have you been treated well, Kuf?" General Toth-Ftari asked, as he had on every visit—which had been almost every day.

"As always," Kuf said. He sometimes wondered if the freep would rather hear that he had been beaten with sticks and called a critter. He found an open space where a chair had been removed and sat down at the table; his head was still above everyone else's but this seemed to matter less in meetings.

"Are we all here?" Raul asked. "Iggy, I know you have reasons for secrecy, but I really want to know what this is all about."

"One of the reasons, I suspect, is a sense of the dramatic," the archbishop said.

Toth-Ftari bowed. "Guilty as always. But also I wanted to make sure the evidence would be seen by enough unprejudiced eyes before it got filtered into a report.

"What I've done is set up a complex search program looking through all the relevant records—mostly camera recordings and transit central records, but also comm calls, credit use, and so forth. The senticide unit would have done the same thing eventually, but they were going to take a few weeks to get around to it.

"For a case like this, where the crime didn't happen on camera, the program starts out with everyone on board as a suspect—that's about seventeen million suspects. Then it takes known facts and probabilities to eliminate everyone who physically couldn't have been there at the time of death, and then weeds that much smaller set for consistency with the facts. It works a lot like a 'detective' in some of your ancient Terran literature.

"When it has one or more suspects, it identifies the checkpoints—cameras, microphones, credit reads, ID-cued doors, whatever—that they would have had to pass through if they were guilty, along with a time range for each checkpoint. Then, if it finds anybody who is consistently in the right places at the right times, it stitches together a collection of shots of them, which lets a sentient observer see if they 'look guilty'—because a machine just can't deal with motive, or tell what's 'suspicious behavior.'

"What I have here—and I myself haven't seen it—is a block of output. Apparently the machine has found only one suspect pathway, and there's somebody in it; we can just hope it won't turn out to be Kuf, or some poor janitor. I remind you that the output will not include the

murder of Phrath'chra and therefore will be purely cir-
cumstantial, maybe not even enough to go to a magis-
trate with. But anyway I think we can assume it will get
Bishop Kuf off the minds of the police and that's a big
step right there."

"If there's only one suspect pathway," Raul asked,
"wouldn't that settle the question completely?"

Toth-Ftari shook his head emphatically, rotating it
more than halfway around. "No. More than one suspect
could be on the same pathway. If you lived in a major
residential complex and killed someone on a major con-
course on your way to work, you'd be on the same path
with a hundred thousand suspects. And the real murderer
might not have been in the pathway at all—if he managed to avoid ID checks for, say, twelve hours, there would
be no physical data for the machine to work with. All we
get is a person or people in a possible pathway at relevant
times."

"Enough!" the archbishop growled. "Run the output
before we all die of curiosity."

The general bowed, stood on one leg, and reached up
with the other to a control panel on the wall. He fiddled
with the controls, slid the record block in, and pushed a
knob. The lights came down and one wall lit up to form
a screen.

A maglev car slid to a fast stop, bright lights flashing
on its side. "Irregular stop—it's a manual override,"
Toth-Ftari noted. "Supposed to be investigated but there
are thousands of those every day."

Ajax Madison, the deputy of the LCP delegation, got
out and looked around, then walked back the other way.
A service door opened to his left and a parcel carrier
glided by. He touched the safety on the service door,
springing it back open, and slipped through.

The camera cut abruptly to a service tunnel somewhere; Madison was walking quickly down it, his shoes
thudding softly. The scene stopped. Toth-Ftari was again
fiddling with the controls. Numbers appeared at the bot-

tom of the screen. "The tunnel takes him directly under the Archbishop's Garden. There are fourteen upward entrances."

The scene started again; a very grainy picture, blown up from a camera a long way away. Madison walked down the tunnel and up into the ceiling as the curved floor rolled away beneath him.

Camera cut: now he was in the Archbishop's Garden, strolling quietly through the hedge maze. The scene stopped. "Within three hundred meters of Phrath'chra's apartment," Toth-Ftari pointed out.

Camera cut again. Madison was on his feet, running; cut again: bursting through the shadows of trees near a small group of buildings. "The one on the right is the guest residence—the rosebush is on the other side." Restart, cut to long shot—a darting figure, clearly Terran, went behind the guest residence. Forty-three seconds later by the clock at the lower left corner of the screen, the same figure emerged, walking quietly around the building. "Too grainy for the machine to make a positive ID, I'm afraid—let's back up and blow up." A moment of darkness, and then a greatly enlarged hazy figure— clearly Madison—emerged from behind the wall.

Cut again, to Madison in another service tunnel, running hard, and again and again to other tunnels. Finally they saw him get into another car among a clump of pines in a simulated forest zone. He was clearly breathing hard and sweating.

"The deputy to the LCP ambassador." Raul sighed. "So much for their peaceful intentions."

There was a long, long silence. Kuf said, "I think I had better speak with him."

Clio laughed, a high-pitched choking noise with an ugly edge. "Well, somebody should. He's been a very bad boy."

No one responded. Kuf pressed the point. "I'm going to request that formally. Let me talk to him alone—on camera and microphone, of course, with plenty of reinforcements right behind the door."

"Why you?" Clio asked, calmer now.

"Because I have an idea, and it's got to be somebody," Kuf explained patiently. This deck was near the bottom of this wing of the station; the gravity was far too heavy, he noticed, and his joints were beginning to ache.

No one seemed to have anything to say, or any other immediate suggestions, but no one wanted to agree with him. It took half an hour before the archbishop reluctantly said that Kuf could see Madison as he wished. By then, the pads of his feet, too, were sore, and more than anything else he just wanted to get back to his bed, whether in prison or in the guest residence.

6

Y OU STILL DON'T have to go through with this," Clio said to Kuf. "There are lots of other ways to handle it. And it doesn't have to be you."

Kuf shook his head emphatically. "The problem here is not that he did it. The problem is why he did it. And I think I know."

"Then why not just tell us?" Toth-Ftari demanded.

"Because I'm not sure enough. And until I am, I don't want anyone to act on the idea. I'll be fine. I'm not a grabber with a weak neck, he's not taking me from behind unexpectedly, and there's a whole platoon of Templars just outside the door. And anyway, my beak is a lot bigger and sharper than anything he can carry through the metal detectors in the corridors. Just make sure everyone is seeing everything—and don't interrupt. I'm going to tell some great big lies and I want you to see how he reacts to them." He reared his head back and breathed out hard, rolling his neck around. "Ugh."

"What's the matter?" Clio asked anxiously.

"Arthritis. Same thing the old king had. Clio, you and I have gotten entirely too old and seen entirely too much."

"Amen," she said, her mouth curling up a little.

"Now," he said, "all of you need to get out of here. You'll want to get good seats in front of the screen and Ajax Madison—" he checked the small screen in the corner—"just went through check three. He'll be here in less than ten minutes."

Clio, Raul, and Toth-Ftari filed out Kuf's front door, got into a car, and rode off to join the archbishop and the Communist ambassador. Kuf let the door slide shut. He darkened the corner screen. For a moment, he wondered what story the archbishop had given Ambassador Kirlov—but since it was hardly relevant, he forgot about it quickly. He sat down to meditate and pray, resisting a stray urge to make faces and gestures at the cameras whose locations he knew.

The evidence was clear enough; what it meant was another question. Camera tracking and searches on the stored information in the transit system net had revealed that Ajax Madison was leading a complete double life. He was easily the most gregarious of the LCP delegation, hanging around in public places all over Arimathea Orbital, always willing to talk to school children or social groups, quick with an interesting folksong or story from his part of Communist space. Children who had seen him in class or on the video wrote letters to him, which he answered carefully. When people approached him in public, he always made time to talk with them, and they usually left impressed with what a nice young man he was.

But at least twice a day, he would slip off to do some bizarre inflammatory act. The riot had been triggered by him—he had encouraged two recently arrived outbound colonists, who did not know who he was, to begin shouting anti-atheist slogans in a bar, then slipped out the back way. He had painted the same slogans on walls, left threatening messages on the doors of officials who would have a hand in negotiating the peace agreement, and leaked distorted stories to the news service reporters; this last, apparently, without realizing that in Christian space all reporters were employed by the Temporal Authority or the Church and had reported it to their superiors at once. All of this obviously aimed at scuttling the peace treaty . . . but no one knew why. Now Kuf would see if his guess was right.

Ajax Madison himself was an odd enough specimen even for a Terran. Clio assured Kuf that Madison was physically attractive and that he seemed to be very sincere in public; privately, Kuf had always felt there was something off about him, something that he had noticed at that first meeting. It was not one of those vague emotional reactions that some of the Terrans seemed to set great stock in, or just a hunch—after some sustained thought, Kuf had realized it was quite specific. When Ajax Madison said something, he somehow always left his listeners with one and only one "reasonable" response to it. And after a while of his conversation, logic itself seemed to compel the outcome—even though it might well be something with which you disagreed.

Superiority in rhetoric was hardly a mortal sin, but it had far too much of power, and too little of genuine reason, about it. When they had talked about it, Brother Raul had finally landed right on the mark; Ajax Madison was a sophist. As such, he was an extraordinarily effective tool for whoever held his handle.

The door dinged softly. Kuf went to it, opened it, and Madison came in. "Thank you for coming," he said.

"My pleasure, Bishop. Though it would have been hard not to come, given your message."

"Oh?" Kuf said. "What about it brought you?"

"The request that I not let anyone know I was coming." Madison's head swiveled around. "May I sit?"

"Surely. Use the padded area if you wish."

The Terran sat down a little awkwardly. Kuf studied him for a moment, and said, "Straight business. We have the search underway. We have a Gate ready to go. We'll destroy ours if you tell us where yours is."

"I don't know—"

"It must be over five hundred lighthours out or we'd
have spotted its flare when it came in."

The Terran's weight did not shift at all, but the muscles
in his thighs tensed and his face warmed slightly. "I take
it you are not talking about my speech to the Women's
Association yesterday."

"No. Though I should say I'm well aware of your less
public activities."

Madison sat silently for a moment. "There are no
doubt people listening to this."

"Yes." There was another long moment, but Madison
didn't say anything, so Kuf went on. "It couldn't be more
than twenty-five or thirty lightdays away, because if you
gave us any more than about sixty days we might get a
retaliating strike under way . . . so let's say seven hundred
lighthours at furthest. Probably somewhere off the plane
of the ecliptic."

"I have no idea what you're talking about."

"We've seen you. We have enough on record to make it
absolutely clear that you've been trying to kill the peace
treaty. You can be quite sure that the ambassador won't
do it now."

"How do you know *I* can't? That I haven't already?"

Kuf snorted. "Because if you could you'd have done it
as soon as you arrived. And it's been too long."

The door slid open. The first through it was Toth-
Ftari. He was followed by several Templars armed with
fletchers, and behind them came the archbishop and Ambassador Kirlov.

Madison rolled forward and came up at Kuf; something in his hand whipped up to Kuf's neck. Kuf struck
downward at the Terran's face, but the Terran's other
hand shoved his beak down and Madison leaped to his
back. "I'll kill him." His voice had an oddly even quality. "Don't move. Stay where you are. We can talk."

Kuf's wings flared in a great, thundering clap in the small room and he bucked forward. He felt something cut into him as Madison flipped forward and hit the floor. He struck downward with beak and claws, tearing Terran flesh, and leaped back. A volley of flechettes splattered into Madison, who lay still.

The world was darkening rapidly; Toth-Ftari was shouting for an ambulance. Clio burst from the crowd and held his head up; incuriously, he realized that major blood vessels must have been cut, to judge from the feel of her hands pressing down. But the cold, searing pain said there had been some poison on the blade as well.

None of that mattered. He twisted his head, looking for Ambassador Kirlov, and spoke directly to her. "Do it now," he said. "Do it now. Give the order. You know by now we have no arms . . ."

Ambassador Kirlov drew something on a chain from around her neck and pressed it in her hand. Kuf saw her face was wet.

He heard questions and recognized the archbishop's voice. Something told him to squeeze with his forepaw after each question. It was very dark now, and he thought he might just fall asleep. He squeezed once again, in answer to the archbishop's last question, and then darkness descended—quietly, peacefully, just a moment of listening with all his attention for a sound that didn't come.

Epilogue

I T DIDN'T MEAN a thing," Clio said. "Everything would be the same today if he were alive. Madison's scheme was dead, Madison was as good as dead— why did Kuf have to die?"

"He didn't have to." Andy Kanegawa kept his eyes on the instruments below the viewport. "He just did. Everyone does sometime." He stretched his legs, wincing at the atrophied muscles. In a bit over a year, supposedly, he would be able to walk in regular grav again; already he had taken a few steps in two-hundredths g. "We're coming into the selected orbit, Excellency, Madam Ambassador."

Through the wide viewport, Arimathea's sun was a tinier disk than it ever was from Orbital or from the planet. But here in this outward leg of a cometary orbit, against the dead blackness of space, millions of stars shone.

"I don't know your sky," Ambassador Kirlov said. "Which is Sol, and which is Randall?"

"The Home System is right there," Andy said, pointing. "And Menkent, Randall's sun, would be somewhere on the other side of the ship from us." He watched the screen as the red actual orbit line converged with the green desired orbit. "Close enough, Excellency."

Archbishop Uterra nodded. "Ambassador Kirlov—" He smiled. "Patience." He licked his lips. "Would you have . . . if Kuf had not—"

She sat so quietly that the no-gee straps floated around her, not touching her at all. "I can't say. Kuf guessed right, of course. The load of cram bombs, in its own gate, was orbiting about five hundred and twenty lighthours out from your sun. One signal for if we got a peace treaty, one for if we didn't. If we didn't . . . the bombs would be arriving about now, almost at the speed of light. Since we did . . ."

"But you didn't have one when you signalled." Uterra's voice was soft, as if he were trying not to cry. Clio reached through her webbing and rested her hand on the back of Andy's neck.

"I have one because I signalled," she said. "And that explosion will be the signal for the—"

Toth-Ftari made that strange "vlaffp" noise the freeps used for anything surprising. "You mean . . . of course. The special opencast code. You couldn't get much more open than a three hundred teraton explosion . . ."

"The point," Ambassador Kirlov said, ignoring Toth-Ftari. "The point the bishop made. I don't know how we missed it in the first place. You don't come to bargain with a gun in your hand. If you want peace, you come peacefully. Poor stupid Ajax Madison was more honest than all of us. He—and whoever sent him—wanted a pre-emptive strike even if he had to die in it . . . but we came here ready to kill, and announcing this was peace . . ."

"All Kuf said was 'Do it,' " the archbishop said quietly. "Do what? Push either button, one to end the world, one to save it . . . all he said was 'Do it.' "

"You know which he meant," Clio said. She did not expect the flatness of her own voice.

"I know," the archbishop said. "I know." Tears streaked down his face now. "We were the last thing he thought of. But who could have blamed him if he'd meant the other, wanted her to blow it all up?" He sighed, his hands thudding hard against the padding. He rose a little against the straps without noticing. "What had we done for him? Destroyed the culture he was born into and helped to enslave his people. How could he forget all we'd done and plead for us?"

"That's a strange question for an archbishop," Clio said.

Uterra laughed a little, but it was a sad sound and afterward everyone was quiet.

"Is this a customary thing to do for the dead?" Kirlov asked, finally.

"From now on, thanks to Dr. Yeremenko, it's what we do with the best of our dead," the archbishop said.

Far out in the darkness, a great new star gleamed for a second or so and was gone. "Won't look like much, even in the nearest star systems, but the instruments will pick it up without trouble," Andy commented. Clio had expected to feel her heart rise with the destruction of the concealed bombs, but she felt only emptiness.

"We might as well begin," the archbishop said.

Andy activated the release sequence. They all bowed their heads. The archbishop spoke the centuries-old words. And from a hopper on the back of the skiff, the remains of Kuf, powdered and dried carefully to preserve the DNA, were sprayed into space, sown into the orbit of the ship. The pressure of the solar wind caught them, and they accelerated outward, to land wherever they might across the next million years.